COVERT OPS

COVERT OPS

FEDERAL AGENTS OF MAGIC™ BOOK FIVE

TR CAMERON   MARTHA CARR   MICHAEL ANDERLE

DISRUPTIVE IMAGINATION

LMBPN Publishing
PMB 196, 2540 South Maryland Pkwy
Las Vegas, NV 89109

First US edition, July 2019
Print ISBN: 978-1-64202-368-8

COVERT OPS - TEAM

Thanks to the JIT Readers

Dave Hicks
Misty Roa
Diane L. Smith
Micky Cocker
Larry Omans
Nicole Emens
Dorothy Lloyd

If we've missed anyone, please let us know!

Editor
The Skyhunter Editing Team

DEDICATIONS

For Dylan

— TR Cameron

To everyone who still believes in magic
and all the possibilities that holds.
To all the readers who make this
entire ride so much fun.
And to my son, Louie and so many wonderful friends who
remind me all the time of what
really matters and how wonderful
life can be in any given moment.

— Martha

To Family, Friends and
Those Who Love
To Read.
May We All Enjoy Grace
To Live The Life We Are
Called.

— Michael

CHAPTER ONE

The matte black multifunction ARES watch on her left wrist emitted three soft pulses, and Kayleigh pushed herself away from the computer terminal. *Three a.m. Damn. I'm working too much.* Her basement apartment was dark and only the glow of monitors spilled faintly into the quiet nothingness around her. She stood and stretched, balanced on her toes, and raised her arms high above her head.

One of the things that had appealed to her about this particular cellar was its extra height, which she concluded meant the habitable space was not an afterthought but part of the original design. *They probably had a mother-in-law they wanted to stash down here or something.*

She laughed quietly as she moved toward the open center of the giant room that formed the center of her living quarters, surrounded by functional spaces and a bedroom. Her bare feet enjoyed the caress of the plush carpet beneath them, and the slight breeze of the house's air conditioning raised bumps on her flesh where the loose shorts and Ramones T-shirt didn't cover it. The back of her neck was protected from the draft by the scrunchie that gathered her long blonde hair. If tomorrow were an office day, she'd feel compelled to head to bed. But since it was the start of the weekend, she had plans that should prove to be far more entertaining.

Kayleigh opened the metal cabinet that ran from floor to ceiling on one wall—identical to those the BAM Pittsburgh agents stored their gear in—and withdrew her gaming rig. The Virtual Reality goggles shared the basic code with the popular models on the consumer market, but she had done a great deal of modding. Nothing that would inappropriately tip the scales in multiplayer combat, of course, merely much-improved aesthetics to create a more engaging experience.

She slipped the eyewear over her head, cursed as the strap pulled at her hair, then pressed the button to pair them with her comm earbuds. Once she'd attached the motion sensors to her ankles, she flicked her feet to seat them properly. The modified joysticks were the last things she withdrew from the cabinet. Her preparations complete, she turned to face the center of the room and spoke the activation phrase with an appropriate clipped British accent. "Engage."

The virtual representation of the space materialized in her display as the system detected the markers that set the action boundaries and created a pulsing circle in the middle to designate the home location and starting point.

Kayleigh paced the square boundary around the room to remind herself of where it was. To warm her legs up, she threw gentle sidekicks and front kicks and bounced a little with each step. She stalked to the center and twisted her hips, rolled her neck, bent over to touch her toes, and straightened with a predator's grin. "Launch Quake."

The snarling guitars and synthesizers of the Nine Inch Nails soundtrack coursed through her like electricity as the game searched for the private server run by one of her college friends. The arena appeared as her character spawned with a trusty Super Nail Gun in her hands. Most players preferred to get close and mix it up, so she chose the role of a distant sniper. The spikes didn't do much damage individually, but the weapon held a large number of them and boasted an impressive rate of fire.

The countdown appeared for the next round and she glanced down to admire her avatar, which was the result of some significant time investment. She'd contributed to the code that altered the original game to allow what she considered proper resolution on her friend's server, and it showed in her character's looks. Her electronic self wore knee-high boots, shiny black leather pants, and a matching corset with shining steel accents. A half-jacket with mid-length sleeves covered her shoulders and fingerless black leather gloves clasped the weapon's grips.

She had selected Scarlett Johansson's face from the *Ghost in the Shell* film, mainly to taunt everyone she played with as general hatred for that movie was almost universal. Worse, she'd topped it with live-action Harley Quinn's multicolored coif, complete with ponytails. In short, the entire image was calculated to rub salt in the wound of anyone she defeated.

The round began and she paced through the basement play space and turned when required to march toward the center. The setup was customized to her specifications. It had taken some getting used to, but she liked the actual movement that accompanied her gaming over simply pressing a button to walk her character forward. She crouched behind a set of boxes marked with the NIN logo and peeked around it.

There, in the far distance, stood an enemy player. His avatar was modeled after one of the characters in *Street Fighter*, and she smiled in recognition. He was a tech she'd worked with at ARES DC. Everyone who had access to the private server was connected to her professionally or personally within a few degrees of separation, given that she knew the owner and had invited several of her former coworkers to join. She sighted carefully on his feet since the nail gun climbed with recoil and pressed the trigger to stitch him with metal spikes from his toes to the crown of his head. He fell back and out of sight—not dead, but definitely damaged.

An amused voice broke through the music. "Nice shot, Kitana." She had chosen her gamer tag in honor of yet another game she loved, Mortal Kombat. "Aiming for the crotch was a little vicious, though."

She grinned. The trash talking was always fairly tame at the beginning and pure filth by the end. No stories she'd ever heard from active agents could compare to the bravado of anonymous people with fake weapons in a virtual world. "It's not like there was anything valuable there."

Whistles, "oohs," and laughs followed, and her opponent joined the conversation. His voice sounded politely confrontational. "Rude. Just rude. Come a little closer so I can plant my ax in your forehead."

Kayleigh laughed. "No one uses handheld weapons, and that's for a reason. It's like asking to be gunned down from a distance."

He chuckled once. "Character concept."

Those magic words shattered any derision sent his way as everyone's shared past in tabletop role-playing games gave character-related decisions a place of honor, even entirely impractical ones. She was also guilty of it and had once played as a mage prone to losing her voice, which had resulted in no end of hilarity for her and an equal level of frustration for her party.

She ran forward in a crouch to cover farther ahead. Another head was barely visible over the top of a stack of boxes across the large cavern, and she put a trio of nails into it before her opponent realized he was under attack and ducked away. A figure she instantly recognized materialized beside her, carrying a rocket launcher. She grinned and opened a private channel. "Hey, Deke, how's tricks?"

He raised a hand and waggled it from side to side, then pointed ahead. Another enemy lurked at the edge of a half-wall that she no doubt thought was solid but which was vulnerable to piercing damage. *As it so happens, I have an affinity for piercing damage.* She nodded and hefted her SNG. They pulled their triggers together. The nail gun startled the woman out from behind the barrier so the rocket could catch her in the chest and obliterate her. Deacon's laughter was as pure and joyful as always. "I love that shit."

"I know you do, boy toy."

He groaned, and she grinned. *He's so easy.* Once upon a time, he had admitted to a deep passion for Madonna as well as many other questionable things from the eighties, so she'd developed a host of nicknames to remind him of that revelation. He hadn't been around the game for a couple of months, and it lifted her spirits to see him again —right until the moment when another enemy's rocket launcher killed them both because they'd lost focus on the competition.

They respawned in the lobby, which featured virtual floating screens to show the viewpoints of the five remaining combatants. Deke sounded half apologetic and half flirty. "Sorry. I know what a distraction I am to you."

She snorted. "Yeah, that. Sure. So, where have you been, stranger?"

He sighed and frustration replaced the other emotions in his voice. "I'm not thrilled with my position at Skyrift. It seemed like a great offer—top-flight and all that. The best tech, cutting-edge, industry leader in essentially everything they choose to dabble in, plus big money. *Big* big money. It turns out that it's filled with assholes."

Kayleigh broke into a laugh. "And you expected corporate culture to be different? Tell me they don't make you wear a suit."

The sound of his rocket launcher reloading in a threatening manner carried across their channel and drew another snort from her. "No, no suits, although I would look damn fine in one. But...ties." He said the word with derision.

"Seriously?"

He clucked his tongue as if to confirm that he couldn't

believe it either. "Seriously. I guess it's because we have government people and industry bigwigs through all the time. Hell, the other day, there was an elf at my building. In a suit, no less."

"Tie?"

"Of course. He also had one of those pins that showed Earth and Oriceran overlapping, but with more of his home planet." Her avatar nodded along with her own motion. The icons were becoming more and more common. Humans wore ones that displayed more of Earth and Oricerans did the opposite. Anik had called them testicle tags, which had immediately caught on with Tony and earned him a slap from Cara. Kayleigh had only groaned but inside, she found it secretly amusing. *It would be better for everyone if Cara and Anik would quit dancing around each other and just do it.* She pushed the stray thought away and forced her mind to rejoin the current moment. "What are you working on?"

There was a hint of reluctance before he spoke that she put down to a momentary desire to keep secrets on behalf of his company. Fortunately, he abandoned his restraint quickly. "A few different projects, actually. My background task, when I'm not engaged with anything else, is magical surveillance of and improving defenses in our computer system."

She nodded. He was one of the few tech mages she'd ever met who was as good at the coding side as he was the magic side. She couldn't imagine what putting those together would be like, and when he'd attempted to explain, it had sounded too similar to *The Matrix* or *Neuromancer* and she'd made him stop trying. On that particular occasion, she recalled with a smile, the distraction had been accomplished by redirecting the girl he had a crush on over to talk to him. Kayleigh Dornan, uber wing woman. "That doesn't sound too bad."

His avatar grinned. It was modeled after Jet Li, one of his favorite actors, and looked entirely incongruous with the formal black Chinese shirt, the Buddhist prayer beads wound around one wrist, and the huge rocket launcher resting on a shoulder. The face was an amalgam of the actor and the man she knew, which struck her as odd each time she noticed it. "The rest of the time, I'm on two other projects. The first is trying to reverse the flow of anti-magic emitters."

She realized instantly what he was getting at. "To make more magic available at a particular place on Earth, right?"

He nodded. "Exactly. There are many people who would pay to be able to access that kind of thing, apparently."

Criminals, especially. I'd better mention that one to Diana and Bryant. Outwardly, she didn't react. "And the other?"

He looked uncomfortable. "Exoskeletons, armed almost entirely with electric and kinetic stun weapons."

She scowled. "Urban pacification?"

Deacon shrugged, and the frown seemed foreign on his virtual features. "I can't see another reason for that partic-ular tech unless we're moving to a gentler, kinder type of war."

When they'd been in college together, they had bonded over shared concerns about government overreach, which very much included actions against citizens. That philos-ophy lay at the core of her reluctance to deploy weaponized drones for fear they might be hacked and used against innocents. *Or that they might be directed by untrustworthy people, which amounts to the same thing in the end.*

Their characters respawned as the round ended and they marched forward together, falling back into team tactics as if he hadn't been away for months. They took turns being the bait, always carefully covered by the other, and their enemies fell one after the other. As the competition reached the final six, Kayleigh turned to him and shot the rocket launcher with her nail gun. It exploded and kicked them both out of the game. As their avatars returned to existence in the lobby, he whined, "Hey. I was doing good there."

"Quit mewling, baby. Such a baby. Baaaaby." That was another long-standing joke and drew a smidgeon of a smile from the odd-looking avatar face. "Listen, here's the thing. The people I work for are interested in adding someone who can do both magic and tech. I'm sure they were thinking more on the tinkering side rather than the computer side since I'm basically awesome."

He barked a laugh. "And humble. Same as always."

She gave him a one-finger salute. "Anyway, it's a good gig with great people. Of course, it won't pay anything near what you make now but you'll never have to worry that you're doing something that might help the bad guys again."

"What bad guys?"

"*Any* bad guys. It's reasonably safe, although not completely."

His avatar's fingers worked their way through the beads

and pushed them absently them along the string that connected them. "It sounds interesting. Are you offering?"

She thought about it for a second, ran through a mental list of the technicians she'd encountered, and decided that other than Emerson, he was easily the most skilled, even if there was some overlap in their abilities. There might be a more complementary colleague out there, but she doubted she'd find a better one. "Yes. Contingent on the boss's approval."

He went still, and she wondered if working for a corporation had surgically removed his formerly dependable impulsivity. Then, he grinned. "I'm in. Go do your confirmation."

She clapped and spun into a cartwheel to show her enthusiasm. He laughed as her avatar mimicked it. Her ponytails swung and the jacket gaped a little more than she'd intended. *Whoops. Corsets and gravity need each other. Well, it's only pixels. It's not like we're pulling a real-life Janet Jackson here.* She pointed at him. "Get your mind out of the gutter. I'll be in touch."

He spread his arms wide with a laugh. "Yeah, it's my fault you chose that avatar, dressed her like that, and decided she was a gymnast."

"Shut up, you." Kayleigh killed the connection with a broad grin and removed the goggles. She immediately realized from the morning sounds above that she'd lost track of time. Her windows were all covered in blackout fabric so she hadn't noticed the sunrise. In the game, she had paid no attention to the pulses on her wrist that informed her of the passing hours while her attention was focused on play.

She yanked on her ponytail to make sure it was tight

and marched up the stairs. Diana sat at the dining room table and a large mug of coffee steamed at her hand. Her bedhead was impressive and strands of dark hair stuck up in every direction. She swiped on a tablet in front of her, one of the secure models Kayleigh had distributed to everyone so they could access important materials outside the base. Her boss and housemate sounded grumpy as she turned to face her. "What? Shouldn't you be sleeping?"

The tech sat diagonally across from her, lifted the mug, and took a large sip. Diana raised a threatening eyebrow, and she laughed in response. "Oh, please. Everyone knows you're useless in the morning."

Her boss mumbled something under her breath that sounded like, "See if you can be that snarky while on fire."

Kayleigh drummed her fingers on the table until her boss paid attention to her again. Diana sighed. "Is there something I can do for you? Perhaps you're planning to move out?" The hope in her voice was clearly inserted to make fun of her. *Ninety-nine percent sure. Okay, Ninety-three.*

She adopted her most innocent look. "I found us a magic tech. He said yes."

The other woman straightened. "You already offered him the job?"

"Contingent on your approval, of course." Kayleigh shrugged. "But this is my area, so I assume my opinion outweighs that of you Luddite types."

Diana frowned. "I embrace technology wholeheartedly."

She tried and failed to contain her snort. "You wouldn't be able to program your watch without my help."

Her boss leaned back and folded her arms. "Only because you designed it that way."

Kayleigh waved to dismiss the thought. "That's irrelevant to the topic at hand. Tell me you confirm my choice and I'll get it done."

"You know, we do have rules."

"That you personally break on a more or less constant basis, miss run-off-to-another-planet-without-backup-to-save-her-friend."

"Good point. Are you absolutely sure he's right for us?"

She nodded. "Positive."

Diana shrugged and picked her coffee up, drank the rest of it, and set the mug back on the table. "Okay. I trust you. But if he doesn't work out, you'll be the target in the next training run. And you're gonna wear one of the painful suits."

The tech laughed. "Deal."

Her boss pushed the mug toward her. "Now, go refill this, coffee thief, and I won't be forced to write you up for breaking the rules." Kayleigh rolled her eyes but took the mug and headed to the kitchen, unable to contain her anticipatory grin. *If you think I'm hard to deal with, wait until you see what trouble Deacon and I get up to together.*

CHAPTER TWO

The summons from Nylotte had come before she'd even finished her morning coffee and after Kayleigh had already stolen far too much of it. Diana rushed to shower and dress in her typical tactical pants, boots, and concert T-shirt ensemble. *The Clash today. Train in Vain, sure. Way to be subtle, subconscious.* She portaled to the Kemana without delay to obey her teacher's call and stepped from the rift into the basement of the Drow's shop.

The underground training space was in twilight as always, lit by fixtures mounted on wooden columns around the periphery. The floor was stone and seemingly changeable at the Dark Elf's whim. It had been filled with glyphs once before and featureless at the other times she'd been there, including today. She scanned the room and discovered her mentor watching her from a darkened corner. The black sheen on her leather pants and boots glistened under the bright red splash of her long silk shirt. Ebony skin and ivory hair completed the picture.

Diana kept her outward visage calm while inside, she scrambled to plan for a surprise attack, but none occurred. Instead, the woman gestured for her student to move to her customary starting position slightly aside from the center of the circle. As she did so, her teacher stepped into her own place a few paces away and raised an eyebrow in query.

She nodded and took a deep, focusing breath.

Nylotte's voice lacked even the hint of softness or caring. *I don't need effusive praise every time or anything, but a hello would be nice now and again.* "Fire." The woman raised her hands and spread her fingers wide, and the dark nails glittered like poison darts on the ends. A jet of flame emerged from each digit and spiraled together to form a large sustained cone that stretched directly toward the agent's head.

Diana swirled her palms from the inside out—*Wax on, wax off, Daniel-san*—and sparks trailed them to outline two giant circles, each nearly her full height. She crouched behind them and allowed her teacher's fire to collide with her own. The flaming assault pushed against her defenses, but her resistance was sufficient to hold it at bay. As soon as the pressures equalized, the Dark Elf increased the flow to shove her back. She stumbled but managed to keep her footing.

The ordinary sounds of the room were buried under the roar of the fire, and Diana almost lost her focus completely when Nylotte spoke loudly into her mind. "Do not resist the power. Instead, make it your own."

Telepathy. Awesome. Exactly what I need—my teacher knocking around in my brain.

"There's hardly any room and already too many of us in here, anyway," her inner voice interjected and she rolled her eyes.

It's always lovely to hear from you but maybe shut the hell up. I'm trying to concentrate here.

She narrowed her focus onto the place where her defense met the Drow's attack and scrutinized it. The differences between their powers registered almost like different octaves of the same note. Or, she realized, different octaves of the same chord was a more accurate description, as each was far more complex than a single note could ever be.

Her teeth gritted in concentration, she searched for a way to connect that vision to the power that threatened to overwhelm her. Suddenly, she recalled playing Rock Band with Kayleigh and Rath, and the images of the game's streaming symbols leapt into her mind. She saw the trail of her own magic on the left and Nylotte's on the right. The notes were different colors and proceeded at slightly varied rates. *Can it really be that simple?* She imagined drawing the two together, speeding up the one that was lagging, and overlapping them in the center.

When they merged into a unified track, she felt the other woman's magic flow into her as pure energy and was able to redirect it out into her own attack. Diana cycled each pulse to continually steal the woman's strength and force it back at her, which required her to increase the power she committed simply to maintain the stalemate. Success was assured, and she couldn't resist the slight grin that stretched her lips.

Without warning, a series of small hailstones struck her from above. She retreated and redirected one of her flame shields when she realized her teacher had quietly switched the attack to ice and banked the projectiles off the ceiling. In the moment that her shield interposed itself, the fire assault ended and a blast of cold pounded into her chest where she'd unthinkingly left herself uncovered. It hurled her against the rear wall and she dropped onto her knees and elbows.

Diana pushed up with a groan and raised her gaze to her teacher's amused expression. The Drow's perfectly white teeth were irritating. "You're progressing well, protégé. But overconfidence still seems to be a problem."

Overconfidence this, wench. She used a blast of force to launch herself from the ground and landed smoothly on her feet. Without pause, she thrust both hands forward to eject high-speed darts of that same power from each finger at her opponent. Nylotte laughed and made a broad gesture to create a curl of ice between them that shattered and consumed the threat. The woman's voice was full of mockery now. "Your skin seems thinner than usual, as well. Sonic."

The agent's eyes widened as her teacher raised her palms and a shrill buzz built in the room. It seemed to ripple through her flesh and immediately alarmed her at the way it made her bones hurt. She could vividly picture the scene—her body would crack and fall apart under the onslaught and her head would roll to land at her benevolent attacker's feet.

Her teeth gritted, Diana closed her eyes and envisioned the protective bubbles she had used before. A force shield appeared an inch away from her skin to dull the effect of the noise. She sensed the soundwaves probe as they sought crevices through which to return. She pushed to extend the shaped barrier outward and layered another false skin inside. The attack dissipated, and the Drow nodded.

"Very good. You're improving. Now, force."

She called her buckler up, ready to turn the incoming strike back on itself, and realized she'd been played. *I really need to learn not to trust her when we're training.* The magical form she most hated—freaking shadow tentacles—whirled in from both sides. The moment of distraction cost her and dark orbs pummeled her shields and forced her to focus on defending against them.

Before she knew it, she hung upside down in the grasp of the half-transparent appendages. Her teacher's voice spoke in her head again. "And yet, you are not yourself. This is an attack you ordinarily would have caught. Relax." The tentacles guided her gently to the floor, and Nylotte summoned the cushions and the low table that traditionally ended their sessions. Diana was pleased to have the practice truncated, as her mind had skittered around like an insect on the water rather than focusing like a shark in the deep. *Great. Now I'm using her metaphors, too.*

Her teacher stepped out of sight momentarily and returned with a tea service. Diana looked carefully to ensure it wasn't the mental-barrier-lowering drink that heralded a trip inside her mind, but this seemed to be a different variety. She took it as a sign that apparently, the Drow had already spent enough time in there to be satisfied.

Nylotte lowered herself to sit in the lotus position on the cushion, then tucked her white hair behind each of her pointed ears. She poured and extended the two cups. Diana accepted the one on the right, as she always did, and they sipped together. It was green tea of some kind, but far more flavorful and vibrant than any she'd ever tasted. Her pleasure must've shown on her face because her teacher grinned.

"It's from the forest that surrounds the bunker we invaded." Diana had a moment of fear that her mentor quickly assuaged. "It's perfectly safe. I am thoroughly acquainted with the various plants that can cause damage, and this does not. In fact, it is a stimulant for both physical power and magical power. You should feel restored after drinking it. Well, somewhat anyway." The woman took another sip, then set the delicate cup on the tray in front of her and rotated it until its position met her expectations. She raised her gaze to Diana's. "So, what is distracting you today? Hopefully not that boyfriend of yours."

She didn't choke on her tea, but only because she'd come to expect almost anything to emerge from the other woman's mouth. "Quit rummaging around in my mind."

Her teacher's laugh was short but enthusiastic. "No rummaging was required. It's right there at the edge of your thoughts. They practically shout about him to anyone with the ability to hear."

She scowled. "Whatever. No, not him. Well, not only him."

"Explain."

Diana sighed. "A friend of ours—technically, our boss— is in the hospital in a coma. The doctors have no confidence that he will emerge from it, so we're stuck waiting."

"One of your least favorite things."

"Admittedly. I would prefer to have everything resolved and in its proper place. Who wouldn't?" She shrugged.

The Drow nodded. "Of course, you refer to the loss of the armor and its use against you."

"Naturally."

"That is worth worrying about but not worth obsessing over until there's something you can do about it."

She laughed, but there was no humor in it. "And when will that be? The next time the mysterious unknown villain steps in to turn our victory into defeat?"

Nylotte scowled. "Don't be dramatic. It was a stalemate, at best. However, I hear the question you are really asking. Yes, there is an action we can take. We can seek Rhazdon's Vengeance."

Diana remembered the woman's description of the sword, Fury, and the daggers, Angel and Demon, all artifacts. "I wouldn't begin to know how."

The Drow grinned. "Fortunately for you, I would and do. The trail begins at Nehlan's bunker, and we shall follow it from there."

"It would be good to have a potent weapon against Rhazdon's defense."

She chuckled. "Be careful what you wish for, my student who forgets that artifacts have a will and purpose of their own. If yours is not in line with theirs, it can provoke a battle far more dangerous than any physical opponent."

Diana shrugged. "There's no sense in worrying about it until we get there, right? Maybe the weapons want nothing more than to carve up the enemy."

Nylotte lifted the teapot and refilled their cups. The

lack of response didn't make her feel any better about the notion of searching for the artifacts, so she changed the subject. "When you whispered in my mind today, it reminded me of something. Last time I was in DC, I visited my old dojo. While I was sparring, I heard a whisper that suggested specific magical counterattacks at each moment."

Her teacher rewarded her with a smile. "That is exactly as it should be. You continue to synchronize with the power inside you. As the connection grows, so will your awareness of it and its awareness of what you are doing. In this case, it recognized that you were training and offered options. If you had been in a battle, it would have manifested as instinct rather than choice."

Diana's eyes widened. "You speak of magic as if it is separate, somehow. Or has a personality of its own."

The Dark Elf shrugged and finished the tea in her cup before she repeated the process of setting it down and positioning it perfectly. "Is that so unusual? You are already the sum of many parts. Your professional voice and instincts, your personal voice and instincts, and your romantic voice and instincts. What are they all if not competing voices that clamor for your attention? Some are simply so familiar that you no longer perceive them as separate. Someday, perhaps, you will bring them all into synthesis. Not many do."

Diana snorted. "Of course you have, O wise one."

Her teacher raised an eyebrow. "No, actually. The reluctance to kill those who annoy me is still a voice I must fight against almost constantly *these days*." Diana had no doubt that she caused the emphasis on her teacher's final words.

Before she could reply, the woman changed the subject completely. "I have spoken to Kienka. It seems your paramour has visited her recently. She says he appears sad, doubtless pining for the love he misses. I can only assume that's you."

She groaned. "So, is that what humans are to you? Something for amusement?"

Nylotte laughed. "No more so than most Oricerans. The Drow have long made a practice of observing the actions of others, and it is true. Your kind does provide a wealth of distraction."

Huh. Arrogant much? "It's easy to forget you have a past beyond your time here in the Kemana and apart from teaching magic and selling objects of power."

The woman stood and gestured for her to rise. "It would be good for you to keep that in the forefront of your mind, especially should you decide to pursue Rhazdon's Vengeance. Don't overlook the fact that I was acquainted with Nehlan as well. If you assume you know the truth of me, you open yourself up to surprise and disappointment."

Point taken, but you're not nearly as enigmatic as you think you are, sister. "Gotcha. Do I get an energy potion for the road?"

A flat stare met the request. "Your level of effort doesn't deserve one. Perhaps next time, you'll train at an intensity worthy of reward."

"Ouch." Diana stepped quickly through the portal Nylotte had created so she would have the last word and re-materialized in the corner of her bedroom always kept vacant for that purpose. She smirked, pleased with herself, right up until the moment her teacher whispered in her head.

"Maybe consider working on your mental defenses, as well, protégé. You don't want random people...what was it, rummaging around in your thoughts."

She fell back onto her bed with a deep sigh. *If the bad guys aren't the death of me, Nylotte will be.*

The Drow's laughter echoed in her skull for several seconds before it faded.

CHAPTER THREE

Bryant squinted against the sparkling sun as he strode toward the entrance to the Capitol Building. He masqueraded as a lobbyist today, complete with false identification that claimed to represent the National Corn Growers' Association. One of the DC techs had whipped it up and delivered it with a laugh. The ID badge actually had cornstalks on either side. He had been doubtful when he saw it. "Is this a real thing?"

The tech had laughed and nodded solemnly. "It very well might be."

He released a long sigh at the memory and tugged on his cuffs to ensure that they extended correctly below the hem of his gray pinstripe suit. A crisp white shirt and dark-blue tie rendered him anonymous among the staffers and politicos who dashed with great gravitas from place to place outside the grand structure. He passed through security without an issue and the metal detector didn't object to either his ARES watch or the charm necklace he wore. It also missed the collapsible wand tucked along his forearm, carefully hidden from view but always ready for a quick release triggered by the sharp twist of his arm in a particular direction. It had taken some time to procure a replacement, despite Diana's continued delivery of captured wands to him. Now, her efforts were more a gesture of affection than a practical action.

The thought of her put a smile on his face. He strode ahead like he owned the place and relied on the map projected in his glasses to get him to where he needed to be. His newly upgraded timepiece had an increased sensor ability that manifested in ghostly images in various shades of orange to represent the people around him based on the heat they generated. He made the twists and turns into the area of the building populated with various conference rooms and finally reached the secure one they always used. Today, a miracle had occurred in the form of a carafe of coffee on the serving table. He extended the watch to examine it, identified no chemical scents other than what was expected, and deemed the brew safe to drink. After the attacks that destroyed his apartment and landed Taggart in the hospital, the acting Special Agent in Charge of ARES took no chances.

He sat at the table and sipped from his cup for only a moment before he rose again to extend a hand to Senator Aaron Finley when he entered the room. Bryant was relieved when the man closed the door behind him, which signaled a solo meeting rather than one that would include the far more annoying members of the oversight committee.

The senator was in a navy power suit with a white shirt and a bright red tie. He retrieved his own heavy mug of coffee and sat across from Bryant. "I'm afraid I don't have much time for chitchat. I have a lobbyist coming to see me."

"What does he want?"

"She, actually, and she's the lead champion for a defense contractor we're using for some special work. So, half-salesperson, half-lobbyist, would be more accurate I guess."

Bryant nodded. "But in any case, too important to give anything less than full attention to."

"Exactly." The man's intense gaze met his. "So, we have a couple of things to talk about. First, the Cube is done."

"I assumed that. Good choice."

Finley laughed. "It's the only possible option, really. First, secrecy failed, then the actual physical defenses failed. I imagine it's back to the drawing board on that one."

"In the meantime?"

The other man took a sip of his coffee and winced at the hot liquid's burn. "Anyone we think we can handle goes to Ultramax, with damn anti-magic emitters strapped to them if we feel the need. Everyone else goes off to Trevilsom."

He shook his head. "Harsh."

"But necessary."

"You'll get no argument from me. What about Warden Murphy?"

Finley gave a small smile. "Classified. But she'll have responsibilities commensurate with her skills."

"Those are some hefty responsibilities."

The smile became a wide grin. "That woman has some impressive skills."

Bryant frowned. "Speaking of impressive women, I have a deep lack of faith in Senator Cyphret. I don't believe she wishes us well."

Finley had already shaken his head before he had finished the observation. "I have the same read on her, and on Tomassi and Clarke, whom you haven't had the distinct displeasure of meeting yet."

"You are correct. So, three clearly against?"

He nodded. "Somers definitely for, and the last one, Ekkles is something a wildcard. Every time I think I understand her, she makes a perfectly logical argument that causes me to realize everything I've assumed is wrong."

Bryant laughed. "Diana can do that, too. It's annoying, isn't it?"

"How is she doing?"

"Personally? As you would expect, given Taggart's hospitalization and the constant danger that surrounds her. Professionally, she's assembled a kick-ass team that works really well together. She was undeniably the right choice for the gig."

"Speaking of right choices, we need to talk about Taggart."

The acting Agent in Charge shook his head. "We really don't."

The look of sympathy on Finley's face disarmed him as the man said softly "Yes, we really do." He waited, and when his companion nodded he continued. "Because, while we all want Carson to get up out of that bed and take the leadership role again, there's no guarantee he will be able to—or even that he'll want to."

A laugh escaped him. "What'll he do—retire?"

Finley shrugged. "There's no way to know, and that's the point. Smart organizations have backup plans."

"And backup plans for their backup plans," Bryant finished, one of Taggart's favorite expressions. *Dammit. I hate this.* "Okay, Senator, what's the plan?" *Maybe it'll be Murphy. That would be good.*

"You're the plan."

He blinked and it took a moment before his sputtering brain caught up to reality. "Come again?"

Finley laughed and tapped his knuckles on the table with each word. "You. Are. The. Plan." He leaned back in his chair and steepled his fingers. "Taggart was quite clear about what should happen in the event that he could no longer lead. The list is a short one, and you're the first name on it."

"Okay. Shit. I really don't want to do that."

He laughed again. "I'm sure he cared about your wishes in the matter about as much as I do. You are needed."

Bryant chuckled with disbelief. "You sound like him, do you know that?"

The senator nodded. "I have an unlimited amount of respect for the man. So when he says it has to be you, it has to be you."

He sighed. "Fine. We need to find someone else to work on the expansion plans, then..." He fell silent when he realized the other man was shaking his head. "We don't?"

Finley leaned forward again and placed his palms flat on the table. "Bryant, what I have to tell you cannot go beyond this room. Not even to your most trusted people."

"Okay."

"Swear it."

Bryant's eyes widened involuntarily. "Okay, I swear. I'll share it with no one."

The other man sighed. "We are in a moment of existential crisis for ARES. Half the oversight committee is very vocal about wanting it shut down. The rest of us argue against that, but where the chips will fall is still unknown. In the meantime, you need to stabilize what we have so we don't lose any more. We have to be ready, in case."

A chill of dread swept through him and turned the warm coffee in his stomach to sharp, frozen spikes. "In case what?"

Finley's voice was grave. "I've shared all you can know right now. That's both me and Taggart talking." The senator rose and stuck a hand out. He stumbled up a moment later, still completely off balance from the conversation, and shook it. The other man looked him directly in the eye. "This won't be easy. I won't lie. It may be the hardest thing either of us has ever faced. But remember, you're not alone. And none of us will give up while there's an ounce of life left."

He nodded. "Senator."

Finley gave him a half-smile. "Special Agent."

The trip back to the office was uneventful, and Bryant sat behind Taggart's desk, burdened by the weight and the unreality of trying to step into his shoes. He was still in the chair a half-hour later, staring off into space while he tried to decide what task to start on first, when he was interrupted by a junior agent. The woman walked in quietly, set a wrapped parcel on the table in front of him, and departed without a word. He saw that it had been delivered by Andercarr and his name was printed on the address label.

He waved his watch over it although he knew they would've done a full examination already anyway. Naturally, he found nothing. He retrieved the knife Taggart kept in a drawer—bigger than a letter opener but smaller than a Bowie—and sliced the padded, tear-resistant sleeve open. A small cube clattered onto the desk, wrapped in black printed paper. He recognized the folding method of the ornamental covering, one that Taggart had shown him long before when the older man revealed his love of origami. It was as verifiable a signature as a DNA test, and his chest tightened at the sight. He poked it at the right place, and the material unfolded to reveal a solid, intricately carved wood-and-metal cube.

What the hell? Bryant turned it over and rolled the object in his hands. *Maybe it's a puzzle box?* He held it up to the light and examined it from all angles but couldn't make sense of it until he saw the tiny image in the corner. It was an ancient symbol meaning ghost or spirit. He slid a finger up his sleeve to touch his wand tip and whispered an incantation. The scent of cinnamon wafted up from the object, his personal signifier of the presence of magic. "Weirder and weirder. Where in the world would Taggart get a magic box, and why would he send it to me?" He only realized he was speaking out loud when a passerby stuck his head through the door and asked him to repeat himself.

He waved the man away, grabbed his messenger bag, and placed the cube carefully inside. His expression thoughtful, he snatched his phone up and dialed a number he had committed to memory. "Kienka, it's Bryant. I need a secure place."

———————

A twenty-minute car ride later, Bryant pulled the standard-issue government sedan into a blessedly free space in a shopping area east of the city proper. He jogged toward the antique shop, barely able to keep himself from running. He'd spent the drive considering all the things the box might portend, and curiosity was eating him alive.

The entrance opened as he reached it and the Drow ushered him into a small room at the back. Before leaving, she whispered, "You owe me," and he nodded in acknowledgment. She closed the door behind her, and he sensed the protective wards snap into place around it. Kienka could provide almost any magical item or service one could desire, including a protected space in which to do magic unwatched by prying eyes of either physical or arcane varieties.

He set the box on a tall table positioned in the center of several metal rings. He did not speak the words to activate them, knowing he didn't need that level of warding and resistant to putting himself further in the Dark Elf's debt. The seal around the room would be sufficient. Bryant twitched his arm in a very particular way, and the base of his wand slid into his waiting palm. He gripped it and flicked it out to full extension, then waved it over the cube and spoke in the language of the symbol on the side, imbuing the word with a magical demand that it activate. A dim blue light emerged from the top in an expanding cone and filled with a mist that coalesced into Taggart's features.

The voice he'd despaired of ever hearing again came from the small figure. "Bryant, if you see this, then I am either dead or missing."

Bryant chuckled. "Or incapacitated. You forgot that one, boss." He dashed away the tear that threatened at the corner of his eye. *You're talking to a magical cube. You've lost it completely.*

The image nodded. "Acknowledged. Or incapacitated." Bryant blinked, confused. "For some time, I have created this simulacrum and worked with our magic techs to fill it with my knowledge and ideas. It's certainly not me"—his familiar laugh echoed out of the tiny projection—"but it is a reasonable facsimile. Now, before we can continue, you must tell me the nickname Diana gave you."

He groaned but realized that few people who might get their hands on the box would know him well enough to answer that particular question. "Bryant Classified."

The figure nodded and smiled. "Very good. I presume that since we did not have an orderly transition of power from me to you, that something is amiss. Thus, it is essential you learn about the organization's ace in the hole. Project Adonis is ARES' emergency fallback plan."

CHAPTER FOUR

Once Diana had returned from her training session, showered again, and dressed, it was already mid-afternoon. The transit to headquarters, even aided by the magical subway, cost her more time, and she finally arrived at work only a couple of hours before her planned departure for the group dinner that evening. She'd tried to arrange at least one social outing a week for her team, and they'd missed the last due to fallout from the attack on the Cube. As a result, it was doubly important she be clear-headed and functional tonight. *Too bad Nylotte doesn't care about that kind of thing.* She snorted at her own whining and took the elevator to the fifth floor.

Cara awaited her in the conference room and had already poured her a cup of coffee. She scooped it up from the table and walked to stand beside her and gaze out over the water. The other woman sipped from her mug. "How goes it, boss?"

Diana thought her second-in-command had not quite been herself lately and was trapped in the indecision between feeling like she should push but not wanting to pry. Once again, she concluded that the situation hadn't reached a level that required intervention, so she relegated it to the box in her mind labeled "waiting." She sighed. "I had a call from Bryant before I came in."

"Does he miss you?" The woman's voice was teasing, and she continued to be amazed at how quickly the word of her burgeoning relationship with Bryant had spread since neither of them had officially told anyone about it.

"Really, who wouldn't?" She paused for the responding laugh before she continued. "He's worried, so we probably need to be, too." Her companion took a slow sip of her coffee, which effectively masked any reaction, and continued to keep her face turned toward the water. Her profile offered no indication of the thoughts hiding in her head. "He says there's some weird stuff going on within the oversight committee and that we're in stabilizing mode. In effect, we're no longer expanding."

"So it's only us, DC, Buffalo, and Hartford?"

She paused for a few fortifying sips of the bitter brew in her cup. "He didn't specify, but I would assume Buffalo is out of the mix. The Remembrance wiped them out, so it would have to start from scratch, which doesn't quite match the whole stabilization theme."

Cara turned and leaned her shoulder against the window to face her squarely. "And?"

Diana sighed. "And, apparently, Taggart left a message for Bryant giving instructions for some kind of worst-case scenario response."

"Shit. That's heavy."

"Plus, I don't think he's told me the whole story. Which,

legitimately, he probably can't since he's the head honcho at the moment."

The other woman chuckled softly. "Perhaps you need lessons in pillow talk, boss."

She grinned and raised an eyebrow. "If there's any energy left for talking, maybe you're doing it wrong."

That inspired a real laugh from Cara, and the sound soothed something inside her. "So, I have a line on our next hire."

Diana gestured toward the table and moved over to fall into one of the chairs. "Hopefully, you haven't made them an offer yet."

The other woman gazed at her with a quizzical expression. "Of course not."

It's good to know someone still cares about existing procedures. She waved a hand and dismissed that part of the conversation. "Tell me."

Her second-in-command took her seat and tapped her watch, and an instant later, Diana's vibrated as the file was transferred. She paged through the pictures while the other woman spoke. "Henry Stills. Air Force. His career so far has had an unusual trajectory. He flew fighters, flew helicopters, and oversaw and performed maintenance on both. Plus, he's sharp with weapons and has black belts in a couple of different martial arts."

He was handsome and built like a truck. Diana thought he might push the size limit of some fighter planes. *Maybe that's why he flies choppers, too.* "That's quite a resume. What does he do in his spare time?"

Cara gestured toward her. "Keep paging through and you'll see. He builds and races cars for fun."

Diana found the images and shook her head. "He is like an advertisement for maleness from the nineteen-seventies."

"Right?"

"So why's he interested in moving on?"

Her companion looked momentarily uncomfortable. "I put Quinn on the task of finding a few candidates, and she pried a little deeper than I expected or intended. There is some romantic stuff that's not quite perfect and some personality conflicts inside his unit that might make him receptive to a change."

She raised a hand palm up. "That's enough info for me, thanks." She narrowed her eyes. "And don't think I don't see what you're doing here."

A mischievously innocent expression dawned on Cara's face. "Why, whatever do you mean?"

"Hiring someone who's an accomplished fighter *and* driver."

The woman let the facade drop with a laugh. "Eventually, boss, you know we'll need to be more mobile. I'm merely planning wisely for that future."

Diana sighed. "Yeah, sure. Anything else from your end?" Cara shook her head. "Okay, it's beyond time that we quit waiting around for these people to screw with us and started screwing with them instead."

"Which people?"

She spread her hands wide as if to indicate the entire world. "Any scumbag who thinks they can use their own magic or purchased magic to make trouble in our city. So, Sloan's group, the jerks above them, and whoever the bastard in the armor was."

Cara held up a trio of fingers. "Only three?"

"Oh, and the oversight committee. I'm not sure what Bryant's up to with them, but we should put some effort into finding out what we can about them as well."

Her second nodded, looked at her watch, and stood. "It's time to make the trek across the river. Are we driving or walking?"

Diana pushed herself to her feet with a groan. "Walking. Staying motionless hurts."

"The Drow bitch?"

"Nylotte, yes."

Her companions scowled. "I hope you don't invest too much trust in her."

She cocked her head to the side in a query. "Is your problem that she's a Dark Elf? I know there's some animosity between our kind and their kind." Her teacher had outed Cara as an elf, and Diana had learned of her own Elven lineage from her mother long before.

"Neither. She's an arrogant wench who's overdue for a good smack-down, that's all."

Diana laughed. "Well, when you put it that way, I'm not sure I can argue."

"Damn straight. Let's get moving. It wouldn't do for the most powerful person on the team to show up any more than fashionably late. Or you, for that matter."

She put a hand over her heart. "Ouch."

They were still laughing and making verbal jabs at one another when they finished the walk across the bridge to the entertainment complex on the opposite shore. Tonight's venue was a Brazilian steakhouse, complete with servers who masqueraded as gauchos and offered various meats on lethal-looking skewers. The restaurant was a single giant open space with a side dish buffet in the middle. They'd made special arrangements to have a reasonably quiet corner to themselves with an adequate number of tables pushed together to seat the entire team. Sloan had made one of his rare appearances—in disguise, of course—and there was an unfamiliar face seated next to Kayleigh. The tech beamed at something the newcomer had said.

He was young-looking, clean-shaven, and had long, wavy dark hair pulled back on the center of his head into what looked like a ponytail. The sides were buzzed short with only enough stubble left to show it was a preference rather than nature. His features were generally soft, but his chin was solid and his cheekbones sharp.

Damn. I can see why Kayleigh likes him. Of course, the fact that he looks like a sixteen-year-old would be a problem for me. By the way the tech laughed at his jokes, Diana assumed it probably wasn't a problem for her. *There should be regulations against hiring your own potential partners.* Then she thought about the spark that had always existed between her and Bryant and decided that perhaps she should simply keep her mouth shut. Her mental voice applauded the decision.

"Always a good choice where you're concerned."

And, as always, shut up, you.

She made a circuit of the table before she sat, greeted each member of her team, and made some kind of physical contact—a hand on the shoulder, a fist bump, and in Anik's case, a solid punch to the upper arm. The others laughed at the man's complaint as she finished and held her hand out to the newcomer. "Diana Sheen."

He stood, natural grace appearing where her instincts suggested gangling discomfort might occur. Her mental voice intruded.

"He's not actually sixteen, you know."

She sighed inwardly. *Shut up, or I'll stun myself into unconsciousness so I don't have to listen to you anymore.* The voice's mocking laughter faded in time for her to hear his name.

"Deacon Addams."

"Welcome aboard."

He nodded eagerly. "I'm beyond happy to be here." Kayleigh had explained his situation and the reasons she thought he'd be a good fit, and Diana was sympathetic.

"Have you met everyone?"

"More or less. I'm still working on names."

She laughed. "Wait until you try to add the call signs. That's when it gets really confusing."

"He'll be Warlock," Kayleigh said quickly. There was neither doubt nor question in her tone. He looked surprised but pleased. Diana merely shook her head. "Acknowledged, Supreme Commander Glam." More laughter followed as she moved to the only open chair remaining—at the head of the table with Cara on her left and Anik on her right. "Everyone, flip your coaster things over to the green side so we can get some food here. Anik, find our server and pick up a few bottles of wine. I trust you to choose good ones, unlike the rest of these people."

The demolitions expert grinned. "The mark of an excellent leader is knowing the capabilities of her team. I'll be back."

They ate and laughed and ate a little more. Rath, who had arrived with Kayleigh and Deacon and sat near them, tried each offering carefully and provided Diana with a surreptitious thumbs-up or thumbs-down. That particular game had become a restaurant staple, and she enjoyed it more than she would admit to anyone else. She burst into laughter as he tried a piece of Parmesan chicken and made a terrible face to go with a double-thumbs-down. She rose under the guise of going to the buffet and bent to whisper in his ear as she passed. "Seriously, why even bother to offer chicken at a place with this much delicious steak?"

"Exactly. Mooooo."

His impersonation was right on the money, and she walked away laughing.

As they neared the meal's end and the more ambitious among them ordered desserts, she poured another half-glass of wine and leaned back, inordinately pleased with the people around her. Deacon recovered from a fit of laughter and raised his hands. "Okay, okay. I think it's important that all of you know who Kayleigh truly is, rather than the false impression she's apparently given you."

The tech elbowed him in the ribs, but he simply moved out of reach with another laugh and leaned on the table. "When we were in college, our football team had a big rivalry with the other team in the state. Details are unimportant. What is important is that a tradition of pranking the other school was an all-important feature of our student experience. So, it was time for the big game, and Kayleigh here had an idea."

She reached a hand out to cover his mouth but he avoided it and lurched out of his chair to stand on the opposite side of Rath from her. "You'll protect me, right, buddy?"

The troll turned to Kayleigh and gave her a ferocious growl and the whole table collapsed into laughter. When it subsided, Deacon continued. "Anyway, she decided that since their mascot was a ram, it would be fun to create a half-sized robot version. Well, it was a fairly innocuous idea at first, but after the third night in a row without sleep, the party got a little loopy."

He paused with the instincts of a showman to allow the suspense to build. He was already laughing and had to force out the final words. "When the other team came out for their opening ceremony, a life-sized robot ram with huge spiral horns ran out of the stands. It seems that someone—and to this day no one has taken credit, but *someone...*"

Deacon stared directly at Kayleigh, who refused to meet his eyes. "Someone had programmed it to charge anyone in the opposing school's colors. It dashed onto the field and did exactly that. They scattered hilariously. The programming kept them safe and sent the ram after a new target if it got too close, but of course, they didn't know that. Our last sight of the robot was as it chased the poor person inside the other team's mascot costume out of the stadium."

The table exploded into laughter again. Kayleigh tried to make arguments in her own defense, but no one had any interest and each attempt made them laugh more. Finally, when it subsided, Diana stepped outside, followed in short order by Cara and Anik. Her second-in-command gave her a grin. "That was a fun night with fun people."

Diana nodded. "The funnest, and the best."

"We're heading over to the hotel bar for a drink. Do you want to join us?"

She shook her head. "I need a walk to clear my head. You all have one for me." *Enjoy it while you can. I'm sure someone will be along to mess it up soon.*

CHAPTER FIVE

Marcus had enjoyed every moment of his first week of freedom since his liberation from the Cube. He mourned the loss of his boss and friend in his own way by submerging himself in a variety of illicit pleasures. He'd been a little untethered and had lost focus on and connection to the world around him when Vincente's lawyer appeared unexpectedly. She'd caught him as he exited his new apartment headed for yet another night of self-abuse, identified herself, and offered to give him a ride to wherever he was going.

During the cross-town trip to his favorite gentlemen's club, she'd revealed that the promise his erstwhile employer had made while they were in prison together was still valid. The man had set everything in motion to provide him with a replacement for his lost limb. That realization—the validation of his trust and the potential to be whole again—had struck him like a bucket of ice over the head. He'd returned immediately to his apartment to detox aggressively in preparation. After days of cleansing, the time had arrived.

His new lieutenant, Murray, had appeared at the appointed moment to pick him up. The man stood outside on the street and held the rear door of the Escalade open for him. His underling was dressed better than he remembered from before in a tailored black suit and matching fitted shirt and tie. The ensemble served to minimize his bulk, and the precision of the cut provided an air of intelligence and competence that he'd formerly lacked. *Either his skills, his wardrobe, or both improved while I was away.*

He nodded as he climbed in, and Mur closed the door behind him. He drove in silence to a recently constructed office park along the river occupied by a number of high-tech firms, a product of the city's ongoing courtship of the science and technology sectors. In the basement of one of the new buildings was a research laboratory funded by a consortium of local universities. What the funders didn't know was that the theoretical developments under investigation had already reached practical application. The researchers had simply chosen to employ them for their own benefit before they revealed their success.

When the elevator opened on the lowest floor, the lobby resembled every hospital Marcus had ever seen. The woman behind the reception desk stood and smoothed her slightly more elegant than professional red dress before she walked around to extend a hand and greet him with a sharp smile. Her mid-height heels matched the outfit perfectly, and her voice held the sultry edge he expected to hear. "Welcome, sir. Before we proceed further, I need to provide some ground rules. No names will be used and no records will be kept. All financial arrangements have already been taken care of. This man has been permitted to accompany you as an assurance of your safety. We expect that after the procedure is finished and you depart, we can rely on both of you for complete discretion. Any failure in that regard would be met with a rapid and decisive response."

Both men nodded. The lawyer had warned him it would be this way and that he should take their warnings seriously.

The woman smiled more broadly and tilted her head toward the door leading into the facility. Her short, straight blonde hair bobbed slightly. On a less beautiful person, the cut might've looked masculine. On her, it merely emphasized the perfection of her features. Marcus wondered for a moment where the organization at the center of all this had found her, then decided that given the lawyer's level of gravitas, the receptionist was very likely more than she seemed. Which, in this place, would make sense.

They left the lobby and its guardian behind and walked down a long corridor before they were intercepted by a trio of people in dark suits—two women and a man. The oldest member of the group spoke first, her curly gray hair and no-nonsense voice a harsh contrast to the woman in scarlet who'd greeted them in the outer room. "Sir, welcome. It is time for your assistant to depart."

Marcus gave him a nod, and Murray left with a wave. She continued, "You'll be here for a week, assuming normal response to the operation. The procedure itself will take most of a day, and you'll spend the following one in a medical coma. After that, we'll wake you and begin the processes of integration and training."

Marcus smiled in anticipation. *It's so Close.* "What are the risks?"

The man chuckled. There was an Ivy League look about him that matched the arrogance in his tone. "Considerable. However, your benefactor believed them within the range of tolerance, and rest assured, we are the best of the best." The woman beside him nodded. She appeared to have the same background. He noted that her nails were clipped short, one of the hallmarks of a practicing surgeon. *Hopefully more accomplishing than practicing.* Her voice was smooth and haughty. "You will be in the most skillful of hands, sir. You need not worry."

There's not much point in worrying unless I prefer to pass up this opportunity. If anything goes wrong, I surely won't wake up to find out about it. He grinned. "I'm all in. Let's do this thing."

He had woken from the coma feeling rested and energetic, which was unexpected. The nurse, who seemed to have no other charge except him, had explained it was due to the drug mixture they employed, which he would need to continue to take for the rest of his life. He'd had a moment of concern at being beholden to the organization, but the arm that rested, still inert, at his side had banished it instantly. It was a high-tech marvel of shiny metal that immediately brought the Terminator to mind. He'd imagined the hand turning to him and pantomiming a mouth. "I *said* I'd be back," which sent him off into gales of laughter. The realization that part of his jubilation was probably chemical didn't faze him. *I could get used to this.* The nurse, a man who looked like he spent every one of his off hours pumping iron, grinned. "It feels great, right?"

Marcus nodded.

"All I know is it's part science, part magic, and all good."

The days since then had followed an unchanging routine. Ten hours of training each day, divided into three sessions. Ten hours of sleeping in one solid block, and the drugs took all choice in the matter away. The rest was divided between relaxing, eating, and other mundane tasks. Each session with the doctors left him craving the next as his new limb became more and more functional.

Finally, though, it was time for his last three hours of practice and imminent departure thereafter. The nurse escorted him into the training room, which featured a wide array of devices, large and small, most of which he still had no idea of their purpose. He sat in the form-fitting white plastic and vinyl chair in the center and they ran through the basic battery of tests and asked him to perform certain tasks with his new appendage. The mental connections had been sluggish at first, the arm's response frustratingly languid, but through practice and the doctors' constant reassurance that it was an ordinary part of the process, he'd gained full control of the limb.

He could use it for all the normal things one might use an arm for with no more difficulty than the one he was born with. The new appendage was stronger and faster, limited only by what his skeletal structure and human musculature were able to support. They'd explained that it would be possible to essentially rebuild him if he so desired, but he'd seen Wolverine movies too many times to want that level of pain and invasiveness.

The arm itself was a technological marvel. In addition to the normal functions—which would've been Nobel-worthy on their own—the doctors had packed an abundance of surprises inside. He was most pleased with the ability of the hand to extend and compress into a blade able to both slice and stab. There were three places in the limb designed to hold modular weapons and choosing from among the many options had been exceedingly difficult. They'd assured him that he could swap them out if they failed to fully satisfy. The metal itself had electronic camouflage that would allow it to pass as skin by sight if he desired. The doctors had offered to sheath it in something very like regular flesh, but he was done with regular *anything*. This was a new beginning, and he intended to make the most of it.

Before his departure, he'd requested a list of other available procedures and had already prioritized potential augmentations once he wrangled the money.

Marcus had returned everyone's fond wishes with matching ones of his own, thrown a broad grin and a wink to the blonde at the desk, and strode outside to find Mur at the car in the company of another man. He advanced with his right hand extended, ready to transform his other limb and stab it through the newcomer's throat if he sensed a hint of menace. The man only nodded, more deeply than necessary as a show of respect, and stammered, "Tommy. I'm Tommy. Ketchum. Tommy Ketchum."

He released the man's grasp and his worries. Murray

had mentioned him previously as a trustworthy soldier. He climbed into the car, and Mur took the driver's position with Sloan in the passenger's seat beside him. His lieutenant twisted to face him. "Boss, Sarah has asked for you. We told her when you'd be out, as you instructed, and she'd like you to come to the warehouse as soon as you can."

Marcus grinned when he imagined the woman's voice as she gave what were likely the real instructions. *Tell him to report straight here—immediately.* He nodded agreement, and they drove the short distance in silence. He was impressed that the third man in the car didn't feel the need to fill the time with empty chatter. Being a blabbermouth was a telltale sign of insecurity, and he wanted no such nonsense around him anymore. Where once he had enjoyed exploiting his underlings' weaknesses and pitted them against each other as a way to confirm his own superiority, his own confidence was now unshakable. At least where humans were concerned.

They pulled into the gravel lot outside the warehouse, and he saw it with unfamiliar eyes. Dilapidated, broken windows stretched high above on the dirty building. It didn't match what he thought of as the new him, but perhaps that would be an effective disguise. He led the way in, Murray a step behind on his right, Sloan two steps behind on his left. His stint in prison had given him the opportunity to focus on stretching his senses, on trying to discern what was happening around him, and he'd come out more accomplished in that area than before he'd gone in. They circulated among the non-magicals and he greeted those he knew and was introduced to others by his escorts. He then made the bold move to cross to the magical side of the room to exchange quiet words with those he'd met before. As he made the rounds, he noted how many of his acquaintances were missing and seemingly replaced by newcomers.

When they'd completed their circuit, Murray led him to the base of the stairs leading to the office. "She'll want you up there." The man turned so his mouth couldn't be seen by anyone in the room except Marcus, and his voice dropped to a whisper. "She's not who you remember, boss. While you were in prison, she was in a nightmare of some kind. I don't know what it was, but she came out different. Crazy. Like, certifiably insane crazy."

He reached out and let his new arm—notably heavier than its former version—land on the man's shoulder. Mur's eyes widened, and he nodded. "She's not the only one who's changed, my friend. Have faith."

The door banged open at the top of the stairs, and he turned and climbed them with a smile. *Nothing will be like it was, and that's a very good thing. For me and mine, at least.*

CHAPTER SIX

S arah watched the former convict climb the stairs and fought to keep the sneer off her face. *His people see him as a hero, rather than a man who was defeated and humiliated. Fools, all of them.* He gave her a nod as he crossed the threshold. "Sarah." His words lacked respect, as did his posture. She considered the temptation to pull her wand and burn him to ash, but two unknowns stopped her. First, she hadn't been able to pierce the veil of secrecy around the hospital that had restored his arm. The questions about that were plentiful and concerning.

Second, and far more importantly, Dreven had insisted she make Marcus part of the next magical meeting, and the window to contact her supposed master was closing rapidly. She stared at the thorn in her side as he slouched across the room and fell into the visitor's chair with a fond laugh. "Vincente could be about to walk through the door, the way this all feels."

She bestowed a thin smile upon him. *Idiot. He's dead. Get used to it.* "Indeed. But things change, even when their outward trappings do not." She moved to the seat on the opposite side of the desk and lowered herself into it. Spinning the chair so he couldn't watch her, she unclasped the locket around her neck and withdrew the coin, then restored the jewelry and swiveled back. The golden disc set off her newly manicured nails well, each covered in a black matte base coat with shining grey runes painted atop it. *Nothing wrong with a little luxury, now and again.* She'd rummaged through Vincente's paperwork until she'd discovered the locations of the group's wealth and had taken a small portion for herself as a reward for assuming the leadership and all the headaches that accompanied it. *Like the cretin across from me.*

The cretin in question gestured at the statuette. "I remember seeing that out when Vincente was still the person who sat behind that desk."

Sarah kept her face neutral but couldn't suppress the slight twitch of annoyance that made her lip rise for an instant. "Vincente is gone, never to return. While mourning certainly has its place, this isn't it." She gestured at the room around them. "Our purpose remains. It is essential that a person of power remain in charge, and that will be me."

He straightened at the provocation but did not speak. She decided to poke him a little more. "After all, it's not like you even have a way to communicate with those above." His eyes went sleepy, a sign of danger in this man. Still, no words emerged from the thin line of his mouth.

She shrugged. "So. We are agreed, then. I will fill the role Vincente once did. You will continue to lead our human forces. Wysse will lead our magical followers. I'm glad we have that settled." Marcus leaned silently back in the chair and gestured toward the object on the desk.

The witch slipped the coin into its holder and the artifact activated. Blue energy crawled up the spiral and coalesced into an image of the wizard who was her contact with the Remembrance. As usual, he wore a long robe and a hood that obscured his features. He turned in a full circle as if he were physically on the desk and looked around the room. *Maybe that's the way it works from his end? It would be strange but possible.*

His deep tones were louder than she'd expected. "Sarah. Marcus. It is good to see the two of you together again. Quite appropriate, in fact." A sense of dread started in her toes, and the icy tingle raised bumps on her flesh as it climbed upward. "Obviously, the loss of Vincente is a significant blow to your organization, which had operated so very well before your battle with the agents that have descended upon your city. However, I believe we can turn that around." She heard many things in his voice—confidence, arrogance, but most of all, possessiveness. It warned her of what was coming an instant before he announced it. *No. Oh, no.*

"I will replace Vincente as the leader of your organization. Sarah, you shall continue to be the conduit for our conversations and are responsible for overseeing the magical beings. Marcus, you will be present for all discussions and are responsible for leading our mundane forces. Under my leadership, the setbacks that have plagued you will be left in the past as we press forward to achieve the goals of the Remembrance. Henceforth, we are to be the tip of the blade for the entire movement, rising above all others."

She carefully avoided Marcus' gaze but caught his expression of unbridled pleasure out of the corner of her eye, nonetheless. He leaned toward the statue to address the glowing image. "What others do you mean?"

Dreven waved a hand as if the question was irrelevant. "Other minions, other cities, other plans and plots and ideas. They cease to be any concern of ours. All that matters are our actions, our will, and our success."

Sarah tried to keep her anger hidden under a neutral tone. "So, what are our plans and plots and ideas, Dreven?"

The grin visible from under his cowl told her she'd failed to hide her feelings. *Asshole.* "You will cause trouble whenever and wherever possible with small attacks—strike and fade away. In this way, you will sow chaos and fear among the people."

She snorted. "That's the opposite of what we've done so far."

Marcus laughed. "Which has gone so well, right? I love this idea. Plus, we can steal stuff."

Sarah shook her head. "It's beneath us."

Dreven frowned. "Nothing I tell you to do is beneath you. You will serve the desires of the Remembrance, or you will be replaced. Permanently. You'll do it because I said you'll do it. Is that abundantly clear?"

The man clapped his hands. "Absolutely. Let's mess people up. I know exactly where to start."

She sighed. "As you say, Dreven." *For now.*

The wizard nodded, and the image vanished. Marcus stood immediately, a wide grin on his face. "I'll go make plans with my folks. They'll know the easy places to strike, which will be a good way to get started quickly." She was still searching for a response when he breezed out of the room and slammed the door behind him.

She quietly returned the magical objects to their storage spots, lost in thought.

The penthouse condo Sarah had acquired after returning from the World in Between was her greatest comfort. The dark memories of that place were always with her, from the fear she ruthlessly controlled to the enduring pain of the wounds she'd received. When she was around others, she kept it all hidden. Here, in her sanctuary, she could let the walls drop a little. *But not too far. And never all the way. That would be...bad.*

The down payment had been made with the contents of Vincente's safe—what had probably been his personal emergency stash. Diamonds, primarily, which she'd managed to sell at a good price by threatening the family of the merchant. It had been inelegant but satisfying. The mortgage was paid through a secret account she siphoned cash from the gang to fund. All in all, a satisfactory arrangement. As long as she kept the money flowing, everyone benefitted. Some more than others, of course, which was fair as some were more deserving.

And none was more deserving than her, given what she'd been through.

She had a corner of the tall building as her own. The long wall faced the park and the fountain where the two rivers met to create the third. The other looked south and the soccer stadium and train tracks were visible over the lower buildings and across the water. It had come fully ready for occupancy, with white furniture and colorful paintings on the walls. The only touches she'd added were the crimson duvet on her king-sized bed and the assortment of sculptures throughout the space depicting warriors, combat, and death. They were a reminder that her current battles were part of a protracted history of conflicts that resulted in greatness, exactly as hers would.

There had been time to corral her hair into a ponytail and change into a pair of soft black pajama pants and a grey sweatshirt with the neck cut off before a discreet knock sounded at the door. The camera feed from the hallway showed a shipping cube in front of the entrance to her apartment. She retrieved it and crossed to the white couch, then sat with one leg folded beneath her and set the object on the glass coffee table. A whispered spell and a wave of her wand freed the inner box from the outer, and a repeat of the process revealed the treasure within.

A magnificent necklace lay inside the container, constructed of faceted gems cut into spherical shapes, each a different color than the ones next to it. There was no clear pattern, and yet it managed to look both beautiful and right, somehow. An ebony card sat beside it, and she flicked her wand to fold it open. Elegant brushwork was revealed, a metallic red that darkened with the pressure on certain letters and spelled out *We must speak*. There was no signature.

Sarah stared at the object and ran the possibilities through her mind. One, it could be from Dreven, another level to his plotting he didn't want Marcus to know about. She discarded that idea with a snort. *That asshole gets his jollies from pitting people against each other. This isn't his style. Besides, he's nowhere near subtle enough to write like that.*

Two, perhaps it was a trap. She had doubtless created enemies inside the gang when she'd chosen Wysse to lead, and an ambitious underling could be attempting to reshuffle the hierarchy. While more likely than the first option, she discounted this one as well. The necklace was almost otherworldly, and she couldn't imagine any of her followers managing to lay hands on it without her knowledge. If there was someone she'd already suspected of acting against her, maybe, but it simply didn't feel right. *Still, if I do decide to put it on, I'll have counterspells prepared.* Necklaces with the ability to choke the life out of their wearers were well within the realm of likelihood, whether magical or technological.

Third, and most interesting, it might be an artifact of some kind. She drew her focus inward and reached for the connection to her bonded magical partner. Its tone in her mind was derisive, something she hadn't heard from it before.

"About time, witchling." Damn, it sounds offended. It's touchy, apparently. *"It is not an artifact in the traditional sense, but it is magic. Most likely, it is meant to be worn as a method of communication. Stop delaying. With every moment we waste with inaction, our power diminishes."* The rush of pleasure that usually accompanied commune with the object buried in her flesh did not appear, and the lack upset her more than she would have expected.

She muttered several spells to ward the room against

physical and magical threats. Another invocation summoned a ring of force tightly around her throat to prevent the necklace from choking her if it suddenly contracted. With a deep breath, she lowered it over her head and set it on her skin. Her vision blurred at a whirling sensation and nausea rose in her stomach. The chaos suddenly resolved to reveal a place that was most definitely not where she'd just been.

The artifact spoke to her immediately. *"You are still in your home. This is a mental projection. There is nothing to fear here."*

An amused voice answered, its sultry tones and timbre revealing it was a woman even before she stepped into sight. "I wouldn't go that far. Many fear me, and rightly so."

The artifact hissed, and Sarah realized she was in the presence of a powerful being who also possessed one of Rhazdon's treasures. It was the only thing that could provoke her own partner so heavily. The woman flowed across the intervening distance to stand before her—tall and thin, sharp-featured, with long dark hair and intense eyes, and clad in a tight black dress that hugged her curves and revealed a substantial amount of cleavage. She snickered internally. *Lady, you might be trying a little too hard with that getup.*

The woman smiled, and the surrounding space seemed to vibrate with her power. Sarah's respect for her increased. When she spoke, that respect doubled. "I am Iressa. I serve on the council that leads the Remembrance. You know Dreven, of course."

She nodded, and the words tumbled from her lips before she captured them. "Unfortunately, I do."

The woman's laugh was appealing in every way a laugh could be. She fought against the pure entrancement that her mind wanted to spiral into. *She's good. But after the World in Between, I'm better.* "That is an appropriate attitude toward him. He has been useful, but it is time changes were made. He will soon be removed from his position of power, and given your recent change in circumstances, I thought you might enjoy helping me accomplish it."

A wide smile spread across Sarah's features. "Oh, yes, I would very much like that."

The woman nodded. "Good. Here's what I need you to do."

CHAPTER SEVEN

Rath was generally happy, despite all the chaos that was happening around him. *Or because of it, maybe.* The other tech, Deacon, knew many movie quotes, and almost all of them were from films the troll hadn't seen. Kayleigh had invited her new coworker to the house for a movie night, and they'd watched what she claimed were classics—*Big Trouble in Little China* and *Buckaroo Banzai.* The first was okay, the second was incredible. Both technicians were uneducated in the Rambo series, though, and had promised to share another evening with him to remedy that.

The sun shone overhead as he and Max made their way toward Emanuel's shop. They hadn't seen the man since they'd dropped the artifact with him for safekeeping, and Rath felt like they owed him a visit. Besides, he enjoyed talking to the elderly wizard who seemed to have considerable knowledge about the early days of magic on Earth to share. He didn't ask for much in exchange, only tales of what the troll remembered from his time on Oriceran, which were minimal at best.

They passed far fewer people than usual as they traveled. While they'd been occupied with fighting off the Remembrance, the semesters had ended at the local schools. The campuses were noticeably quieter, and the entire atmosphere of the area had become more relaxed. *Good time for a break, for all of us.* The only place that wasn't more relaxed was wherever Diana was. He didn't realize that he frowned at the thought until he noticed the passersby gave Max a wider berth. He banished the outward sign of his worry with a sigh. Attempts to get her to train away the bad energy had been met with postponements that never arrived. *She's too deep inside to choose an escape path. It'll take something big to shock her out of it.* He chuckled. *I can be big. She won't like it if I have to be the one to drag her free.*

They reached the shop and breezed in through the screen door to find Manny in his normal place in the front room. His face stretched into a wide grin at the sight of them. "Hello, Rath and Max. It's so good to see you!" He gestured toward the chair beside him, and the troll dismounted, grew to his three-foot form, and scrambled into it. "Are you on patrol?"

The troll shook his head. "Uh-uh. Coming to visit you."

A note of caution entered the man's voice. "Is there trouble?"

"Nope. Wanted to say hi."

He grinned. "Excellent. You picked a great day for it, actually. Charlotte will be here in"—he checked his watch, which was a strangely chunky antique-looking device on his left wrist—"about twenty minutes. She's bringing our newest addition to the group to see the place."

Rath cocked his head to the side. "You have a new person?"

He nodded. "We do. He was auditing one of her classes and made the effort to connect. She discovered that he has the right mindset and impressive skills to boot."

"Boot?"

He chuckled. "Merely a figure of speech. It means...uh, in addition. Or as well."

"Got it. Hadn't heard that one."

Manny grinned. "Watch more westerns."

The troll laughed. "Will put on the list."

The front door banged open earlier than expected, and they both turned as Professor Charlotte entered with another man. He had close-cropped grey hair, a trimmed mustache and beard, and wore khaki shorts and a green collared shirt with a pony logo on it. His eyes were slightly wider than the others' and his skin tone a little darker, which called to mind a much older Bruce Lee. His posture was so perfect that Rath straightened involuntarily. He had a wide grin and a strange analytical look. His teaching friend cleared that oddity up immediately, and the man's gaze shifted to her while she spoke. "This is Lian Chan, one of my students. And he's deaf but reads lips really well."

The man grinned. "Way to give away my secret, Charlotte." He took a step to the side that would allow him to see if any of them began to speak. Rath and Emanuel greeted him. "You're the first troll I've had the good fortune to meet in person. I must say, you're bigger than I expected." He held two fingers up at about the distance his smallest form would fill and laughed, a pleasant sound that seemed free of worry.

"Am in what friends call normal mode. Have tiny mode and fighting mode."

"Perhaps I'll get to see those sometime."

Rath nodded. "Sure."

Professor Charlotte stepped up beside him. "I'm glad you're here since I wanted the two of you to meet. Lip reading is not Chan's only skill, nor his best one."

His interest sparked, the troll turned a quizzical look on the older man, who smiled again. "I'm fairly good at throwing things."

The woman snorted. "That's a typically humble gross understatement." She pulled out a bag of grapes from her giant purse-tote bag—Rath still had no idea why she needed such a large one—and plucked two, then handed one to him and one to Chan. She pointed at a portrait on the kitchen wall two rooms away. "So, my normal-mode friend, can you hit the painting from here?"

He hopped off the chair and judged the distance. The fruit was a little light to make it that far, so it would have to be arced upward. He took a couple more seconds to determine the angles, then heaved it at the target. It struck the wall about three inches below the bottom of the frame, which was about a foot and three inches lower than he'd intended. He scowled. "Trick grape."

The others broke into laughter, and the professor patted him on the shoulder. "Yes, I deliberately sabotaged your throw. Whatever makes you feel better, Rath." He turned a grin to her and skipped out of the way. Chan moved into the position he'd vacated, faced the painting squarely, and stepped back with his right foot. He held the grape between two fingers of his left hand and brought it across his chest near his opposite ribs. In a move that was so smooth it seemed almost unnoticeable, he flicked the tiny orb away. Its arc was much shallower than Rath had attempted and it struck the figure in the eye and exploded from the force of impact.

Without conscious intention, Rath's mouth said, "Oooooooohhhh."

Professor Charlotte grinned. "The best part is that he could make that throw another dozen times with no more effort than what you've seen and perfect accuracy." She knelt to meet his gaze directly. "There's only so much the four of us can do to help you, Rath, but we all want to. The others gave me permission to ask Chan if he would train you, and he said yes. So, if you're interested, and if he's still willing, then...." Her voice trailed off.

The man standing above them had folded his arms and gripped his opposing elbows with his hands. "Willing. Very. As long as Rath proves to be as virtuous as you've claimed."

Happiness erupted from deep within as the opportunity filled a need he hadn't even realized existed. "Interested. Very. As long as Max can watch."

Laughter circled the room as they all assured him he wouldn't have to abandon his partner. They talked for a while more, and the man gave him an address, a date, and a time for his first lesson. Rath left as late as he could to be punctual for the meeting at headquarters but far earlier than he wanted to. *Excellent. Will be better fighter. Must Train.*

The shift in mood from Emanuel's shop to Kayleigh's lab could not have been more pronounced. Dim lighting was provided by work lights, while the main illumination in the room was off, which fitted the emotional atmosphere perfectly. The tech was subdued and Diana was downright grim. Even Deacon, who sat nearby with noise-canceling headphones on while he worked on a computer program, seemed less bouncy than usual. His fingers on the keyboard produced a constant percussive undertone Rath found soothing.

The conversation, though, was anything but relaxed.

Kayleigh sat on a tall chair on the opposite side of the table from them and sounded like she was in pain as she spoke. "I've put together what you asked for, boss, but I have to say again, this is a bad, terrible, really awful idea."

Diana sighed beside him, seated on a high stool of her own. He stood on his and swiveled his head from one to the other as they talked. "I'm aware of your feelings on the matter. Tell me what you have."

The tech pointed a finger at one of the small devices spread on the worktable in front of her. It looked like a tiny cube of black licorice with toothpicks protruding from it. "That's an audio sensor with enough range to pick up any sound in a normal room." She gestured around them at the lab. "So, for a space this big, you'd need three of them."

Diana scowled. "That's the best you can do?"

She folded her arms and frost entered her tone. "You asked for hidden microphones. If you're willing to tolerate the risk of something more visible, I am able to make it more sensitive. Of course, that would be fairly idiotic, given what you have in mind, so perhaps you should accept that I know what I'm doing, hmm?" Rath blinked, and he was glad that the words hadn't been aimed at him.

The target of the verbal reprimand blinked as well. "Okay, I hear you. Back down, woman. None of us is happy about this."

The woman sighed and pointed at the next device. "Camera with a fisheye lens. Placed in a corner, it will provide a good sight of half a standard room with the correct processing on the receiving end to deal with the artifacts around the edges."

Diana nodded. "Okay. So what's the trouble?"

"Which trouble do you want to discuss first? The installation trouble or the continuing secrecy trouble?" The blonde raised a palm. "Right, back down, sorry. I hate this."

"We all hate this. Tell me about the installation."

"Since the warehouse is occupied at all hours, it'll have to be done from the roof. We can only hope that there aren't active defenses on it. They probably didn't think that far ahead." *That explains why I'm here. Spider Gwen and Spider Troll are on the case.* "We'll need Sloan to give us a time window if possible, or at least a heads-up when the office is empty. Then it's merely drilling and a little putty."

"It sounds reasonable so far."

"The bigger problem is when the devices transmit. Even though they'll be set up to capture and store and only send information when they haven't detected nearby presences for a certain amount of time, I can't predict what kind of sensors they might have for that. I can tell you that the same device planted here would be identified right away. And that's assuming they don't go up to the roof for some reason and see the repeater that we'll leave behind to boost the signal."

Diana nodded. "They won't have our level of tech, though."

Kayleigh countered, "They have magic. I can't do a damn thing to hide them from the right kind of magic. And no, Deacon can't either. I asked. Covering them in illusion is a zero-sum game when they have the power to detect illusions. That's only useful against non-magicals."

Deacon's voice called out, "Like you."

She scowled at him. "A, you should be working, not listening in. B, bite me." Diana struggled to hold in her grin and Rath didn't even try, which annoyed the tech that much more. "And C, you all suck. Every last one of you."

Her boss locked gazes with her. "So, you don't like it but it's doable, is that right?"

She sighed. "Yes. Danger at the install for Rath, and danger ongoing for Sloan. If they find the stuff, they'll know they have a spy among them."

The Special Agent in Charge of ARES Pittsburgh stood with a nod. "The decision is on me. You've done your best. Now work with Rath so he's ready to do the installation. I'll signal Sloan that he needs to get in touch for a chat." She strode briskly from the room.

The troll turned to Kayleigh and gave her a grin and a thumbs-up. "We're good. No problem. Everything will be fine. Do what Buckaroo says—be cool, but care."

She laughed. "Is this my life now? Anything I share with

you gets thrown back at me like a motivational poster with a cat on it?"

He grinned. "Yes to both."

Finally, she smiled in return. "Thanks, buddy."

"Anytime."

CHAPTER EIGHT

Cara crept carefully along the illuminated path that her AI, Quinn, had drawn onto the display in her glasses. It showed the arcs of the security cameras and the ranges of the sound and motion sensors scattered around the location. There were several icons to tell her where to hold and wait for notification as some of the devices were moving. *Thank you, Kayleigh, for making life so much easier.*

She pressed the stud to lock her mic open once she'd completed her instructions to and discussion with Quinn. "About thirty seconds away from being in position."

"Affirmative," Tony replied immediately. "Me and Hercules here are ready to charge in the back on your command."

The deep voice of the team's newest member—who preferred to be called Hank rather than his given name Henry—was preceded by a low chuckle. "That's an interesting callsign choice you've given me, Stark. Are you feeling…inadequate?" The two men had instantly struck up a fast friendship based on mutual insult, as near as she could tell. It was so stereotypical. *Boys. Honestly.* She laughed inwardly.

The next voices were less confident but made up for it with enthusiasm. "Starsky, all good." That was James Maxis, the policeman of the duo.

"Hutch, even better." And that was Vicki Greene, his policewoman partner. They were on their first run with Two Worlds Security and were not privy to the ARES half of the organization in any way. Cara and Hank wore their illusion necklaces so as to not betray the connection.

She paused when she reached the icon, then sprinted forward at Quinn's chime to avoid the paths of several moving sensors before she stopped in the last safe area before the entry door. The building was four stories high and to all outward appearances, was a typical indoor storage facility. Their intelligence had revealed that one of the levels was actually the base for a pair of wizards who were distantly linked to the Prince of Plunder. *And when we find that bastard, it'll be pure pleasure to make him spill every secret he has before we send him on to Trevilsom.*

Diana had shared the decision to freeze ARES' expansion that resulted from the Cube jailbreak, which fueled the anger Cara felt at the escape of her personal nemesis, the one-armed man. She'd itched for a fight ever since and had jumped at the chance to apprehend the bounty. Rath had wanted to come too, but with the off-duty police officers along, it would have been too obvious a connection back to BAM.

"Okay, people, exactly like we planned it. I take the front and Stark and Hercules take the rear thirty seconds later. Starsky and Hutch stop any runners." A drone high above provided overwatch and fed into handhelds that the pair carried. Having non-agents along had raised numerous questions they didn't yet have answers for, including how much tech they could share without revealing enough to endanger the team. She waited for a few more beats until the sensors swept past, raised her stun rifle, and fired at the camera overlooking the main entrance. With that disabled, she dashed forward and slapped three explosive packages Anik had prepared for her onto the door and spun aside. The shaped charges blew and the barrier swung free, its locks destroyed and the metal twisted from the detonation.

She arced outward to avoid the other cameras' lines of sight, then ran ahead and leapt at the door with a side kick. It slammed inward and her momentum carried her through the guard who had rushed to investigate. He fell back with a cry of pain. She swiveled to avoid landing on him and followed with a blast from the stun rifle to put him out. The expanded view in her glasses showed no other immediate enemies.

Advance scans from Kayleigh's drones had revealed that the first, second, and fourth floors were identical. Each had a double-wide hallway around the perimeter, with single-car garage-sized storage units along the inside. At the back center of the building, a staircase climbed from level to level. A freight elevator protruded from the left side of the facility but getting locked down within it would put a definite crimp in their plan, so they'd chosen to avoid that route.

She stood and ran toward the right. Tony announced, "Moving," and an instant later, a crash sounded from the back of the building. She turned the corner and came face to face with a rent-a-cop who held a pistol extended in shaking arms. Cara reacted instantly and swung her left leg up in an inside-out crescent to knock the weapon aside a second before it discharged. The round ricocheted off the concrete wall. She fired the stun gun without aiming, and the blast caught the uniformed woman a glancing blow. It knocked her to one knee and she fumbled for the taser on her belt, which earned her both Cara's respect and another volley from the rifle. She slumped the short distance to the ground. The bounty hunter knelt and checked her pulse to ensure the double dose of energy hadn't overwhelmed her heart, but the beat was strong and steady.

"Heading up to two," Tony announced.

"Right behind you, Stark."

The presence of the big man at his side—several inches taller and with muscles that would make Arnold envious—wasn't as reassuring as it could have been. In a close-quarters fight, he'd choose Hank over almost anyone other than Cara or Diana, a clone of himself included. But the long hallways took away the advantage of his physical might and his shooting, while good, had proven less formidable than most other members of the team at their last excursion to the range. *He's nowhere near my level with a pistol. Decent with a rifle, though.*

The other man's bulk made Tony feel like he had only a fourth of the hallway to himself. A guard appeared ahead, and the agent's stun blast connected with the target a full second before Hank's did. The man fell and another turned the corner beyond him, saw what was going on, and ducked back. The two agents charged together and his partner proved faster as well. *Fine. He's a specimen. Let's see him shoot with his offhand.* A gunshot boomed as the big man rounded the corner, and Tony followed to find him grappling with the other man. "Yo, Hercules, quit playing around and get some distance." Hank shoved the uniformed defender away, and Tony dropped him with a burst from the nonlethal rifle. "Good work."

Their leader sounded out of breath over the comm. "Another one down. That's two for me."

Tony replied, "And two for us."

"So, that's all but one of those Quinn identified as hourly guards. You finish clearing this floor. I'll go up to three. Once you're done, head up and take care of four."

"Are you sure you want to go into the danger zone alone?"

Cara laughed. "Don't worry, I'll only take care of the periphery. I won't go in until we're together."

Hank's chuckle was filled with satisfaction. "I wouldn't want to miss the good stuff."

Tony shook his head. "There's always more than enough danger for us all, my friend." The third floor was essentially a bunker, according to the scans. Once inside the huge area created out of what had been separate storage units on the other floors, an outer hallway funneled around twice before it opened into several large rooms. They'd been unable to get anything more than that from the drone, and Kayleigh and Deacon agreed that there must be some kind of physical or electronic shielding present. Or both. Or magic. Or all three. When they'd shared that finding, Tony had laughed and commented about how incredibly helpful they both were, which earned him a few snarky words from each of them in return.

They turned the corner and discovered two enemies, which could only mean that at least one of them was a criminal. "Left," Tony called and fired his weapon at the opponent on that side. A shield shimmered into being and the stun blast washed over it and failed to penetrate to his target. Hank's attack met the same fate. "Contact, two defenders."

Tony dropped the stun gun and it clattered on the floor as he yanked the Armalite up from his chest. Pre-loaded with anti-magic bullets, the rifle spat rounds at his opponent as the recoil raised the barrel. The man was already dropping, and he felt his aim pushed to the ceiling as his foe's magic grabbed it. When it started to bend around to the right and toward his partner, he pressed the button to eject the magazine and let the weapon fall. "Careful. Mental grabby hands over there."

He drew the pistol at his hip quickly and fired two triple-taps at his prone adversary. The target's response wasn't fast enough, and the anti-magic rounds drilled through his hasty shield and into his chest and skull. Tony shifted his aim to the other opponent, only to find that Hank had closed to melee distance. The man delivered three torso punches followed by a hook to his opponent's head, which caused him to stagger and positioned him perfectly for the left uppercut that lifted him from his feet and dropped him bonelessly into a crumpled heap.

Tony looked at his teammate with respect in his eyes. "Damn. Nice."

The big man blew on his knuckles. "He was easy. I didn't even need to use any boost."

"Humble, too. You have it all, man."

His deep laugh accompanied their progression through the rest of the floor, and they climbed to the top. The drone above was able to scan there and showed four heat signatures, all on the move toward their location. Cara announced, "Third clear, waiting on you bozos." The men shook their heads at one another and Tony pointed his partner to the right and moved to the left.

He crouched next to the wall and waited about ten feet back from the corner. His rifle was raised to his eye level, and as soon as the first man appeared, he pulled the trigger. The modded AR-15s the cover security company used possessed extra-sensitive triggers to make up for the lack of burst or automatic fire. He had three shots on the way before the body they'd struck fell from the first. The second target managed to conjure a shield and dive aside, but Tony tracked his dodge and dispatched him with another two anti-magic bullets. He met up with Hank, who looked none the worse for wear after he'd taken care of his own enemies, and they descended to join Cara.

She had already prepared her last set of explosives that would get them into the labyrinth, and Quinn awaited the command to detonate. The entry into the protected section was a standard garage-door-sized barrier, but one her sensors indicated was far thicker than the rest. The glasses couldn't penetrate it, so there was no telling what lay inside. She carried a pair of flashbangs on her belt and sonics on her left hip, plus her pistol, rifle, and backup Ruger. The time for the stun guns was past, and hers rested near the staircase at the back.

The men joined her and nodded to indicate their readiness. She returned it and gave the command. "Quinn, detonate."

They had agreed that speed would be essential in order to avoid getting cut down in the defensive hallway, so she was in motion before the smoke had cleared. The shaped charges had blown off a portion of the door, and she crouched to peer through the opening. Their greatest fear during the planning session was the potential for automated defenses and she was ready to magically mangle any turret she saw, but none were present.

"On the move." She darted into the narrow hallway, which was barely wide enough for her to run in. *Hank will have to come through sideways. That's gonna suck. Heh. The fun never ends.* The corridor extended for the full length of the building toward the front, with a turn to the right far ahead. She ran with her rifle held at the ready across her chest and her finger along the guard and increased her speed into a sprint. The thud of boots behind her confirmed that the others followed.

Their first adversary appeared before she reached the end and stepped out with a wand in one hand and a heavy riot shield in the other. He released a cone of flame down the hallway at chest height, everything but his arm protected by the shield. She slid, unable to evade in any other way, and hoped her teammates were paying attention. Despite the awkwardness of the narrow passage, she extended the rifle and pulled the trigger in a frenzy. The mage cowered behind his shelter, which proved strong enough to deflect her rounds. *Dammit. I know all the reasons why we don't carry armor-piercing rounds. But it sure would be nice sometimes. I guess we'll have to go with Plan B.*

She retrieved, primed, and threw a sonic grenade in a single motion. Her aim wasn't perfect with her left hand, but close usually counted with explosives, gas, or sound. She took some professional pride in the way it banked off the ceiling and the wall to detonate behind her enemy and swamp him with a barrage of noise powerful enough to rupture eardrums. When her earpieces once again picked up external noises, his screams suggested the weapon might have done exactly that. She scrambled to her feet, stepped over the fallen shield, and touched her shock glove to his temple. It sparked, and his eyes rolled back in his head.

Hank's deep voice commented, "How gentle of you."

She chuckled softly. "There's no need to do more damage than absolutely necessary. Karma will get ya."

Tony laughed as if she'd made a joke. "Karma, right."

Cara made a mental note to explain the concept to him at a later date as she peeked around the corner. The hallway running along the front of the building was suspiciously empty and twice as wide as the previous one. "Quinn, anything?"

The AI's tone was sassy. "If there was, it would already be displayed."

She rolled her eyes. *Even my electronic teammates need a*

good slapping. "Stark, Hercules, something doesn't feel right about this. Flashbang out." She hurled the object, braced herself for the concussion, and stepped into the hallway as it detonated. A shimmer three-quarters of the way down confirmed her caution. "There's an illusion or force wall ahead." She raised her rifle and sprayed the barrier with anti-magic bullets, which caused it to drop and reveal a witch and a mage behind it. They were dressed like characters out of a vampire roleplay, sporting rich robes, blindingly white shirts with ruffles, sparkling jewelry, and perfectly coiffed hair. They must have had vests hidden under the costumes, though, because they were stunned but not visibly bleeding. She aimed at their heads as they staggered back around the corner, but the rounds smacked into the far wall without any success.

"Damn. Okay, two magicals at least beyond the next turn." Tony squeezed past her as she ejected the depleted magazine and slapped a replacement into the rifle. He had lost his teasing edge, apparently rightfully concerned about any opponent she hadn't managed to take down. He got close enough to throw, and the grenade left his hand and bounced into the hallway beyond. "Sonic out." He hurtled around the corner and she followed a few steps behind.

The grenade had accomplished exactly nothing as it activated near the mouth of the corridor and the enemies were most of the way down it. She knelt and fired at them, adding her own bullets to the ones Tony was already firing, and heard the chatter of Hank's gun above her. Their foes fell, punctured and moaning from the pain of multiple wounds to their limbs. Miraculously, none of them had managed a headshot. She stalked down the hallway and resisted the urge to kick them in the head and instead, tapped them with her shock gloves to put them out. "Quinn, roll ambulances."

"Affirmative."

Cara turned the corner, anger replacing her good sense, and saw nothing ahead. She fired a few rounds as a test, but they encountered nothing as well. The next turn would take them toward the front of the building again and close to where they'd entered. She touched the wall beside her. "They're probably on the other side of this. We should have brought more explosives." She thought back to the battle at the Cube. "Quinn, would sonic grenades be able to compromise this surface?"

The AI paused before replying, presumably running calculations. "Yes. If you have four and place them at these precise locations, it would weaken the barrier by about half."

She groaned. "Well, that won't do it."

Hank cracked his knuckles and rolled his neck. "I can provide enough boom to finish it off. Do it."

"Seriously? It's that strong?" She raised an eyebrow.

He laughed. "That's what all the ladies say." Cara stared at him until his smile was replaced by a frown that she read as concerned. "Yes. It is. You take care of your part, and I'll handle the rest."

He handed her his pair of sonic grenades, and she used gaffer's tape to stick them to the walls in the designated places, thanks to an AR overlay Quinn provided. Tony delivered his and she used her last one and attached them as well. They stood a few feet away in case something unexpected happened, and the AI detonated them. When the vibrations stopped, Quinn confirmed the wall had been damaged.

Hank stepped across from it and squared his shoulders. Cara nudged Tony and mouthed, "Watch this." The big man pushed his back against the solid wall, then took a long stride forward and delivered a front kick to the target surface. A loud crack heralded an expanding cloud of dust and shrapnel as the barrier disintegrated under the impact. He continued into the room with a shout, and more noise answered him from inside.

"Go, go, go," she yelled as she dashed after him. Stones from the wall had disabled several defenders, who moaned and thrashed on the floor. Hank had closed with the nearest upright foe and held his opponent's rifle at bay with one hand while he punched him repeatedly in the head with the other. There were two left standing, both of whom held riot shields in front of them and had backed into a corner, their wands sticking over the top.

Enough of this. With a sigh, she let her Armalite fall on its strap, extended her hands, and hurled darts of fire out of each of her fingers. They traveled the short distance to her opponents and burned through both the shields and the legs behind them. The sight of their protective barriers falling on top of them was funny enough to inspire laughter as the wave of exhaustion from the double draw on her magic surged over. She staggered back a step and slid down the wall.

Tony called "Runners, at least three," but didn't pursue.

She managed to say, "Be careful out there, you two," before she had to close her eyes and focus on not passing out. *Shit. My reserves are even more depleted than I thought.*

The weight that had pressed on her for weeks suddenly grew heavier. *Current methods aren't working anymore. I need to find better ones. I will find better ones.*

Her partners searched noisily for items that Diana needed to make her teacher happy or others that might be directly useful to the team or easily sold. Eventually, the call came from below that Starsky and Hutch had corralled the escapees. She laughed. "Great job, Wonder Twins." She pushed herself up the wall and stood unsteadily, leaning against it. "Quinn, transport."

"The police are on their way."

"I've always loved their music." She snorted at her own joke.

The AI didn't respond, but Tony did. He took her arm carefully and led her from the room while he tried to hide his concern. "You should sleep a little more, maybe."

"I'll sleep when I'm dead."

She pretended not to hear his whispered "That's what I'm afraid of."

CHAPTER NINE

What does one pack to visit another planet? Diana stared at the open locker in front of her and shook her head. The bottom level of the base was empty aside from her at the moment, everyone else out on information-gathering tasks as part of the "kick the Remembrance's ass" initiative. Her duties for the day ran along the same lines but were of a rather different nature.

She decided to wear the vest, just in case, but hid it under a black uniform shirt. The tactical pants and combat boots she already wore matched the top. She snapped her utility belt closed over it all and tied the holster down to her right leg. Her gaze settled on the grenades, but she realized she had no idea whether they'd operate as expected on Oriceran. *It's something to discuss with Kayleigh. Or Nylotte. Or both. But not together.* She smirked at the image of putting the two most annoying people in her life in proximity to one another but discarded it as far too dangerous for everyone involved.

Still chuckling, she inserted a magazine of anti-magic

bullets into her Glock and slid it into its holster. The Ruger rested in its home on the back of the belt. She slotted two spare pistol mags into the holders at her waist. Without the carbine magazines and the grenades, the belt felt light and empty. She had the Bowie knife, but it was trapped under her shirt and thus mostly irrelevant. *If it gets down to melee range, I'll use magic anyway.*

The agent was in no way prepared to portal directly to Oriceran on her own so instead, she opened a rift to the basement of Nylotte's shop and stepped through. The Drow was gathering her own equipment and placed several objects Diana had never seen into a large courier bag that rested on her hip with a strap across her chest. She was clad entirely in black and wore heavy denim pants, boots that rose to her knees, and a top that buttoned down the left side and looked rather martial. She gave her teacher a half-grin. "You look like you're dressed for a fight. Should I be worried?"

The Dark Elf laughed. "This old thing?" She gestured at her outfit with a smile that told her she was secretly pleased with the compliment. "No, I don't think we'll find any trouble awaiting us. But it doesn't hurt to be sure."

She nodded. "Somehow, in all of our conversations, I never asked whether explosives work the same on your home planet as they do here."

Her mentor grinned, showing her teeth so she looked vaguely like a shark. "Your home planet as well, if we take lineage into account. But no matter. Yes, they should function the same, although many of the creatures on that world would be more resistant to their effects."

Dammit. I should've brought some. Oh well, live and learn.

Hopefully both. She clapped her hands. "Okay, then, shall we get this show on the road?"

In lieu of a reply, Nylotte strode to the center of the space and motioned her forward. The floor featured the embedded rings again, and the outermost shimmered with a protective purple barrier as soon as she stepped across it. She raised an eyebrow and her companion replied, "Well it's best to err on the side of caution when we can, right?"

"That doesn't fill me with confidence."

"I wasn't aware that was my job. Here, let me try." She put a patronizing singsong into her voice. "It's okay, Diana. Everything will be fine. The pretty shield is only there to make you happy."

Diana snorted involuntarily and broke into a laugh. "Wow. Your bedside manner is atrocious."

Without another comment, the Drow summoned the rift and stepped through the opening to Oriceran. The agent tapped her belt to verify the metal vials with her healing and energy potions were where they were supposed to be and followed.

After the strange distortion of time and space and the disorientation that always accompanied portal travel for her, Diana's vision cleared to show a hallway. It struck her as familiar, and she turned to find the damaged door and marked wall that confirmed their location outside the chamber in which they'd fought and defeated Nehlan. She wondered why they hadn't portaled into there since it had clearly been designed for that purpose and realized Nylotte was already explaining. "There are some odd barriers in that room. I noticed them when we last visited. Trying to portal into it without permission might activate nasty things so I thought it best to avoid it. I left my anchor point here last time, but once we've had a proper look at the place, we'll select a different location."

Diana nodded and followed her teacher as she walked in the opposite direction. She recognized the dining room which they had run through while rescuing Lisa. The Dark Elf gestured around the well-appointed chamber with its elegant furniture and impressive chandelier. "This was an important place for Nehlan. He, like you, had problems concealing his thoughts when excited, and during my single visit here I could tell there was something untoward going on. The foods he offered me were laced with a subtle poison. Because I know this area thoroughly, it was familiar enough that I could detect it without him knowing." She chuckled. "He was no doubt frustrated at my lack of appetite that day. His human servants watched us the whole time—an elderly pair that I presume were a couple. He had broken their minds and transformed them into little more than obedient flesh with no free will. But I dispatched them when we were here last."

Diana stopped walking and grabbed her teacher's arm. "You what?"

The Drow looked down at her and rolled her eyes in annoyance. "No, I didn't kill them. If I had, you would've heard the words 'I killed them' rather than the ones I used. I am always precise."

She squeezed a little harder. "Precision can be as important a part of concealing the truth as an outright lie."

A grin spread across Nylotte's features. "My. You are learning. How wonderful." She brushed her hand away as if her grip was nothing more than a nuisance. "I transported them back to Earth. Human doctors would be useless to repair this type of damage, so I put them in the hands of the Fixer." She started to walk again, and Diana hastened to catch up.

"I've heard of that person. Some sort of magical sheriff, right? Kind of like the Lone Ranger?"

Her teacher clicked her tongue. "I have no idea what you're talking about, and if you try to explain, I will teleport you into the deep forest and leave you there. If we accept that sheriff is a synonym for do-gooder, and that the lone whatever you speak of is as pretentious as can be, then it is an excellent description of that being."

"So, you don't like him?"

She waved a hand airily. "I neither like nor dislike him. He has his uses." The woman muttered something she thought sounded like "troublemaking troll," but it was lost in the shock of entering the kitchen.

Diana had never seen such a large space for food preparation and imagined it was bigger than that of most restaurants. "Wow."

The Drow gave a laugh that was simultaneously amused and condescending. "Our dear departed Nehlan liked to present himself as a gourmet. I wasn't privy to all his secrets, but I assume he would have had no idea what to do in this space and simply hired or coerced others into cooking for him."

"Well, in any case, it's a nice kitchen." She noticed that several of the items had labels from Earth, most notably the Viking range and the Gaggenau ovens. "Hey, wait. These aren't from Oriceran."

Nylotte shook her head in clear disappointment and pointed toward the other exit from the room. "There is a thriving black market for things from your planet and a whole host of beings who spend their time merging technology and magic in useful ways. How could you not have intuited that, given your occupation?"

Diana immediately thought of Deacon and nodded. It made sense but she'd never considered it all the way through. Her teacher named rooms hidden behind closed doors as they passed. "Closet. Bathroom. Closet. Another closet." They came to a T-shaped intersection, and Nylotte chose the right side. "We'll check out the less soiled areas first."

An opulent red door lay at the end of the hall, and the Drow stopped several feet from it. She raised her palms and spoke some words Diana didn't understand. The barrier glowed in response. She sighed. "Who puts this many wards on a bedroom?" She fluttered her fingers and delivered more arcane commands, and after a minute or so, the magical telltales on the handle vanished. The agent expected her to step forward and enter but instead, she snapped a command. "Create a force shield in front of me, then open the door with your magic."

This is a strange time to suddenly start teaching, but okay. She did as instructed, flicked the latch, and pushed the door wide with her telekinesis. An onslaught emerged from the opening—a fan of fire at head level, spikes of ice at knee height, and what appeared to be crossbow bolts firing in a line that spanned the width of the hallway at their stomachs. She grunted with the effort of maintaining her shield but managed and only let it fall once the danger had passed.

"Good work, protégé." Nylotte allowed the barrier she'd created behind Diana's to become visible and melt away before she strode forward into the space. To the left was a dressing corner, with racks of robes hanging in an indented section of the wall. To the right, an open door led to an en suite bathroom. The rest of the near half of the room was empty, which allowed an unimpeded view of the tapestry woven into the sumptuous carpet. It displayed a battle scene, and each area she focused her eyes on looked more violent and bloody than the last.

The Drow made a tsking sound. "The ancient battle against Rhazdon. A little on the nose, really." She strode toward the bed that occupied the back half of the space, with four great posts supporting a canopy above and easily large enough to fit a half-dozen people in relative comfort. *More, if they overlapped.* She shuddered and banished that line of thought.

Her teacher slowly approached a tall table in the rear corner that seemed empty. She waved her hands and cast a spell, and an ornate wooden box engraved with elegant symbols filled in with precious gems appeared. The Dark Elf tapped a long finger on her chin. "My, what have we here?"

She stared at the box for about thirty seconds and her unfocused eyes indicated her use of magical perceptions rather than mundane ones. When she spoke again, it was only to mutter, "Idiot." She raised a hand and the box's lid popped open. A small snick sounded as a needle stabbed out from the latch. "Apparently, he was so excited with his poisons that he forgot magic was a thing." She waved for Diana to draw near.

Inside the box lay a matching set of jewelry made of strange beads connected to one another with expensive-looking metal links and settings. There were six rings, two bracelets, and a necklace. The former objects seemed finished, while the latter had five settings without stones attached. "What is it?"

"Nehlan had been siphoning power and storing it in those stones. If he'd managed to complete it, this set would've been a formidable magic item."

Diana nodded. "Can you destroy it?"

"Can I? Certainly. But should I, is the question. There may be a way to finish it without incurring any further costs." The darkness that filled the final word was eloquent.

"This wasn't made by willing people, either, was it?" It wasn't a question, and her teacher did not correct her. *Bastard. I wish we could kill him again. Along with anyone who thought trapping life forces to create artifacts was a good idea. I'm looking at you, Rhazdon.*

Nylotte breezed from the room. "Now, it's time to take a look at the less savory parts of the house."

There are less savory parts? She discovered her teacher wasn't exaggerating when they reached the next room. It was apparently a research lab, judging by the strap-festooned metal chair in the middle and the variety of instruments hanging from the wall. A single door led onward, and the enduring aura of pain in the adjoining space caused her to stumble. Even the Drow shook her head. "Torture room." The central feature was another chair, this one with spikes that could be applied once a victim was in place. It was surrounded by far crueler-looking implements on the walls.

They passed through it to a final chamber, which at first glance resembled an ordinary office. *He would have to walk through those rooms every time he wanted to come here. Definitely a sick puppy.* It had a reading chair, attractive lightning sources, and a large desk that looked like wood but of a kind she'd never seen.

Her teacher caught her gazing at it. "From the dark forest nearby. It has been shaped by magic, rather than cut, as it is highly resistant to blades."

"It sounds like a good material for armor. Was it?"

Her teacher gave a small laugh. "It has an unfortunate side effect, as those who spend too much time near the trees or the wood gradually lose their sanity."

Diana raised an eyebrow. "That is unfortunate. Is that what happened to him?"

The woman's eyes defocused as she stared at the desk, then she shook her head. "No, the object is encased in a series of sheaths so thin they're essentially invisible. He clearly loved this item." She trailed her fingers along it. "I can see why. It is an accomplishment. Nehlan was driven and focused, to be sure. To his detriment, he was also a twisted moron." She closed her eyes and turned in a slow circle, then pointed at a cabinet on the far side of the room. "There." With a gesture, the doors parted to reveal a heavy vault behind the facade. It was about the size of a gun safe on Earth but appeared to have been crafted from the same dark, madness-inducing trees.

The agent frowned. "Can you open it?" Nylotte nodded, extended a hand, and tore the door from the front. Diana laughed as pieces of the locking mechanism erupted like shrapnel. "Well, I guess there's no need to always be subtle." She walked to stand before the safe and saw something thoroughly unexpected. Nestled in a small, lidless box was an iPod resting on a red velvet cushion. She picked it up and swiped to activate it. No passcode had been set. *She's right, he was kind of a moron.* It held nothing other than a series of videos.

She tapped the last, and an image appeared showing the room they were in. Nehlan's back was in the foreground, but he'd clearly positioned the device to focus on the desk where, floating above a small statue, the projection of a hooded man spoke. "To find the sword, we must start at the courtyard."

Nehlan's voice, entirely odd to hear given that he was no longer among the living, gave a sharp laugh. "That's unexpected."

The hooded figure inclined his head. "Even to me. But it is convenient. Begin your search there."

"Yes, master."

The figure vanished, and the recording ended. Diana looked at Nylotte. "It has to be Fury, right?"

The Drow nodded and they shared a look of concern. "It is too much of a coincidence to be anything else. It is unsettling that they are already on the path. I will follow this lead and prepare an appropriate landing place for portals. His bedroom, I think."

"While you're at it, can you destroy that bed?"

Nylotte laughed. "I know, it's gross, right? I'll keep the

frame but will replace everything else. This shall be my base of operations for a time, so don't look for me at the shop. It will also serve as a foothold on Oriceran for you."

"Why would I need that?"

Her teacher shrugged and the concerned expression settled on her features again. "You are pulling on threads of a knot you cannot see. There's no telling how complex it might be or where the strands will lead. You would be smart to consider that you might require a defensive place on this planet. And perhaps a better equipped one on yours."

Diana's eyebrows drew together in a frown. "You're serious."

"I have never been more serious."

An involuntary shudder swept through her. "Okay, make it so. I'll track leads on Earth." *Dammit. When I tell Kayleigh this, she'll have an army of robots marching around the perimeter of our yard.* She snorted internally when she recalled Tony's comment. *And then, Skynet.*

CHAPTER TEN

S loan's cover identity was moving up in the world. Tommy Ketchum was now able to afford his own wheels. Unfortunately, they were not good wheels. The well-used Nissan sedan from a decade and a half ago struggled to climb the hill toward the gang's headquarters and for a moment, he worried he'd have to get out and push in order to reach the top. He achieved the plateau that marked the halfway point, and his mind wandered to the job at hand.

Bugging the warehouse shouldn't be that tough. There are a number of corners to stick them in, and the devices are small. The office, though...that's another matter entirely.

His car complained its way up the second part of the hill, and he finally pulled into the gravel lot. He parked it away from the other cars lest it get jealous of their better looks and cease working altogether. Once he'd exited, he slammed the door—the only way to ensure the latch would catch—and headed inside.

Even now, an hour or so past dusk, the place was busy.

Small groups of non-magicals gathered to the left while the witches and wizards clustered to the right. Some were conversing, some playing cards, and he was reasonably sure that the clattering from the far left was a dice game in progress. The building was essentially a clubhouse for criminals, which was amusing when you really thought about it. *More people than I'd like, but still probably the best amount of darkness out there to protect Rath and time before Sarah leaves and the real defenses kick in.*

He was dressed to escape notice in dirty jeans, converse shoes, and a large black hoodie. His hair was a mess but he hadn't pulled the hood over his head since that might draw attention. Tommy Ketchum wasn't too concerned about his looks on most days, only about the next scheme and the next party. Sloan wished, at least once, that he could impersonate someone who cared about looking attractive and dressing well. *Or at least someone committed to showering daily, at a minimum.*

As he wandered through the room, he kept his gaze moving and his ears attentive and pushed gently to encourage his magic to give him a clue. As usual, it was indifferent to his priorities. With a groan, he bent to read the labels on the stacked boxes and used the action as cover to toss one of the sticky bugs into a darkened corner. He repeated the process along the back wall, then made the turn to the front and distributed several more. When he reached the front wall, an arrogant voice spoke from behind. "What are you doing over here all by yourself, dirtbag?"

Sloan straightened and arched his back with a groan. "I heard that hidden somewhere around here is a crate of guns. Good guns. Better than what I have, anyway." He turned to regard the wand-holding man in the ill-fitting black suit. *Maybe try robes next time.* He plastered a gullible smile on his face. "Have you seen any?"

The wizard laughed. "As if I would require such a thing." He raised his brown wooden wand and waved it dramatically. "This has all the power I could ever want or need. Far better than any gun you might find."

Let me have some anti-magic bullets and we'll see if you still think so, you pretentious twit. His sarcasm didn't reach his face, however, and he shrugged. "Okay, I'll keep looking. Thanks." The man turned away with a sound of disgust and rejoined his little circle of supporters. *It's like high school all over again with the cliques and the bullies.* He had finished his circuit of the room and returned to the center when his magic gave him a flash of insight.

The leader of the magical members of the group, Wysse, was cloistered with several other witches, all of them in identical slinky black dresses and with similarly styled ebony hair. Taken alone, it was a decent look. As an effort to ingratiate themselves to Sarah, however, it was sycophantic enough to be nauseating. He couldn't hear her thoughts but he felt her disdain toward the humans in the room clearly. Her ire was focused on one person in particular, and it registered on his senses as a threat. *And, hopefully, an opportunity for Rath.* He pressed the appropriate buttons on the phone hidden in the pocket of his sweatshirt to alert the team to prepare for action.

He saw the target of her hatred across the room and walked over to him with his hand extended. "Marcus, how are you?"

The man gave him a firm shake. "Excellent, Tommy, good to see you again." Beside him, Murray nodded and he returned the gesture.

Sloan let the discomfort the woman's mind had caused him show on his face. He stepped forward and lowered his voice so only Marcus and Mur would hear him. "The witch over there—the one in charge—I heard her saying some nasty things about you to her girls. I'd watch out for her."

The leader of the humans in the warehouse frowned and looked at the gaggle of witches. "What's her problem?"

He shrugged and gave a timid laugh. "She seems to think you're less human now that you have the new arm. And not in a good way." He had flashed on Marcus before and believed anything that suggested the modification made him weaker would be an instant spark. He was not disappointed by the man's reaction.

The undercover agent trailed the human leader as he strode over to the witch, who saw him coming and stepped forward to face him. Her people fanned out behind her, and the man grinned. "Is there something you'd like to say to me, Wysse?"

She put her hands on her hips and absently tapped the wand held in long fingers against her leg. "I'm sure I don't know what you're talking about."

Sloan palmed his phone and walked carefully behind Mur. His gaze darted repeatedly to the door of the office above. Marcus removed his jacket, handed it to a nearby lackey, and put his metal arm on display. His reply was acerbic and bordered on nasty. "No? Nothing about this?" He rotated and flexed the limb.

The woman scowled at him. "Now that you mention it,

I wondered what it was like to be less than a real man. Although that might be something you were familiar with even before you had that thing glued on."

He laughed and several of the suck-ups near him echoed the sound. But it had an edge to it that held promise. "Well, you know, it does have some interesting features. Maybe you'd enjoy seeing one?"

She folded her arms and matched his mocking grin—clearly reluctant to lose face before her followers—and now tapped the wand against her opposite arm. The staccato beat was like a threat. "If we must."

"What do you think of this?" He pointed the limb at the women and a panel on the top rose to reveal a weapon barrel. Before she could react, the stunner discharged a blast of energy to spear the witch beside her with electricity. The unsuspecting woman fell with a heavy thud. The barrel retracted with a quiet click, and silence reigned for several long moments.

She snarled, "Prick," and waved her wand. A burst of force hurled him back, and he landed with a painful thud on his back. He leapt upward with rage in his eyes, but his attack was forestalled by a sharp voice from above. "Marcus. Wysse. Stop it this instant." Sarah had emerged from her office and marched down the stairs. Sloan pressed the button to give the team the go signal and faded a little more into the background on quiet feet.

The chief witch marched between them and turned first to address Marcus. "You should know better. What are you thinking? Perhaps we should have a word with…him… about this?" Sloan was surprised to see the man's face turn pale and more shocked at the head-shake that lacked his customary bravado.

Sarah nodded, stared at him for several more seconds, then turned to Wysse. "You have made your first mistake. There will not be a second. You do not need to respect the man, but you must respect his position, which is technically above your own." Marcus had mentioned her de facto demotion to Mur, who had revealed it to Sloan, but it was clear that the witch had not shared it with any of the magical members of the gang. *Interesting. There is some politics going on there. I wonder why she feels like she can get away with that.*

His phone vibrated to signal the successful installation of the surveillance equipment, and he slunk toward the door. He'd accomplished what was needed, and it was time to get away from the crazy people at the top of the group's hierarchy. *Marcus, Wysse, and especially Sarah. She is absolutely crazy.*

CHAPTER ELEVEN

Diana stepped off the magical train at the Market Square Starbucks and climbed the stairs to emerge from the hidden access at the end of a supposedly closed hallway. She had ordered ahead, and her vanilla flat white was waiting. She exchanged nods and grins with one of the baristas and hurried out the door toward headquarters.

It was a sunny afternoon and the sharp light from above cast everything into a kind of visual purity that she managed to see all too rarely. She had broken into a jog before she realized what she was doing and deliberately slowed her pace. *If I can't have a beach vacation, I need to at least slow the hell down and enjoy the sunlight on the few days when it's so perfect.*

They were meeting in Kayleigh's lab again. The space had evolved into surveillance central as the tech's systems tracked the feeds from the warehouse as well as all the other sources throughout the city. Diana was the last to arrive, and she overheard Cara talking to the tech about an eighteen-wheeler. *Seriously, enough with the mobile armory, woman. You need to clear your mind. It's like a broken record in there.* She slid into one of the high seats around the work-table and took a large sip of her coffee.

Her second in command scowled at her. "Where's mine?"

She shrugged. "At the store, I presume."

"You didn't bring enough for the whole class?"

"Heh. There was no class in this room until I got here."

Kayleigh rolled her eyes. "Good one, boss. You're downright hilarious. So, on to actual intelligent conversation. The bugs in the warehouse are all active."

Diana interrupted. "Wait, actually, let's close some open loops before we create more. Is Deacon all set? Does he need anything there?"

The tech blinked, clearly surprised at the turn in the discussion. *Ha. I'll show you who's intelligent.* "So far, so good. We'll want to outfit a space for him—probably the rest of the floor. I know you thought it would be medical way back when, but since we don't have a medic, it seems silly to leave it vacant."

"That's what we thought way back when, too. Also, if you do anything that makes me feel old again, I'll lock you in your apartment with Rath and an unlimited supply of Coke and Twizzlers. For him, not for you."

The threat had no visible effect and Kayleigh resumed speaking. "Other than that, Deacon will need supplies and that kind of stuff, but nothing too out of the ordinary. I'm sure Nylotte can get whatever he requires."

Oh, touché. "I'm sure she can," Diana responded dryly. "I'll have her contact you directly for payment." She turned to Cara. "How about Hank?"

"He's doing well—held his own during our bounty run and has been looking good in training since. He needs to up his shooting game, but that's the case with anyone who joins us because we're so awesome." She laughed but they all knew it was true. "His magic is cool, too."

Diana had heard the story of how he'd broken through the wall like the Kool-Aid man and itched to see it for herself. "All right. Get his paperwork finalized. Put in a clause that the words 'mobile armory' may never cross his lips, singly or in combination." She enjoyed the scowl the woman gave her and turned back to Kayleigh. "Okay, tell me about the surveillance."

The tech nodded. "We have a good signal. Most of the stuff from downstairs collected by the bugs Sloan distributed is garbage. Petty nonsense, really, although some of it is really disgusting. We should consider burning the building down with them in it." Her boss looked to see if she was kidding and couldn't tell. "The feed from the office, though? That's gold."

"Do tell."

"They're after the Prince of Plunder."

Diana and Cara spoke at the same time with the same palpable level of surprise. "What?"

"Yep. In addition to causing trouble wherever they can, they've found the damn pirate and the witch wants him."

"For another big event like the jailbreak?" Cara sounded angry. *Again. She sounds angry a lot lately.*

Kayleigh shook her head. "I guess you might call it a big event, especially if you happen to be the Prince. She wants him dead."

The words jerked Diana's attention back to the issue at

hand. "Well, that's no good. We need to have a chat with him."

Her second-in-command growled. "At the very least. In a dark room. Involving a lead pipe. He definitely needs to live until I can—*we* can—have some quality time with him."

Kayleigh slid a tablet across the table. It spun into perfect alignment in front of the two agents. On it was an image of the exterior of an industrial building. "He's basically in a castle. They're sequestered in this factory, which is both still active and as dangerous as hell." A slideshow launched and short clips played showing robotic welders, autonomous forklifts, and a variety of other pieces of equipment that could easily be turned into threats.

Cara folded her arms and tilted her chin defiantly. "Then we storm the damn castle, rip the gates down, and pull him out of there by his scrawny little pirate beard."

Diana laughed. "While I have absolutely no issue with the sentiment, that could be easier said than done."

Kayleigh tapped her watch. "And don't forget, time is ticking. It might take them a week to get ready, or they might move tonight. There's no telling with that group of morons."

Cara gave her boss a pointed look. "Yeah, when your boss is insane, things can be unpredictable."

She replied with a single-finger salute and turned back to the tech. "Okay, what can you and Deacon do for us?"

The blonde shrugged. "We can get blueprints, of course. We can scan the area to make sure there's nothing obvious that might cause trouble. We can try to hack the computer system, but it's likely that the place is actually a number of separate systems. Most of them are and that becomes a little more problematic. Once we're in, Alfred can assist."

Diana tapped her fingers together, deep in thought. It was clear they'd have to do something, but the conservative part of her wondered if they could catch him in transit or on a job, rather than face every defense he might have put in their way.

Cara rapped her knuckles on the table. "Hello, Earth to Sheen, come in, space cadet."

She scowled. *To hell with it. This is what we do.* "Get the team together. We go in tonight. Be ready to roll at midnight and we can strike during the very early morning lull. All hands on deck for this one, other than Sloan."

Kayleigh nodded. "About that…do you think it's time to pull him out?"

"He's too valuable where he is." Diana sighed. If we get a sign that they're suspicious, we'll do it. Until then, leave him in place. Give him a warning about tonight, though." An email would find its way to his inbox with coded language to alert him to be extra vigilant.

"Okay." Her tone suggested that it was not even close to okay, but they all knew that the need for inside information was paramount.

"We're doing all we can at the moment to keep him safe, correct?"

She nodded.

"He's a professional. He knows the risks. More importantly, he knows how to read people. He would tell us that he'll know when the time is right to leave."

Neither woman responded. Kayleigh clearly had issues with the notion that her technology put Sloan at risk, even though it hadn't been her decision to use it. Cara wore her focused look that she got when a fight was ahead, but several hours too early. Diana shook her head and stood. She thought she should say something to reassure them and get them back on track, but nothing came. *This thing needs to go right, or people will start letting their emotions overcome their logic.* She headed to the core to begin planning.

CHAPTER TWELVE

Diana managed a nap between completing her individual planning session and the set time for gathering in the core. When the clock struck midnight, she splashed water on her face and shook off the drowsiness. She took the elevator down to the basement and walked slowly toward her assembled team. Pride welled inside her at the sight of all of them gathered and clearly ready to take on any challenge.

They exchanged jibes and insults, and even Rath was in on the action in his role as judge. Seeing him happy always bolstered her spirits. During moments of great introspection, she wondered if the universe hadn't put them together deliberately to fill a need that neither of them knew existed. *Most women get boyfriends. Me, I get a troll.* She laughed inwardly. *I definitely have the better deal. No offense, Bryant.*

The group fell silent as she approached and mirth gave way to focus. She nodded her approval and stepped beside the display table. The technicians stood on one side of it and the remainder of the team gathered on the other sides. Rath had pulled a chair up to stand on. It was almost a little crowded—a positive sign for her branch of ARES. She cleared her throat. "As I'm sure you already know, it's time for some payback. Tonight, we capture the Prince of Plunder, who was a thorn in our side even before he played such a pivotal role in the breakout from the Cube." She raised a hand toward the techs. "Kayleigh and Deacon, spell it out for us."

The blonde spoke while her partner manipulated the display. They worked together seamlessly as if they'd been co-conspirators for years rather than weeks. From a satellite view of the site, their visual perspective zoomed to the access road that led from the nearby streets to the location and rolled slowly along it. "The factory is in reclaimed space from a steel mill, which is good for them and bad for us. County records show that when they cleared the old buildings and constructed this one, they were quite optimistic about how many other factories would locate in close proximity. They claimed five, minimum. It turns out the real number was 'nobody likes you,' and this is the only building in the area."

Anik nodded. "Damn. Not good for a stealth approach."

Cara sounded doubtful. "Chopper?"

Kayleigh shook her head. "Again, no cover. If they saw you coming and had even a single shoulder-mounted rocket…well, Deacon and I would be really lonely."

"Stealth chopper?"

Diana rolled her eyes at her second-in-command. "We don't have one of those at the moment, I'm afraid. I'm not sure anyone does."

The newest agent spoke up, his deep voice soft in the confined space. "There are some out there, but none we can get in time for this. And getting permission would be a nightmare."

The tech jumped into the silence. "So, basically, we have to assume the enemy will be aware that we're coming from the moment the SUVs appear on the access road. They'll have between twenty and thirty seconds to prepare while you drive up, assuming you drive like you stole them."

"While I don't personally enjoy crawling through the woods and such, would an approach on foot make more sense?" Tony was clearly reluctant to share his suggestion.

Deacon shook his head and waved to activate a multi-colored overlay on the map. "As you can see, the location is well-equipped with sensors—many sensors." Each variety was a different color, and the projected detection ranges and directions were mapped. There wasn't a single approach that wasn't fully covered. "Before you ask, yes, we could knock them out with the stun drone we've gotten operational. But that's not a great plan, either. It doesn't guarantee secrecy, and it might set off more active coun-termeasures."

Diana's eyes widened at the revelation that they now had an armed drone. Before she could comment on it, Kayleigh took the floor. "We will use the drone, though. We'll run it ahead of the vehicles to either fry or trip the defenses along the road. Deacon has found a way to configure the stunner to impersonate a ground vehicle. Assuming it survives, it will be tasked to assist with any escapees."

Cara growled. "There won't be any."

Rath grinned at the woman. "Slippy pirate is slippy." The combination of the Pittsburgh word for "slippery" and the general image of a buccaneer in such a state was enough to draw laughter from everyone around the table.

The agent in charge nodded. "Hope for the best, plan for the worst. The drone will be our backup plan for runners. Rath will be the main plan." The troll looked at her, and she grinned at him. "You're the only one of us who can fly, so it has to be you." He gave her a fangy grin and a thumbs-up.

"The regular drones will arrive on site as soon as you deploy, of course." Kayleigh clarified. "They'll be spotters if anyone does make a run for it. They've already verified that there's no underground exit from the space. So, if someone does try to escape, we'll be able to see them with the thermal sights on the drone. We've also outfitted one to launch Rath's invisible tracers if things go really awry."

Anik laughed. "You two are very productive. You seem to complement each other well." Diana didn't miss the irritated look Cara threw at him, and she resolved that after they apprehended the Prince, she'd get over her resistance and force the woman to tell her what was going on. *Everything that's going on.*

The techs exchanged smiles, then focused again on the display table. A pair of SUVs appeared and hurtled along the access road. One stopped at the front, and the other veered around the side of the building to head toward the back. Deacon was apologetic. "We modeled it for two teams, a guess as to what you'd want. We can change the model easily though."

Diana shook her head. "Two teams make sense since there are two main entrances. Agreed?"

Everyone nodded, and Cara spoke. "Yep. Two teams. I call Hank."

"Well, since my primary choice will be on top of the building doing his Batman impersonation, I guess I'll go with Tony."

Rath grinned. "Bat-Troll."

"I stand corrected. So, we're set."

Anik frowned. "Hey. Over here. Can you see me? Have I achieved invisibility?"

Diana raised a hand to the techs. "Deacon, would you explain to our resident demolitions man what he'll be doing?"

The tech nodded, and the table zoomed in to a ground view of the building and rotated slowly around it. "See all those doors? We need to stop them from being doors."

Anik rubbed his palms together. "Now you're talking. Blow them in?"

Diana shook her head. "No, seal them up. Welding rig."

He sighed. "Boring."

"But essential."

"But boring."

She rolled her eyes. "Well, if you finish quickly, you can come in and join the fun."

He smiled. "Good deal. But I get to be on Hank and Cara's team."

"I wouldn't have it any other way." He frowned, not exactly sure what she meant by that, and she turned to the techs again. "Let's see if we can get through the rest without any more interruptions from the peanut gallery, shall we?"

Kayleigh gestured, and Deacon adjusted the controls to zoom into the building itself. The roof vanished and the floor plan appeared. "Okay, so...the place is a functioning factory, mainly robotic. You'll have welders working, loads of steel being moved from place to place, autonomous forklifts and other vehicles, and possibly even actual robots wandering about. It's damn high-tech." She sounded jealous or at least desirous of similar equipment for her own use. "Long story short, it's not a great place to fight. Far too much cover, tons of hot hardware around to mess with thermal sighting, and the ever-present possibility that one of the robots is actually a Terminator."

Tony nodded dramatically, his arms folded. "Exactly like I've been saying."

Diana sighed. "Okay, it'll suck. Is there anything you can do about that, smarty-pants tech types?"

Deacon laughed. "Yes. We'll have a few new toys for you to deploy that will enable us to be of some assistance during the op. But that doesn't change the fact that we're basically taking on an enemy in their stronghold."

She clapped. "That's something we're good at. They won't know what hit them. Let's get geared up, people."

Hank sidled up to her as they relocated to the equipping area. "You know, if we had a large vehicle—say a semi—and put changeable skins on it, we could possibly roll right up without freaking them out."

Diana frowned and folded her arms. "And what do you think would be inside this vehicle?"

The big man grinned. "Probably some equipment—lockers, that kind of thing."

"Cara told you to say that."

He laughed. "No, but her opinions are very clear on the matter. The thing is, we could most likely do a basic version of it with off-the-rack parts. It wouldn't be too difficult. A month or so, and I could have it rolling."

She sighed. "Okay, it's on the table. But that's as far as I'm willing to go." They separated and headed for different sections of the equipping area. Diana alternated between getting herself set up and helping Rath into his patrol gear. She bent close and whispered, "You stay safe, you hear me?"

He grinned at her. "I will if you will."

"Deal." She gave him a high-five that was more a mid-five for her and finished strapping her armor pieces on. That secure, she retrieved magazines from the locker, loaded her carbine and pistol with anti-magic ammo, and divided her backups between that and standard bullets. She had slipped the last in when Cara stepped beside her and spoke softly, avoiding eye contact with her gaze fixed ahead.

"Listen, boss, I get rules and all. But we're invading a damn metalworking factory. There'll be a ton of stuff around that they can use as shields. Plus, there are no innocents to get in the way. If ever there was a time that armor-piercing ammo was called for, this is it."

Diana frowned while she considered the suggestion. On the one hand were the rules. On the other, Cara was right, and it was never bad to have an edge. She sighed. "Okay. Two mags each for you and me—one pistol and one rifle.

But be careful. Those things can punch through our vests as easily as they can an enemy's cover. If you shoot our new guy, we might find it hard to replace him."

The woman laughed and sounded a little like her normal self. She grabbed the magazines with the red stripes, handed two to her boss, and retained two for herself. Her gaze was still lowered as she walked away. Diana shook her head and banished the worry from her mind. *Later.* She slipped the mags into the slots on her belt that would require the most effort to retrieve them from to ensure that she didn't accidentally load them.

She turned, ready to tell everyone to head to the cars, but was interrupted by Deacon who rushed over with a case in each hand. Both were roughly three times as wide as a standard briefcase. They looked heavy, based on the way he lurched toward her. "Toys. Get them inside and plan to spend a minute or two deploying them. We'll give you instructions then."

She raised an eyebrow. "Anything fun?"

He grinned. "Well, we think so. But they won't make anything go boom, so you probably won't."

"Hey, no stereotyping. We're quite cerebral."

"Sure, sure. When you're ready to help us build the next one, you let me know."

She laughed. "Well, maybe not *that* cerebral."

He turned, dashed away with a wave, and headed to his workspace above. This was their first run with both techs, and they had decided he would work out of the lab while Kayleigh took her regular place in the core. Diana had no idea what they planned as far as a division of responsibilities but was sure they'd operate in the best way possible.

She gazed at her team, all fully outfitted and waiting for her command, and realized she was completely confident in each of her agents individually—and even more so when they were together. *Whatever comes, we can handle it.* She grinned at them. "You people rock. I couldn't ask for better sisters and brothers in arms. Let's go capture ourselves a pirate."

CHAPTER THIRTEEN

Cara swung the wheel hard to stay on the road as the SUVs barreled toward the factory. The chain-link fence had offered no resistance to her vehicle when she'd simply powered through it, and they assumed that the enemies inside were now aware of the incoming assault. After some deliberation, the team had brought three cars. She and Hank were in the first, the second held Diana, Tony, and Rath, and Anik was alone in the third. Kayleigh had checked to make sure Sloan wasn't nearby, but his phone showed him in the Remembrance faction warehouse, as usual. *At least we don't have that to worry about. Which, of course, leaves only about two thousand other things.*

She shook her head, but the growling in her mind wouldn't be dislodged. Ever since the events at the Cube, a growing part of her brain had stabbed continually at her and tried to break her down. No matter what, she wouldn't give into it but couldn't deny that a definitive win would have a positive impact on her mood.

Hank yelled a warning, and she wrenched the wheel

again to avoid a duck, of all things, that waddled serenely across the road. She wasn't sure who she wanted to shoot first—the animal for causing the trouble or him for deciding it would be better to risk both their lives than to hit it. She muttered threats at both and pressed harder on the accelerator to skid around the final corner that led to the back opening into the facility.

Her partner was out his door before the SUV had stopped moving, and she joined him a few seconds later. They retrieved heavy weapons from the trunk. She strapped her carbine over her chest and snatched up a pair of flashbangs to carry while the newest ARES agent attached his rifle and selected a large shotgun. Tony had made the choice on that weapon for the team. He'd selected the Kalashnikov KS-12T for its semi-auto firing and ten-shot magazine but frequently and loudly expressed his desire for a custom version. Diana had explained that until they had a gunsmith in-house, he'd need to use off-the-rack gear. Hank held the big weapon in one hand as he stuck a backup magazine into his belt, then nodded his readiness.

She activated her microphone. "Back, good to go."

Diana's voice replied immediately. "Front, good to go. Anik and Rath are getting into position now. Glam?"

Kayleigh, clearly excited, spoke quickly. "Warlock and I are good to go."

"Okay. Rock and roll. Let's get us a pirate." The boss sounded irritated, which was well in line with her second-in-command's own feelings about their target.

Cara and Hank broke into a jog toward the door as the first defenses materialized. Two men in mismatched camo gear—*Seriously? In a damn warehouse?*—appeared from behind each side of the opening, rifles held to their shoulders. She curved left and her partner went right, dashed in a zigzag route to avoid the initial bursts, and took position on the opposite sides of the metal walls from their opponents. "Flashbangs out." She threw one grenade at a diagonal across the gap and risked exposing her arm to toss the other inside the building close to her position. They detonated, and she ran forward. Hank's shotgun boomed a second before her carbine's triple burst and both enemies, already stunned by the grenades, fell.

She grinned for the first time in what felt like a long while. It made her face muscles twinge. "Initial opposition down. Moving in."

Diana replied, "Same here." She and Tony checked in a circle around them to be sure that no immediate reinforcements were inbound before each set down the case they carried and laid it on its side. They knelt together and popped the catches. In Tony's box were four heavy-looking spheres. Hers held a pair of miniature drones, fragile objects folded in upon themselves for transport.

Deacon spoke to Tony first. "Stark, take those out of the box and set them on the ground wherever." As the first one touched the concrete floor of the warehouse, lights began to blink on it. It rolled in all four directions, a few feet each, and returned to its center point. After a short pause, it raced away into the factory. They repeated the process with the other three.

The former detective sounded amused. "What exactly are those toys, Warlock?"

"Sensor spheres. They'll help us map the space. However, they're crap at climbing stairs."

Kayleigh jumped in. "Which is why we'll free the two drones in your case, boss. Be gentle with them. Those things are still way too fragile." Diana knew they were experimental, something the techs had worked on together. The level of sophistication required to function in three dimensions demanded delicate components. She detached one from the power cable that connected it to the container and placed it in a clear space. Beside her, the last ball rolled away and Tony stood and scanned the area. The barrel of his shotgun traversed the space in tandem with his gaze.

The four fans on each were stacked in two pairs in collapsed mode, and they unfolded as she watched. Lights glimmered on the back as the device performed its startup diagnostic, then with a whir, the machine elevated and rotated a full turn. "The feed is fine," Kayleigh reported. "Set out the other one and you're free to move about."

Diana followed her instructions and stood. A panel appeared on the right of her display with a wireframe map of the facility that became more detailed with each passing moment. Gunfire barked deeper within, and Warlock cursed. "Bastards. Someone shot one of the spheres."

"Don't worry, we'll get payback for that, too." Tony sounded as irritated as Deacon did.

She shook her head. "Khan, status."

The demolitions expert was out of breath. "Your end is done. I'm starting on the right side."

"Friday, are you able to show me the enemies?" Red dots appeared in her display to mark where the drones and spheres had detected members of the opposition. "Okay, then. Time to clear these idiots out. Glam, if you can locate our primary target, that would be good."

"I'm on it. Wherever he's hiding, my canaries will find him."

———

Cara crept around the side of a machine on her approach to one of the red dots in her display and Hank trailed a few steps behind. She'd ordered him to stay far enough away that her stealth wouldn't be compromised. *We should have suppressors for this kind of op. Something to discuss with the boss later.*

On both her left and right were long machines, each with a roll of steel mounted on the end nearest their entry point. A track of some kind pulled the metal along a waist-high channel toward four robotic arms equipped with cutting lasers, presumably programmable for different shapes. Her target was on the other side of the machine to the right, near the first set of waving mechanical arms. Their articulation kept them from expanding very far outward, but his positioning still smacked of confidence she would have lacked with those giant appendages in motion nearby.

It also made the final part of the approach difficult. She reached a position behind him on the opposite side of the machine and ducked as he started yet another full turn with his weapon extended. The loud entrances from either side had clearly spread the alarm throughout the building, but she didn't want to reveal her position by shooting him. When he turned away from her again, she moved. With her right hand on the machine in the small space between the moving metal and the edge, she vaulted forward and aimed her kick at the back of his head. Her heels connected with his skull exactly as planned, propelled him forward, and dropped him on his face. That was the upside.

The downside was the way his weapon careened from his hand and landed in a machine across the aisle. Laser cutters on that side sliced into it and the ammunition sparked and exploded. The resulting burst of noise confirmed her position far better than if she'd stood on top of one of the machines and yelled. *Dammit. Bad luck atop bad luck.* "Get moving, Hank. We'll have company." Her partner made the leap over the equipment with slightly less grace than she had and was at her side as a trio of enemies appeared ahead. Two men with rifles flanked a woman with a wand. She was dressed all in red, a striking image in the otherwise black and grey factory.

The crimson witch's voice dripped with faux sweetness. "Welcome to our home. You're just in time for the barbecue." She pointed her wand at Hank and a cone of flame seared across the distance between them. He rolled in the only direction he could—toward his teammate—and the fire tracked him. Cara lunged and slid under it, then jerked upright on the far side with her carbine extended. A triple burst eliminated the rifle wielder on the left of the woman, but rounds from his weapon battered her vest and flung her onto her rear. Hank's gun barked, followed quickly by a shout of pain that sounded male. The spent shell clattered across the floor in a strange instant of silence before a piece of cut metal detached from the machine nearest her with a loud scraping sound.

She hurled herself onto her back, and the sharp-edged plate missed her by inches. It stopped in front of the witch in time to intercept the next two shots from Hank's shotgun, which failed to penetrate and instead, richocheted wildly. The metal careened away from the witch and into Hank and knocked him off his feet. His partner scrambled up and fired at their adversary, but she was already in motion to evade and ducked into the cover of another piece of equipment behind her former position. The second man lay on the ground with a wicked wound in his leg from the shotgun, but when he saw her advance toward the witch's hiding place, he tried to reach for his weapon. She knelt and punched him in the head, and the impact and the stun from her gloves combined to knock him out.

As she stood, she realized she was glad that the sneaking around was over and the outright fighting had begun. "Come out, come out, wherever you are, Red Riding Hood. The big bad wolf is here to end you."

———

Diana raced toward the man ahead of her, who was armed with a wand. She raised her rifle and fired, but the bullets went through his head without stopping. In the instant that her mind registered the illusion, a giant piece of metal struck her from the left side, where her hidden foe had presumably waited for her to enter his line of sight before he dispelled his duplicate and hurled the object at her. The impact catapulted her into Tony, and the two of them landed hard in a tangle of limbs.

Her instinctive reflex was to cast a force shield around them both, and that was all that saved them. A rain of bullets bounced off it before another large slab of metal pounded into it. Her energy trickled away as she maintained the defense and she struggled to untangle herself from her partner and used him as leverage to rise. Her magical foe was supported by two men who fired at her. The former gestured with his wand to levitate an even larger piece of steel, and the other two had paused to change magazines. They all wore predatory looks on their faces. She realized why when the first bullet plunged through her defense without slowing and buried itself in her vest.

"The bastards have anti-magic bullets." Her shout was accompanied by a grunt of effort as she yanked the piece of metal out of her foe's grip with a rage-fueled burst of magic and hurled it at the shooters. It plowed into them at a downward angle and crushed them under it. Her body registered that several rounds had hit her and that she likely had at least one fractured or broken rib, judging by the way breathing hurt. She put it from her mind and focused on the adversary to her left. He brought his wand to bear, and she reached out with her telekinesis and tried to rip it from his grasp. She failed, but it bought Tony the time he needed. His shotgun barked twice in quick succession and the enemy mage toppled and lay still in an expanding puddle of red.

The detective's lip was bloody and split from where

she'd hit him with her rifle when they collided. "Asshole. He deserved worse."

Diana nodded. "These guys suck. Glam, any guidance?"

There was a delay before Kayleigh responded. "We only have one canary and one sphere left, so we're trying to keep them in the shadows. But there is a second floor with a number of catwalks leading to a section that's all offices and control centers. Our guess is that he's in there, but we haven't actually located him yet."

"Give me a path." The most direct route illuminated on her glasses, and she nodded. It was ahead and to the right, near the midpoint of the factory, which meant having to fight their way through more chaff before they reached the wheat, no doubt. She looked at her partner, and he gave her a nod. "Okay, we're moving forward."

CHAPTER FOURTEEN

Cara lined up the witch she was stalking in her sights. The woman's feet were exposed under the edge of the equipment she hid behind. The chase had been a good one but she'd expended most of a magazine prior to that moment. She raised her rifle barrel to chest height and pulled the trigger. The carbine clicked empty, but the armor-piercing bullet drilled through the machine panel and the woman behind it. She fell soundlessly but with a look of shock frozen on her face.

The agent nodded in satisfaction and echoed Diana's last words. "Give me a path." Her glasses showed that the staircase to the second level was forward and to the left, at the center of the facility according to the map. She grinned at the thought of eliminating a few more of the scumbags, and her smile widened at the idea of finding the pirate. It would be a pleasure to pummel him until he revealed where the people who hired him to help with the prison breakout were hiding.

They knew each enemy position in advance on their

way to the center, thanks to the remaining sphere rolling around on their side of the building. As the red dots moved, they were able to react accordingly and fire at their opponents as they stepped from cover. A mage who used a piece of steel as a shield had presented a momentary problem until Hank fired at the small gap between the floor and his defensive barrier. He'd yelped in pain and dropped the metal on himself, which led to another scream and ongoing moans of agony from the weight of the slab atop him. The partners had exchanged looks that threatened to turn into adrenaline-fueled giggles, so they faced resolutely forward and continued to move deeper into the facility.

They reached the center at the same time as Diana and Tony, who arrived at a run. Cara asked, "Are you having fun?"

The former detective quipped, "We were until we found you here. The pirate is ours."

She shook her head. "Oh, hell no. He's mine."

Hank shrugged. "Well, since she's my partner, I'll have to back her up on this. Plus, we were here first."

Diana raced past them and ran to the staircase. "Yeah, but we're faster."

They pounded up after her. The stairs switched back on themselves twice and finally ended on a second level about three stories up. Below, the factory floor was dotted with fallen enemies, either dead or severely wounded. Impressively, they'd managed not to destroy any of the factory's equipment, which for a BAM mission showed a significant degree of restraint. *Yet.* Diana grinned. *The night's still young.*

At the top of the metal staircase, catwalks led left and right along the wall of the warehouse, with connectors to the opposite side about halfway toward the far wall. She turned and saw that an actual floor had been built out over a portion of the factory, with walls to create an enclosed area. The crossing pieces connected to another catwalk that ran in front of the constructed office area. The only entrance to that space was in the center of the walkway. Long windows extended down each side of the structure, most likely the control spaces Kayleigh had mentioned.

Diana went right, so Cara dashed left. She knew that on most days, she was faster than the boss, which should bring her to the pirate first if he was back there. However, the defenders who attacked her seemed determined to make things more complicated than they should be. She stopped at the crosswalk and studied her adversaries. They had rushed out at the sight of the ARES agents and carried large metal shields that protected them on three sides. One was halfway across, another three-quarters of the way across, and one awaited them on the rear catwalk. She gestured for Hank to take the long way around—which would at least force the rearmost ones to decide on which approach to defend—and Diana did the same with Tony.

Those at the back reacted as she'd anticipated and scurried down to position themselves at the corners. Kayleigh's voice broke through the quiet on the comms. "I'm not sure if you've noticed, but there are firing notches in those shields." Cara magnified her glasses and confirmed that the tech was correct.

"Damn. Look at them, all prepared and stuff." Tony and Hank had halted their advance at the news as neither had much in the way of defense against fire that might come from behind the shields. The good news was that the items themselves looked heavy and unwieldy enough that the people protected by them probably only had pistols. *Hopefully, anyway.* The bad news was that she'd been too careless with her AP ammo and had none left to penetrate the shields. "So, it's essentially a stalemate at the moment. I say we charge 'em."

"Cara, you've always wanted to fly, right?" The boss had the tone in her voice that she got when she thought fast about something that would probably end in disaster.

Diana calculated the angles for both her and her second-in-command when the other woman replied and sounded more than a little dubious. "Uh...yes?"

"Okay, here's your chance. I'll drop you behind the back one."

"Holy hell. Okay." Cara lowered her rifle, drew the Bowie knife from the back of her vest, and lowered herself into a crouch. "I'm ready when you are."

Diana focused her mind, envisioned her internal pathways, and directed power to both her force magic and telekinesis. With the former, she hurled Cara forward. The woman kept her limbs curled tightly, which made it easier to adjust her trajectory gently. She dispersed the magic and relied on momentum to carry her the rest of the way. The agent's boots struck the metal only inches away from where she'd intended and about two feet behind the rearmost defender on her catwalk.

Shouts of alarm accompanied the landing, and Cara whirled to her right as Diana launched herself over her foes in the same way. She had much better control of her own flight and was able to use her body weight and magic together to maintain the proper angles. When she landed, she tumbled ahead to avoid the attack of the defender, who had identified the maneuver quickly enough to try to intercept her.

She rolled up into a crouch, spun with a hiss of pain triggered by her damaged ribs, and thrust her right arm forward to punch the air. A blast of force smacked into the defender's midsection, doubled him over, and forced him onto one knee. *Damn. That was a little too high.* She lunged into a follow-up attack and punched him in the temple to remove him from the fight. Her assault had positioned her perfectly and she grinned, extended her arms, and rammed the nearest shield into the one beyond it. The defender who had rushed toward her bounced off the piece of metal she'd set into motion and rebounded into his own shield. She didn't wait to see if he got up but pivoted and reached for fire to release it at the man on the far end of the catwalk.

"Damn it to hell," Cara cursed. Out of the corner of her eye, she'd watched her knife—thrown with all her might at the enemy nearest Hank—fall short of its target by several feet. That hadn't stopped her turn toward the man who brought his pistol to bear on her. *If he'd reacted faster, I'd be toast. I guess he didn't expect me to do a super-jump to get behind him.*

To be fair, though, I didn't either. She snorted at the inane meanderings of her mind and lunged forward at the end of her spin, grasped his wrist with her right hand, and shoved the gun away from her.

He pulled the trigger and the bullet ricocheted behind her with a loud smack. She punched his triceps with her left hand, and he jerked from the pain and the shock the glove delivered. Her fist was already in motion to swing in a vicious backhand at his face. He jerked away in time to take the blow on his jaw rather than his temple. She felt something break, but any sound he made before he fell unconscious was lost in the loud snap of the shock discharge.

Cara stepped forward into the three-sided shield to avoid any counterfire from the man she'd tried to harm with her knife throw and drew her pistol from its holster. A deft twist slid it into the firing slot, and she pulled the trigger until the magazine was empty. She crouched to peer through the hole and saw that her nearest opponent was very much out of action. His vest had caught a few of the rounds, but the way she'd rotated the gun had resulted in wounds to a leg and an arm. *And that's why smart people wear armor there, too, boys and girls.*

She felt the vibrations before she heard the footfalls on the catwalk and turned quickly. The other man on her side had abandoned his shield to make a direct attack. He had already pulled the trigger when she flung a hand out and launched flaming darts from her fingertips. They seared through his vest and into his body, and he collapsed instantly. She did as well but a line of blazing pain drew itself along her thigh, just below the armor plate. It was a through and through but still hurt like someone had poured acid into her leg. She fumbled for a compression bandage and by the time she had it in position, Hank was there to help her finish securing it.

He nodded toward her belt. "Healing potion?"

She shook her head. "I'm not damaged enough and don't want to waste it. When you have something that could mean the difference between life and death, you don't use it on a flesh wound. Even one that hurts like a bastard."

She stood with a groan from the pain and discovered that while she couldn't put her full weight on it, she could limp along well enough. Hank extended her knife to her with a grin. "That might have been the worst throw I've seen in quite some time."

"Shut it, new guy." She took the weapon from him and shoved it back into its sheath but wasn't able to banish the smile that accompanied the words. He laughed and waved an arm to gesture for her to lead. She did so, painfully aware that her boss had already dispatched the defenders on her side and dashed into the office area.

"Son of a bitch, they shot my last canary." Kayleigh's voice was harsh in Diana's ear. "I will come down there and kick their asses personally, every goddammed one of them."

She shook her head with a grin at the tech's ire and continued to stalk into the office space. She and Tony had cleared the control booths first and found both empty. The thermal displays on their glasses revealed bodies ahead, but without triangulation from the techs' toys or more agents, pinpointing their exact position was difficult. They could be around the corner or on the other side of a wall, and the display couldn't tell the difference. Diana dialed the detection down to minimum active mode, which gave a generalized glow but didn't interfere with her vision.

The lights had been doused, which left the area almost completely dark. The night-vision function of the glasses was robust enough to compensate, and the main features were clear. Two intersections lay before them in the hallway, one roughly in the middle of the space and one at the back wall. There were no visible doors so presumably, the remaining enemies were down either one or both of those paths. There was no telling which one might hold the pirate, and she desperately wanted to find him herself since the last time it had been Cara who grabbed him while she lay bleeding on the floor. *The bastard has earned some personal payback from me.*

She frowned at the sudden realization that the defenses had been unexpectedly light, but before she could say anything, figures emerged from each of the four hallways, completely undetected by her heat sensors. "Contact," she yelled as the four wands they held spat death and destruction directly at her and Tony.

CHAPTER FIFTEEN

The aggressors in the front dropped to a knee to allow those behind to attack as well. Diana summoned a force shield that filled the hallway, and it intercepted the attacks. Her mind cataloged them—*one ice, one force, one fire, and one damn shadow*—while her energy trickled slowly away. At four-on-one odds, magically speaking, she wouldn't be able to counter their power with her own for very long.

Nylotte's voice whispered in her mind, fortunately merely a memory rather than the woman communicating telepathically with her. *Make it your own.* She focused on the different sensations and found the force attack, then allowed that power to trickle through, grasped it, and cycled it into her own shield. It worked but it needed all the focus she could spare, and even that wasn't adequate. She freed up enough brainpower to speak.

"Tony. Lower left. About a foot." His face turned thoughtful like he planned his moves, and he nodded. She reached within, modified her shield, and opened it where she'd indicated. The former detective dropped his shotgun and sank to his stomach as he drew and extended his rifle on the way. After a second of stabilization, he pulled the trigger four times to deliver bullets into both feet of the mages nearest him.

Their attacks fell with them, which left her to face only ice and shadow, neither of which she was strong enough to be able to co-opt. Those in front fired at Tony and Diana closed the barrier again. She sensed Cara and Hank moving in from behind. "Make sure you're under cover. I can't hold this much longer."

Cara's voice was filled with pain. "I can blast them with magic once you drop the shield."

"You sound like that will put you all the way out. Maybe go with bullets instead."

"Yeah, that's a good—" An odd noise followed, and Diana looked over her shoulder to see that her second had fallen, the bandage around her leg scarlet and soaked with her blood.

"Idiot. You need to think about yourself sometimes." She scowled. "Stark, take her back and feed her the potion. Make sure there's nothing in the wound that can be sealed inside as it heals. Hank, you're with me." With no way to know what was ahead, she decided having the option of magic would be a good thing. She focused ahead again, and the newest agent stepped beside her.

"What's the plan, boss?"

"I'll break the shield into four and throw it at them. It should block their attacks until it reaches them. They'll probably deflect or nullify it before it does damage, but that's not the point. You go left, and I go right, head down the corridor, and look for cover. If they're stupid enough to follow, shoot 'em. When you're halfway down, stop and wait for instructions. If you see a door, move past it so they can't come at you from behind." She was aware that someone from the far hallway could circle if the whole thing connected but was willing to gamble it didn't.

"Go." She quartered the shield and hurled the four individual pieces. The enemies acted as she'd anticipated and blocked the attack with their own magic, but it gave them the necessary time to reposition. Diana was glad to see her guess was right, as the hallway ended at a wall. There was a door about halfway down, and she dashed past it before she turned back about twelve feet or so from the intersection.

She watched for someone dumb enough to stick their heads out, but no one did. "You throw sonics. Let me know when you're ready with two." A moment passed while she prepared her own grenades.

Hank sounded eager. "Ready."

"Execute." She heard the clatter a few seconds later as his ordnance struck the intersection and threw her own. His detonated, the wicked aural attack an effective tactic to make wizards and witches lose focus. Her earpieces protected her from the noise, so she also didn't hear the results of her own contribution to the assault—a pair of fragmentation grenades. When her ear protection allowed sound again, silence reigned.

After waiting for a moment to listen carefully, she strode forward, and the other agent mirrored her on the opposite side. They peeked around the corners of the hallway to confirm that the attack had worked as she'd envisioned it. The sonics had removed their defenses, and the fragmentation grenades had inflicted a series of wounds. All four were eliminated. She shook her head. "This guy does not surround himself with the cream of the crop."

"What would you have done?" He sounded genuinely interested.

Diana thought about it for a second, then shrugged. "I wouldn't have clustered together in such a small space if I could help it. But I definitely would have dashed out of the intersection as soon as the sonics landed."

"It might have been difficult if you were shot in the feet."

She chuckled as she waved him toward the door on his side and jogged to the other one. "Good point. Still, I'd like to think I wouldn't find myself in that situation." She extended the tiny camera in her left sleeve under the door and the feed appeared in her glasses. The room was filled with cubicles but apparently empty. She retrieved a flash-bang and a roll of gaffer's tape that was included in each belt's supply of miscellaneous items and secured the grenade to the door. If someone was hiding inside, she'd hear it when they came out.

Hank reported that his room was clear, and she helped him to rig that door as well. They returned to the intersection, and she considered her options. As far as they knew, there were only a couple more rooms in the facility if their initial scans and the blueprints were both correct. It was safe to assume that at least one would hold their target and a number of guards. There was no way to tell what challenges the other might hold.

Anik's voice came as a surprise. "Doors are done."

Diana replied, "Okay. Get into position to go after runners if necessary."

"Affirmative."

"Glam, any read on the rooms nearest us?"

Kayleigh sounded highly irritated. "No. I've tried to use Rath for triangulation—he's directly above you at the moment, actually—but something is messing with the sensors in that section. Maybe they built it with radioactive materials or shielding."

Hank almost yelped in alarm. "You're telling us this now?"

The tech was dismissive. "It's a joke. Mostly. Chill. We always check for that kind of thing, and nothing environmentally harmful is present other than the goons with the guns and the magic and the 'hey, hey, it hurts me.'"

Diana laughed. "Professor Frink. Nice impersonation. Maybe we should change your callsign. But on to serious matters." She pointed down the hallway to the left. "I'll take a look. You stay here and guard the other way." Her steps were slow and careful as she searched for traps and triggers but discovered none. *Odd. I'd expected a more entrenched defense.*

When she reached the door, she lay on her stomach next to it to snake the camera beneath. It showed a barricade made of office furniture and metal scavenged from the factory floor below. The room was deeper than anticipated, which suggested she'd lost her bearings on the structure's dimensions. The tiny microphone picked murmurs up, and she heard the Prince of Plunder's voice.

Kayleigh confirmed it a moment later. "Alfred says that's him."

She stood and put her back to the wall on the far side of the door. "Tell Alfred thanks. Hercules, move up to the other side of this door. Stark, is Croft stable?"

"I'm fine but I can't stand yet." Cara sounded seriously annoyed. "If anyone comes near me, I'll shoot them, stab them, and roast them with fire for pissing me off."

Their leader couldn't contain a chuckle, which earned her another growl from her second-in-command. "Right. Stark, come up to the far intersection and guard the hallway in case there are surprises from the other room."

Hank had retrieved his shotgun and held it in the ready position, aimed at the door handle. She positioned herself at an angle from the door with her back against the opposite wall. "You shoot it, and I'll blast it in. We'll follow immediately. You go right and I'll go left." He nodded.

Diana reached for her magic and readied it, then nodded. "Go." He pulled the trigger and she followed with a blast an instant later. The door flung open. He dashed into the room and she followed a step behind, moved left, and scanned for enemies. Time slowed as her magic sense warned her something was wrong, and her illusion detection bracelet froze around her wrist. *Not good.* She shouted a command to dispel the magic, and the false image fell away to reveal the strangest weapon she'd ever seen.

Someone—presumably the pirate and his crew—had put four of the mechanical arms from the factory below on a turntable. With their entrance into the room, the contraption had activated and now began to move. The limbs ended with the cutting lasers and featured a kind of sensor package on top. The robotic appendages moved into position with the lasers closest to her and those closest to Hank arcing to bear on them. There was no time for subtlety, so she grasped the first idea and put it into action. She ran to her left and cast a sustained channel of fire into the center of the device. The laser cutters tracked her, but she was faster than the turntable and it apparently wasn't smart enough to change direction.

As if she'd called for it with her thought, another of the arms rotated toward her. She growled and reached deep for her magic to release a massive wash of fire into the middle. Small detonations followed—presumably, important pieces had overloaded or melted or something—and it fell silent. She panted, then realized Tony was yelling over the comms. "They're on the run. The pirate and four others. And they have illusions active so they look exactly like him."

Diana snarled her fury and frustration and launched into a sprint with Hank at her heels. *Dammit, you bastard. You will not get away.*

Rath listened to the chase inside the factory over the comms as he tracked the heat signatures. Now that the fugitives were out of the office area, they were visible. Two moved to the front and two to the back. He'd heard the deep satisfaction in Cara's voice as she'd eliminated one of them, then the frustration that replaced it when the illusion vanished to reveal he wasn't the right pirate.

Diana pursued the pair who raced toward the front, and Tony and Hank raced after those who headed to the rear. He considered where he might make the most difference and decided that their leader didn't need backup. Besides, Anik waited in that direction as well. He ran along the centerline of the rooftop toward the back of the building. "Gwen, all systems ready?" He'd checked at least a dozen times but still wanted to hear her say it.

"Affirmative. It's all good."

He grinned. Her personality grew stronger every time they patrolled together. Below, one of the heat signatures stopped and darted behind an object on the floor plan. Rath toggled his microphone. "Rear ambush. Careful."

Tony replied, "Thanks, Rambo. It'll take us a second, but we'll get him."

It wouldn't make sense to stop running if he was the Prince, and it wouldn't make sense for someone to sacrifice themselves for anyone other than the Prince. Which means...

The troll grinned at the turn of events. He kept pace as he loped above the target, then launched himself into the darkness as the pirate exited the factory. The low light function of his goggles worked perfectly, and Gwen put an outline around his quarry as an added bonus. The man paused briefly before he veered aside on an odd vector across the grass at an angle from the building.

A drone whizzed overhead, and Kayleigh spoke into his ear. "The one nearest you is running on a line toward what is probably an outbuilding. It's fairly far away and not even part of this facility, but he might have hidden a car there or something."

"Got it." Rath banked, his flight silent as he rode the currents and wove to match pace with his target. When he judged that everything was right, he swooped at the fleeing buccaneer. He retracted the wings about ten feet off the ground and plummeted toward his foe. His calculations were perfect, and the troll thunked into the pirate's back heels-first and hurled the man onto his face. To his credit, the enemy recovered quickly, stood, and extended a wand with a snarl. Before he could cast, Rath's batons struck him in sequence—left leg, right leg, left rib, right arm—and culminated with a double thrust into his chest. The Prince lost consciousness as the stun batons discharged and he landed heavily in the dirt.

He looked down at his captive with a cheerful smile. "Happy trails, pirate."

Kayleigh laughed and delivered her next comment with the perfect amount of sarcasm. "Come out to the coast. We'll get together, have a few laughs."

The troll grinned. He was always happy when someone recognized one of his action-movie quotes, and his new housemate was getting better and better at it. Of course, it helped that they had watched *Die Hard* together only a few days before.

Tony and Hank arrived, lifted the stirring pirate, and put one of his arms around each of their necks to drag him to the car. Rath trailed them happily as he tossed the man's wand in the air and caught it a few times. The chatter on the comms was all positive. They had minimal injuries, their objective was achieved, and police and ambulances were on their way to deal with the low-level defenders inside the factory. The prisoner would be taken to a safe house Bryant had acquired to use as a transit point for prisoners headed to Ultramax or Trevilsom.

Everything was perfect, right up until a bullet—fired from so far away that they didn't even hear it—drove through the Prince's heart and killed him instantly.

CHAPTER SIXTEEN

D reven materialized in the ruined courtyard already in motion toward his position. He concentrated on transforming the intense rage on his face to a more neutral expression. His excursion to Nehlan's bunker had not gone as planned.

In fact, it had almost killed him.

The portal to the landing room had worked well, as always, but as he stepped through, a plethora of defenses activated. The wicked spells sought not only to end him but also to maintain the connection he'd created so that if he did escape, he could be followed. It had required most of his impressive skills in magic to break free of the trap, and the battle had taken longer than it had seemed, which made him late to this meeting.

Ahead, the other four were already gathered and each offered their companions an almost identical sour look. If the situation hadn't been so unpleasant, it would have been funny. But after their recent failures, mirth was far beyond him. Even Iressa's beauty—which he ordinarily would have taken great pleasure in—seemed simply one more threat to add to the growing list.

He nodded at the others as he stepped into the leadership position. Dreven raised his arm and drew the cross in the sky that would summon the sight and sound barrier to protect their conversation from all kinds of potential surveillance. Their plans were safe within it, except from one another. He had a strong feeling that the common cause which had previously bound them was frayed, possibly to the point of breaking. It might be that only the threat of his own superior would be enough to keep the group on task.

Rather than listen to their complaints, he spoke first. "The humans have achieved a foothold on Oriceran."

The Dwarf, Jarkko, snarled his reply. "How could this happen? My target, the man in their capital city, has been taken off the board as planned."

Pesharn nodded. The Kilomea looked smug. "I did my part to set up the prison break, as did Ushev." She gestured at the underground gnome on her right, who declined to communicate.

If those two are in accord, times truly are as dangerous as they seem.

It was the darkly beautiful witch's turn to speak, and the grin on her face told him she'd seen what he had planned and was about to turn it on his head. "My own plans were flawlessly executed, save for one tiny detail. Dreven's target pulled mine away before the trap was sprung." She twisted to challenge him directly. "How did your people fail to preserve our secrecy?" Her words were calm and seemingly innocent, but the betrayal they carried struck deep.

Not because he hadn't expected it—and had even counted on it—but because he'd hoped for more time to accomplish his own betrayal of her first. He held his arms wide to suggest he was hiding nothing. "The attack on the leader of the group defending the prison was unsuccessful in that it did not eliminate the woman. It was, however, successful in that it did delay the deployment of the team long enough for our most important people to escape." *An exaggeration, but they wouldn't know that.*

Iressa spoke out of turn, a deep violation of the compact that bound them together. "So, what you're saying is that you failed and brought the entire plan down with you." Never had her sharp features seemed so threatening, despite his frequent desire to abandon caution and risk being cut by them.

"Another view would be that you delayed too long in taking care of your target, and his presence turned the tables in the effort to eliminate mine." She opened her mouth to retort and he interrupted her when he turned to the others. "In any case, the details of the past are irrelevant. We must focus on the future, and I have news of great concern about that."

Jarkko nodded. "Begin with the humans' foothold on this planet." The other two signaled their agreement, and the woman simply stared at him, her arms folded across her chest and a twist to her lips that promised his destruction. He raised his gaze in the hope that he might see something in her eyes he could exploit, but she was as sane and controlled as always. In many ways, the witch was the female version of him, or he the male version of her. That similarity would bring them to blows one day. He had always known it and imagined that behind her seductive words, she had as well.

He cleared his throat and pushed those worries back for a later time. "There is a bunker hidden deep within the Dark Forest. The humans have taken it as their own. How they found it is unknown." *They found it because Nehlan was a fool, and I equally a fool to trust him.* "The defenses they have placed on it are formidable. Working together we could, perhaps, assault it, but that is not necessary. The fact that they have claimed it, though, suggests they may be here for a reason. They might be seeking Rhazdon's Vengeance."

The dwarf scowled. Beside him, the Kilomea's desire for the weapons was palpable in her expression and the way her fists repeatedly clenched and unclenched. She managed to keep most of the emotion out of her words. "We cannot risk such powerful artifacts falling into the hands of our enemies, be they human or anything else."

Ushev scowled. "How did the humans obtain this insight? How can they be aware of the items?"

Iressa inserted herself smoothly into the silence that followed his question. "Somehow, somewhere, there must be someone from this planet working with them. An individual with knowledge beyond that carried by most."

Dreven barked a laugh. "Surely you aren't suggesting that one of us or one of our people is to blame?" The others were quick to shake their heads, and she shrugged. "Good. I really am glad our paranoia has not reached that level yet. Clearly, we now have two priorities. First, we must continue to cause trouble for these humans on their own planet to keep them off balance and distract them from their pursuit of the weapons. Second, we must seek the items ourselves."

Jarkko nodded. "I am not one for treasure hunts. I am, however, one for causing trouble."

The Kilomea laughed. "As am I. But I require assurance that once found, the distribution of the weapons will be discussed fairly among us. If they are to be rewards for those who find them, I choose to hunt instead."

Ushev shrugged. "I am good at finding lost things, and I have no problem with deciding as a group how they are bestowed thereafter."

Iressa grinned. "I feel the same as he does."

Dreven was sure the woman would take the discovery of the weapons as an opportunity to break with the rest and steal them for herself. *Because that is one of my potential plans, also.* "I will join the hunt as well and agree that we should decide their subsequent owners by consensus here in the circle in the same way that we have made all the decisions that led us to this point."

Nods of agreement followed, and they disbanded. Dreven watched the witch as she sauntered away. The tight dress no longer evoked any desire in him other than a need for shelter from her machinations. Once they had departed, he jogged to his departure position and conjured a portal, then stepped through it to his personal place of safety.

He had always considered Nehlan's choice of a bunker in the middle of nowhere to be overly dramatic. While it did enjoy the protection of anonymity, hidden as it was among the forbidding trees, it was a very obvious target once one knew its location. As events had shown, it was also at risk of being captured and used by the enemy.

His secure room was different. It had neither doors nor windows and could only be reached by portal or by breaking through the wall that separated it from his public home in the middle of the sprawling city. It was the proverbial grain of sand in a dune, obscured by the teeming activity that surrounded it. His landing location was in an empty corner. Across the room, in the opposite corner, a trio of plants grew in large pots to clean the air and impart a semblance of life to the space.

In the third corner, across from the plants, a leather wingback chair stood beside a small table. A lamp was perfectly positioned for reading, and a warming pot rested beside it. When necessary, a modest expenditure of magic to heat the stone at its center would radiate warmth through the pot and into the room beyond. The vessel was imbued with a scent he particularly enjoyed, floral and subtle. The final corner held a stand for his robes and a narrow wardrobe with several outfits appropriate for a variety of occasions.

A writing table with a chair stood in the middle of the chamber. It had been a gift from Nehlan and was shaped from the mind-damaging wood that made up the forest surrounding the bunker. He spun a magic tendril at it to confirm that his protections were still in place. The item was too beautiful to part with but too potentially dangerous to allow himself to become complacent. *Much like Iressa.*

Dreven removed his outer robe and hung it on a hook,

then sank gratefully into the chair. He activated the warmer and inhaled deeply, eased by the luxurious scent it generated. There was enough time for a nap before another obligation required his attention. He made a gentle motion with his wand and a footstool slid from the wall to its proper position under his feet.

As he slipped into sleep, one single thought accompanied him. *What will that clever witch do next?*

CHAPTER SEVENTEEN

C ara had slept like the dead after the events at the factory thanks to the healing potion. When she'd finally awoken after almost twenty-four hours in dreamland, she'd been running late for her meeting with Diana. She texted an apology, rushed through her morning routine, and abandoned the idea of drying her hair in favor of an extra cup of coffee to get her moving.

She dressed in jeans and a T-shirt, plus her own set of the boots Kayleigh had initially made only for herself and Diana. After the pathetic knife throw in the last battle, she was determined to spend some time working on that skill. *Among others.* She slipped on her black motorcycle jacket, zipped it to the neck, and retrieved her black helmet.

She wove her Arch KRGT-1 through the back streets of the small neighborhoods closest to the city's warehouse district. Riding was the most Zen thing she did, and her mind was free to wander while she navigated the turns and stop signs. She'd been aware all along of the rage and anger inside her since the battle at the Cube but had lacked a plan to deal with it. During the last battle, she'd had the first inkling of an idea, and it gelled during the ride to the restaurant.

Pamela's Diner was at the edge of the strip district, and everything they made was fantastic. They alternated between it and Deluca's, which was closer to the city's downtown, for their breakfast meetings. This one had more space and more comfortable seating. The other had a kind of eternal feel that put you immediately at ease like you were a part of a history that reached back through the years.

She parked and brought the helmet with her. Her boss was already seated and sipped her coffee with an irritated expression on her face. Cara sat opposite her and twisted to hang her headgear over the chair. She gave her breakfast partner a falsely happy grin. "S'up, boss woman?"

Diana didn't raise her head and merely swiveled her eyes upward to glare. "What are you so chipper about? You've been a sad sack for an eternity."

"Ouch. Harsh. True, but damn. You're not pulling any punches today, huh?"

Her superior sighed. "I'll say something personal, and after I have, will deny ever having said it." She paused, then like she released a burden, exhaled slowly. "Bryant is an asshole for making me miss him this much." Her head remained lowered in either conscious or subconscious self-defense.

At another time, when she hadn't been a "sad sack" for so long herself, she might have played it off as a joke or used it as a way to tease. But she felt the pain and felt its echo inside her. *Different causes, similar results.*

She put her hand on top of Diana's. The other woman didn't react but didn't pull away either. They stayed like that for more than a minute until the overly perky waiter arrived to take their order. When he left, Cara shook her head. "I have literally never wanted to shoot anyone as much as I want to shoot him for being so happy."

Diana laughed. "I hear you, sister. So, how goes the recovery?"

"Well, I'm still tired." She shrugged. "You know how those potions sap your energy."

"Yeah. And you took serious damage."

"Which really is a key part of the job description."

Her boss shook her head sharply. "No, it isn't, and that's something we all have to remember. Taking care of yourself is important. We're not here to sacrifice ourselves for short-term gains. If there's one thing Nylotte has beaten into me—repeatedly—it's the need to maintain a stable foundation at all times."

Cara ran her hands through her hair. The moment she'd dreaded for a while had arrived. Her internal arguments had vacillated wildly from the moment when she'd failed to stop the prisoners from escaping the Cube, but she always returned to the same thing. Saying the words, however, turned out to be much harder than thinking them. She'd spent so many years building up a resistance to the idea and had focused on developing her skills in other areas to make up for it. But it was time—maybe past time—to become whole.

She blurted the truth before she could stop herself. "I want you to teach me to be better at my magic."

Diana's head snapped up in surprise. "What did you say?"

"You. Magic. Teach me."

"Where did this come from?"

While she'd hoped there wouldn't be questions, she had also been sure that merely accepting things instead of badgering them to death wasn't a part of Diana's personality. "I need to be able to use it without having it knock me out. It's always been a last resort for me. But it would have been really useful during the battle at the Cube and again at the factory. I've watched you become better with yours and thought maybe you could help me improve."

Her boss narrowed her eyes at her. "Let's put a pin in that for a second. While we're being honest, what the hell is up with you and Anik? Because I see some stress there."

Cara rolled her eyes. "Seriously?"

"Yes."

"I didn't realize we were having girlfriend time." She sighed. "Okay, there's no deal between Anik and me. I think there was about to be, but then Hank arrived and everything froze. It's my carefully considered guess that our demolitions man thinks the new guy and I are a thing —or were a thing, maybe, since I'm the one who brought him in."

"Are you or were you?"

She laughed. "If you really knew him, you'd realize what a ridiculous question that is. But, no, we're not a thing, nor were we ever. Nor will we be."

Diana shrugged. "So what's the issue?"

"Performance anxiety? Who the hell knows? Anik probably has his own issues like all of us. If he stepped up, I'd be willing to see where it goes. But I won't chase him. Life is not a rom-com, and I don't need anyone to complete me." She grinned. "But it's fine that you do."

The curse words in response went unsaid as their server delivered their meals, and once he'd left, they broke into laughter together. They took a few bites without further conversation before her boss answered the initial question. "No, I won't train you. I'm not equipped to do so. But what I will do is ask Nylotte if she'll teach us both."

Cara groaned. "Nope, no way. Forget I asked. It's totally good."

Diana laughed. "Too late. I'm your boss. You'll do it."

"I'll resign."

"I'll shoot you."

The woman pointed a finger at her. "That's coercion. I don't think boss-types like you are supposed to do that."

She raised an eyebrow at the extended digit. "I'm somewhat old-school with none of this touchy-feely empowerment nonsense. If I say jump, you jump."

"Or you'll use force magic to throw me across the room anyway. Yeah, I get it." *Well, it probably won't be a total disaster, right?* "Sure. Let's do it."

Her boss grinned. "It just so happens I was headed there after this. We'll go together."

Cara put a smile on her face and cursed silently at having said anything.

Diana had a moment of reservation about what she was about to do, then shrugged. *If it's a bad idea, she'll refuse. It never hurts to ask, right?* Nylotte was waiting as they stepped through the portal and raised an eyebrow at the sight of the extra person. She spoke before the Drow had a chance to say something unkind. "Cara is interested in learning to use her magic better. I thought you might be willing to take her on if she trained with me, as I'd be able to learn different things that way."

The Dark Elf laughed. "Oh, very persuasive, my student." Her sarcasm was not masked in the least. She shifted her gaze to Cara and studied her from head to toe with a look of mild distaste. "You ask a lot."

Her second-in-command bristled but didn't reply. Nylotte raised an elegant eyebrow and looked at Diana. "Are you aware that she is different?"

"Different than what? We're all different. You're a Drow. I'm an elf. She's an elf." Her teacher shook her head slowly. She couldn't imagine what she was talking about. "Do you mean that she's not as powerful or something? Or that her magic is unique?"

Nylotte sighed, motioned toward the center of the space, and summoned three cushions this time. She disappeared for a moment and returned with an unusual tea set Diana hadn't seen before with two cups the color of ivory and one of deep jade. She poured and extended the two matching cups to Diana, who selected the rightmost, as always, and sniffed it. *It's not the brain-bending-brew. Thank God.* Her teacher reserved the other white one for herself and handed the green one to Cara.

It struck her like a punch between the eyes. *Two white. One green.* Her mind refused to acknowledge it and immediately babbled a denial. She felt her teacher's eyes upon her and vaguely noticed Cara's confusion. Finally, her inner voice spoke in the most soothing tones it had ever used.

"Okay, don't panic. It doesn't matter. But you need to say the words in order to accept it."

No, no, I don't. I don't want to. It can't be.

"It doesn't matter. You are who you are. So reach deep, suck it up, and say it."

She raised her gaze from her cup to her teacher's matching one. "I'm…Drow and Cara is not."

For once, Nylotte did not take the opportunity to mock her. "Correct, my student."

Cara's mouth had dropped open and the teacher stretched out a long finger and tapped her on the chin. Her teeth clicked as she jerked it closed, and she gave an incredulous laugh. "Wow. Damn, boss. That's a major brain-twister." She snapped her fingers. "I always sensed you were evil. Can I call you dark boss now?"

The joke broke the lock in Diana's head, and she laughed gratefully. "No. And Drow aren't evil. You know that."

"Well, y'all are really kind of jerks fairly often, you know?"

"Don't judge me by Nylotte."

This time, it was her mentor who laughed. "Well, that went better than I'd feared. I wondered how long it would take you to realize the truth."

Diana considered going down that path of conversation but rejected it. *What is simply is. Nothing else about it matters.* Instead, she asked, "So does that mean you can't train Cara or you won't train her?"

The Dark Elf folded her arms. "It means I'm willing to do so, but it will come at a cost. For you, my protege, part of my motivation has been to support one of my own kind. Whatever variety of elf your friend might be, it is not what we are so that does not apply."

"Fine. Done. Name your price."

She smiled thinly. "Oh, please. You know by now it doesn't work that way."

Diana grinned. "I almost had you, though."

Nylotte laughed. "Not even close. You are but the apprentice, whereas I am the master."

Cara sounded concerned when she rejoined the conversation. "Boss, maybe this isn't such a great idea."

"Psh. It's fine." She turned to the Drow. "So, no time like the present, right? Make with the teaching."

The wide grin on her teacher's face suggested that she might not enjoy receiving what she'd asked for, but it was too late to go back. *Really, what's the worst that can happen?*

CHAPTER EIGHTEEN

Every muscle, tendon, and bone in Diana's body hurt by the time Nylotte had consistently used her as a living target to train the other woman. At the end of the session, the Dark Elf created a portal back to the base and sent Cara on her way. She had even given her part of an energy potion since they had only been able to make minimal inroads into helping her control the amount of power she expended.

Diana held the cup of tea in her hands and savored the smell of the energizing brew. Her teacher had been correct about its ability to restore both physical and magical strength, although if she had to fight at that moment, she'd need to down a full energy potion simply to be able to stand.

Her mentor gazed levelly at her. "So, how does it feel to know your true origin?"

Diana shrugged. "At first, it was a shock. Now, it's simply another thing that doesn't warrant worrying about. I'm comfortable with who I am."

"And you're not upset that your mother didn't tell you?"

"I'm sure she had her reasons. It probably had to do with the fear that people would assume things about me rather than judge me by what I do."

Nylotte's grin showed her perfect teeth. "What a forward-thinking individual. She must have been very smart."

"She is still very smart."

"What a pity it didn't rub off."

Diana rolled her eyes. "How about we change the subject? What are your thoughts on the blades?"

She set the cup down with a sigh. "I think we're in a race."

A frown accompanied her reply. "Explain."

"The enemy knows about them, and if they have any brains at all, they have reviewed the evidence and concluded that we—or rather you—know about them too. That will spur them to action."

"Like trying to kill me or kidnap my friends again?"

Nylotte shrugged. "I wouldn't put it past them. No one can reach your Lisa while my associates are watching her, so that's not something to worry about. But your boyfriend, perhaps." She never missed an opportunity to jab at Bryant.

She sighed. "I'll warn him, but he can take care of himself. So, what's next?"

"We search for them, of course. I'll handle the first part and seek information on Oriceran. It is most likely that they will still be on that planet rather than this one. There's no evidence to suggest they ever crossed over."

"Does that mean you'll be away a lot?"

The Drow laughed. "It does not. Nice try, though. Your training continues and you'll need to be here when I work with the other one too. I have people making inquiries and tracking down stories and hints about the movement of the weapons. Eventually, something will bubble to the surface, and when it does, we'll move on it."

Diana sighed. "So, wait and try not to be killed, is that the plan?"

"In addition to whatever trouble might occur here, yes."

"Awesome."

Nylotte gestured for her to rise, and she pushed herself up with a groan. *Thank heavens. I need a nap.* Her teacher said the worst words she'd ever spoken. "Now, it's time for your training."

Rath had visited the Griffins the day after the battle at the factory and discussed the unexpected and upsetting end to their interactions with the pirate. They had been sympathetic but unable to shed any light on the matter. It had continued to bother him as he and Max patrolled the neighborhood around their house and searched for any signs of trouble. There were none to be found.

Still, the way the Prince of Plunder had met his end bothered him. He'd planned to discuss it with Diana, but she'd staggered through the portal from her training session with barely enough energy to eat cold Chinese takeout leftovers and collapse on the couch. Instead, he'd taken the magical subway into town to see if Kayleigh was in her lab.

She smiled as he entered. "What's up, Rath?"

He jumped up on the chair across the workbench from her. "Nothing. What working on?" There were pieces of equipment scattered around the table.

The tech scowled. "More canaries. That damn pirate crew blew up the two I had. I need to make them tougher but I'm not sure how." He sighed, and she set the piece in her hands down and focused squarely on him. "Spill, troll."

He laughed, a few quick sounds. Her knack for getting right to things was something he always appreciated. "Upset about the Prince."

"I get that. We could have learned a lot from him."

After a nod of agreement, he shook his head. "Yes. But not that. Who shot him?"

She shrugged. "I've sent drones everywhere but have no results yet. Everyone's been too busy to dig into it, although I think Tony is working his contacts at the police station. No one has anything yet as far as I know." She tilted her head away and spoke a little louder. "Alfred, is all that correct?"

The AI's English accent answered immediately. "Indeed so. Agent Khan is also reaching out to his military connections, but as yet, no definitive answer has been discovered. I have searched all the ARES databases, but to no avail."

She picked up a different piece of equipment that looked like part of the fans that helped the tiny scout drones to fly. "So, there you have it. We have nothing. Nada. Bupkis. Zilch."

"Not good enough." Rath jumped down from the chair. "Gonna find something."

"Stay safe, and good luck."

He gave her a thumbs-up as he headed out the door toward the equipment area.

An hour later, he had made his way to the furthest boundary Gwen could calculate for where the shot had come from. His AI coordinated with Alfred, and they created a list of possible locations in a cone that spread out from the factory. There were five potential buildings on the same side of the river and numerous others on the opposite side.

Rath really hoped he wouldn't need to cross it, although the idea of gliding over the water held some appeal. He climbed the highest of the structures the AI had marked—which, coincidentally, was also the farthest from where the battle took place—and reached the roof. He paced while Gwen scanned and highlighted objects in yellow as they came into focus. He found bird feathers, the remains of a nest, a potato chip bag that initially gave him hope but led to nothing useful, and a dead rat. He slipped the bag into an evidence pouch in case but had no faith that it would turn into anything.

"Launch point, please." Even though he could physically see it, the troll believed in using the tools he was given. The AI marked a spot on the roof and created a series of virtual rings in his goggles to display the optimal route to make use of the prevailing winds. A less perfect but possible path was displayed in a more subdued shade of yellow. Rath leapt from the rooftop and his wings deployed from their container. He rocked gently to bank into alignment with the ring and glided forward. It was an amazing feeling to float unseen high above the world. All too soon, he was over the other building and had to retract the appendages, land, and roll to the side to dissipate the remaining energy.

When he stood, he sensed something about his surroundings that was different. He paced the perimeter of the rectangle, an empty space that surrounded ventilation equipment in the center with a staircase leading down. He realized it was a scent in the air that he recognized from Emerson's lab long before and many occasions since. *Gun oil.* He headed for the best position from which to cover the back of the factory and found the roof somewhat scuffed where the sniper must have lain in wait. He gazed out, magnified the view in his goggles, and confirmed that the position had sight lines on both the front and back of the building. *I wonder if they were merely waiting, or if they knew about our raid?*

He saw the faintly polished rings where the weapon's bipod feet had rested and nodded. It was very clear that he'd found the place. *Step in the right direction.* "Gwen, deep analysis." He turned slowly in a circle and studied the surface. Then, he did the same thing with his chin a little higher to give the AI a wider radius, and one again a little farther out. He repeated it until his head was angled slightly up before the confirmation chime sounded in his ear.

"Standby, processing." A few moments later, the AI showed him a picture of a section of the roof with something strange on it. He searched until he found it. Folded into a cylinder inside a vent was a stylized playing card. He held it up for a good look at it and noticed the skeleton head in place of the face. It was a Jack of Diamonds. *Jack for Prince, Diamonds for Plunder. Clever.*

A crackle from his right was followed by the squelch of a walkie-talkie. Rath spun with a frown. If whatever object made that sound had been active a few moments before, Gwen would have sensed it, which meant someone had noticed him. The troll grabbed the communication device from its hiding place and dashed down the stairs, which would keep him protected from most angles. A deep voice, clearly processed and masked, spoke. "I wondered which one of you it would be. I'm glad it was you. The raid was expertly done."

"Who are you?"

The man on the other end of the comms laughed. "Come on, now. You don't think it'll be that easy, do you? Let's simply say I'm an independent contractor with a particular dislike for criminals."

"We needed him."

"That's probably why I was hired to eliminate him. Sorry about that. It wasn't my intention to interfere with your group. Our goals are the same, more or less."

The troll growled. "Except you work for bad guys."

The voice on the comms sighed. "It's difficult to tell who's who these days, I'll give you that. But, ultimately, as long as the end result is a low-life loses and I get paid, I consider it all good. I simply wanted to be sure to send my apologies for this one, since I imagine our paths will cross again."

"What should I call you?"

There was a drawn-out pause. In his goggles, Gwen displayed the source's signal, which bounced around in different directions every few seconds. *Masking his location, too. Impressive tech.* Finally, the man answered, and the disguise had been discarded. His voice was deep, raspy, and sounded older than most of the people in Rath's orbit. "Call me Amadeo. Good luck with your work, troll. But tell your team that if they see me, they'd better get out of the way. I won't take kindly to any interference." The line dropped and he looked at the card again.

More trouble ahead. I need to show this to Diana. But at least we have something to go on, now.

CHAPTER NINETEEN

K ayleigh was deep in the guts of the new model of her canary. Her glasses showed a blown-up view, courtesy of Alfred the AI, who was closer than ever to being able to intuit what she wanted before she asked for it. As she tapped her multitool on the tiny motor that drove one of the fans, the schematic appeared on the left side of her vision and the actual state of the device appeared on the right. The large sensor pod that hung above the table provided the data in real time.

She cursed softly and more or less consistently as she worked, a habit she'd picked up since coming to Pittsburgh and being the only one in the lab. Alfred occasionally commented on it, but the standard response—"Screw off or I'll turn you into a coffeepot"—seemed to keep the interval between the corrective nudges large enough that she didn't need to take real action.

"Come here, you little bastard," she muttered as she slid the tool in to twist the bolt that constrained the motor from outputting more energy than the fan could handle.

The whole thing was extremely delicate, something she'd try to improve in the next version. For now, her goal was simply to make it faster and enhance the AI to help it avoid incoming fire.

She'd managed to set it when Deacon yelled at her from three feet away. "Boo!" Kayleigh closed her eyes, pushed her anger down, and set the multitool gently on the work surface to avoid stabbing him with it. When she had regained full control, she opened her eyes and grinned.

"Nice try. The next one's mine." He groaned and smacked the table. The last time, she'd waited until the very early hours of the morning when he was finishing a twenty-hour marathon of coding to slip a black plastic spider into his coffee. Half the cup had spilled on him when he noticed it and bolted to his feet in panic. She replayed the video of his shriek to amuse herself on at least a daily basis. "What's up?"

He sat down across from her. "Do you have time to talk?"

She checked her watch. It was two in the morning. She'd lost track of the hours yet again. "Yeah, but not here. Let's take a ride."

———

They agreed to sing along to the radio rather than discuss business on the way. Twenty minutes later, they were seated in a booth at the breakfast place Diana had introduced her to. It was cracked vinyl, trapped in the nineteen-fifties, cash-only, and absolutely delicious. She ordered a Vanilla Coke and a western omelet with rye toast. Deacon went with coffee, regular Coke, and the meat-lover's special with wheat toast. Kayleigh grinned at the choice and recalled the various eating fads he'd adopted in college—Atkins, then vegetarian, briefly Vegan, and something that prioritized mushrooms. Mushroom teas, mushroom soups, and giant mushrooms cooked like steaks. His adventurousness, in food and everything else, came with a side order of blessedly brief total commitment.

As the server departed, she leaned forward. "Okay, what's the deal?"

He looked furtively to his left and right, and she was struck by how much it suddenly felt like they were in a spy movie. "I've worked some angles to find out more about the people on the oversight committee. And there's a lot there."

"Like what?"

"Let's start with the positives. Sam Somers is clearly in our corner. Nothing in his background shows anything to worry about. Aaron Finley, as well. He's definitely on our side." He fell silent.

"If this pause means we're done with the good news, I have to say this is much less encouraging than I might have hoped."

His response was delayed as the server refilled his coffee, then he leaned forward again. "Cassandra Ekkles is about as close to true neutral as the group's members get. She's supported some things Taggart wanted and blocked others. Her in-person appearances are exceedingly rare, as she splits her time between her congressional office and her brownstone."

Kayleigh tapped a fingernail against her teeth. "Family? Any pressure points?"

He shook his head. "Everything I've found suggests she's exactly what she purports to be. A public servant beholden to no one other than her constituents."

"Huh. It'd be better for us if she was explicitly pro-ARES but I can't really argue with that degree of integrity."

"Right? And, as you might have guessed, that's the end of the good stuff."

His revelations of bad news were delayed by the arrival of their late-night breakfast. Each dug in, and she watched his face. As expected, a look of pleasure washed over it at the quality of the food. There was no talking for a while as neither wanted to let the delicious meal grow cold for something as mundane as business talk.

Finally, when they'd mostly finished and had their drinks refilled, he brushed crumbs from his hands and leaned forward. She nibbled on her last piece of buttered toast as he spoke. "Let's start with the least offensive of the bunch. Winston Tomassi."

Kayleigh interjected, "Diana's mentioned him. He sounds like a total douchebag."

Deacon laughed. "I believe most people would agree with that characterization. He's a rich kid, which isn't a problem in itself, but it allowed him to grow up caring only about other rich kids. How he got elected in Louisiana is a matter of some uncertainty, as he doesn't really fit the profile of the state. In any case, he did get elected and has spent his time working tirelessly for those with considerable money."

"I thought you said he was the least offensive?"

"The pivotal word is least. His motivations are very clear, though. He's in it for the cash, and for the cash his influence will bring him when he leaves the Senate. My guess is that he'll serve two terms, maximum, before he becomes a lobbyist." He shook his head and his hair flopped to one side. "So, his position on any ARES issue will always be colored by how he can turn it to his monetary advantage."

"So, he's ripe for payoffs and blackmail?"

"Actually not, according to everything I've dug up. He has money and a plan to acquire more of it. His family life is stable, so he doesn't worry about alimony, child support, and that kind of thing. No, I don't think he's likely to be influenced by outside sources. He has the extreme self-confidence that major wealth can bring. Probably, if someone tried it, he'd laugh at them. Unless, of course, what they wanted was already in line with his plans."

"Okay. So, next on the ladder of evil?"

"Janet Cyphret."

Her mouth dropped open. "You're kidding me."

Deacon grinned. "That's exactly the reaction I expected you to have."

Kayleigh pointed the corner of her toast at him. "You're messing with me now. I've seen the woman on television. Neutral evil at best but probably chaotic evil. I can't even picture how someone could be worse."

"We'll get to that. Anyway, she's downright anti-ARES, as you know. I went looking for the reasons behind it and had to dig deep. It turns out that she had a brother who was in the FBI but he was kicked out. The sealed files I was able to crack suggest he was generally a good agent who occasionally crossed the line and took things that lay around whenever they made a collar."

"That doesn't seem like a reason to hate ARES."

"On one occasion, he did it in the office of a lawyer they were collecting for questioning. He discovered a book of some kind that listed a group of people taking bribes."

"And the means by which he acquired it blew the prosecution?"

"Worse. He apparently decided to go vigilante and used the information as a way to pit the criminals against each other. All this led to a significant number of injuries and several deaths. Eventually, one of the jerks on the list was apprehended by a different agency, and the whole thing came out."

Kayleigh shook her head. She was sympathetic to the concept but not to the manner in which it had been handled. She'd have taken the book to Diana with a plan instead of going it alone. "Ouch."

"Yeah. He was drummed out and more or less blacklisted, then went to Afghanistan with one of the large security contractors." She felt it coming before he said it, and her stomach dropped. "He died there—an IED."

She sighed. "So, she has a strong reason to hate the FBI and anyone even remotely associated with them. Like ARES. Okay, I can see where that might give her the slightest justification for being an obstructionist wench if you look at it through her eyes."

He nodded. "Right. Exactly."

She straightened and braced herself for more bad news. "And the cream of the crop?"

"Zachariah Clarke, Senior Senator from North Dakota."

"North freaking Dakota? Seriously?"

"Seriously. Okay, get this. Zachariah has made a name for himself as an upright, religious man which plays well to the more traditional members of his populace. He has a stay-at-home wife, three sons who are all working their way up various corporate ladders, and teaches Sunday School when he's in his hometown."

"He seems a decent sort so far."

"And that's basically how everyone sees him. The media like him because he's willing to comment on any issue at all. His party likes him because he is always there with a proper vote on the big issues. But the other party likes him too because he's centrist and willing to work with them on anything that's not a hard no for the people in his state as long as it's not a top-shelf issue. He's even refused pork-barrel giveaways to North Dakota."

"Okay. So, I still don't hear evil here. Neutral good, maybe, or lawful neutral at the worst."

"It turns out he's owned by someone in the Chinese government. Apparently, he did very bad things on a trip there. I was able to crack his phone, and that's how they contact him. It took some serious digging and a not fully authorized dip into the NSA databases that I will forever deny, but I traced it back to their intelligence service. He has shared considerable information with them."

Kayleigh was stunned at the news. It didn't make sense. "About ARES?"

He shook his head. "About everything. Literally, every single thing he knows goes to them."

"Dang. They have to have some really valuable information on him."

"Honestly, I can't even imagine. His life must be a hell of cognitive dissonance, playing the good guy while he knows he's the villain."

She frowned. "I don't see why that makes him a problem on the committee."

Deacon sighed. "That's the worst part. I only saw one reference so I can't call it definitive, and I haven't been able to find another source. But hidden in one of the communications was an instruction for communicating directly with a person named Dreven. That wasn't a big deal in itself. But when I searched for that in his phone, I discovered contact info for someone we know—Nehlan."

Her anger spiked. "The bastard who kidnapped Diana's friend."

He nodded. "Good old Zachariah had fed him secrets for months before that based on the timestamps on what I found."

Kayleigh drummed her fingers on the table. "Is it enough to burn him?"

Deacon shook his head. "No way. I'm sure they have a failsafe to destroy the phone, which means the evidence trail is gone. It's only there at all because he knows nothing about actual information security."

"So, basically, we have a traitor on our hands whom we can't get rid of easily." She drummed her fingers on the table again, then snapped them. "Can we spoof him? Turn him into our tool?"

He grinned. "Now you're talking. Maybe, although that's a two-way play—or three-way, if you include needing to keep the Remembrance folks buying in as well as China. It's certainly worth looking at, though. The bigger question at the moment is do we share this with Diana? Or with her boss?"

She shook her head. "They both have enough going on right now. Let's watch, listen, and see if we can worm ourselves in deeper."

He raised a coy eyebrow at her. "I like how you think."

The tech rewarded the notably bad effort at flirting by firing her cloth napkin into his face. "As a reward for being the least cool person ever, you get to pay the bill." He laughed as she walked away. If there was a little extra sway in her hips as she did it, well, there was no harm in showing him what skilled teasing looked like.

CHAPTER TWENTY

M urray's shining truck pulled up alongside the curb near the bar that used to be their hangout, and Sloan yanked its heavy passenger door open. A hop, slide, and slam later, they were in motion again. He had no idea where they were headed, only that Mur had said, "Pick you up in an hour," and he had obeyed, as always.

Frankly, being Tommy Ketchum is now a little annoying. If he were one of my underlings, I probably would have offed him by now. Thinking of his alias in the third person helped Sloan keep a proper perspective on things, but he tried not to do it too often. He'd heard stories during training from retired undercover agents who cautioned against being too into character or too out of character. The right balance was key, they'd insisted, to avoid the pitfalls that lay on both sides of that thin, thin line.

He'd not given it much credence at the time, but after years in the field, he'd personally confirmed that every word the retirees had said was true. His magic gave him an edge, but it was haphazard enough that he didn't feel comfortable enough to rely on it. He blinked and brought himself back to the present moment. As casually as possible, he looked at the other man, who continued to dress well and seemed more comfortable in his new role with each passing day.

Marcus's return no doubt had something to do with that. Murray was not the kind of man who fared well without consistent leadership but was in his element as a middle manager. The radio played softly in the background—some mashup of hip-hop and country about a horse and a road—and he raised his voice to talk over it. "Where are we off to this fine day?" It wasn't an exaggeration, as Pittsburgh was experiencing one of its rare not-a-cloud-in-the-sky moments.

Mur spun the wheel to turn right, then immediately reversed it in a turn to the left that took them into one of the city's many tunnels. This one was shorter than the others and led to a bridge. They crossed it and turned onto the south side's main road before his boss responded. "Marcus wants to see us."

"Both of us, specifically?" He made sure the proper note of concern was present in the question.

The other man chuckled. "Well, me, anyway. But unless someone tells me not to include you, I like having you with me. You see things differently than I do sometimes, and that might be important when dealing with the big guy." He paused and continued in a more somber tone. "I believe in Marcus and in the plans he has for the group. But the dude was in the hardest prison around, lost his damn arm and the leader he followed, and came back as some kind of part-machine. That's gotta take a toll. So, I think the more of us that look out for him, the better."

Sloan nodded. "You know I'm in. Whatever it takes."

Mur turned to smile at him. "You're a good man, Ketch. I'm glad Teddy brought you into the group." There was a moment of shared silence for their friend, who had fallen during the stadium battle in Philadelphia. It was one of the reasons Murray had a personal chip on his shoulder where Sarah, the lead witch, was concerned, in addition to the palpable dislike that Marcus had for the woman. She'd let too many people die for minimal gain on that operation.

They pulled off the main road and into a narrow, one-way street with closely packed houses on both sides. In the older neighborhoods, they'd built up and back instead of sideways, which always looked weird to him. *This place has personality.* He laughed fondly inside. *Most of it weird.*

Mur stopped the truck outside a home that was indistinguishable from the rest. The front door opened as they approached, and a member of the gang that Sloan recognized waved them forward. The pistol on his hip was expected, but the sawed-off shotgun in the hand he'd hidden behind the door wasn't. *Interesting. Apparently, Marcus feels the need for protection.* The man tilted his chin toward the stairs leading to the basement, and they descended without exchanging words.

The staircase turned to the left halfway down, and another armed guard was seated at the bottom, facing any traffic that might come down them. He stood to intercept but returned to his seat at a calm, "Let them through," from Marcus. The gang's leader sat in the middle of the room at a high square pub table with a laptop in front of him. He nodded at the chair beside him, and Murray took it, leaving Sloan to climb onto the next one across from the boss, who clicked a few more times and closed the machine.

He met both their gazes in turn with a nod and a small smile. "Gentlemen. Thank you for coming."

Mur's answer was quicker. "Sure, boss."

Sloan followed with "No problem, sir." *Gotta remember, Tommy Ketchum is intimidated by this guy and will try to look good.* He straightened and locked his gaze on Marcus.

There was the slightest of mechanical whirs as the man raised his left arm and scratched his face with it, but nothing that would have carried beyond a few feet. The agent would give a lot to know the details about and the origins of the limb, but all he had were rumors and guesses, each more ludicrous than the last. It was a hot topic for drunken conversations among the gang members.

Their boss put his elbows on the table and steepled his fingers. "Some things have come to my attention that will be good for us. And I need you two to take care of a few things. Murray, because I trust you. Tommy, because he thinks highly enough of you to have brought you today. You'll probably need a couple more. It'll be dangerous."

Marcus shook his head. "I'm getting ahead of myself. I do that sometimes when I'm excited, and damn." He slapped his hands down on the table with a grin. "I. Am. Excited. It's time to give that witch the reward she's so rightly earned. And it starts right here, right now." He held his index finger up. "First, Sarah got demoted. That had to hurt, and it was a damn pleasure to watch. She didn't let on, of course, but unless she lost all her emotions somehow, she's pissed." He held up a second finger. "However, the fact that Dreven says she's not the leader doesn't really mean she's not the leader since he's not actually here to enforce it. Her power base is still what it was. That's unchanged. Words don't make a thing so, you know?"

They nodded and he continued as he raised a third finger. "He also said that I'm the equal of Sarah, but if you look around, it doesn't seem like that, does it? To an outsider walking into the warehouse for the first time, who would be the magical leader with the same power as me?"

Mur, with reluctance in his tone, voiced a response. "Wysse. The one she put in charge."

His leader pointed all three extended fingers at him. "Exactly. Now, let's examine a few other pieces of important knowledge." He set the hand with the raised fingers on the table and used the other one with the index finger raised. "First, we have a clear enemy in this town, and they're trying to find and eliminate us. We've seen them a few times, so we know what kind of gear they carry, which is a very useful piece of information to have."

He raised another finger. "Second, my people have discovered that there are listening devices planted in the warehouse." Ice shot through Sloan, but his professional experience served to keep his face locked and immobile while the internal spasm passed. *How the hell did they find them? That is not good.* He turned to look at Murray, who reacted appropriately.

Mur sputtered as he spoke and anger overwhelmed him. "Are you saying Sarah is listening to us? Do we need to take precautions like throw our phones away or something?" The undercover agent nodded because he imagined Tommy Ketchum would.

Marcus shook his head. "I'm having them looked at, but the technology is good and you'd think the witch would use magic. No, my guess is that the aforementioned enemy has discovered where we gather. It wouldn't be too hard to find out since we've been there for months. Fortunately, the important conversations usually don't happen downstairs, and it would be much harder for them to put the things in the office."

Sloan kept his voice neutral. "Have you told her to check it out?"

The man grinned and shook his head as he lowered his hand. "No, my friend. When you add all those parts together, do you know what it equals? It equals opportunity. And I'll need you two when I make the first move."

Murray still sounded angry. "Tell us what you need, boss."

"Three things, all in a row. We'll kick it off by killing the pet witch and reminding Sarah that she's not the boss of everyone. With Wysse gone, she'll have to either take that position again for herself—making her equal to me—or appoint someone else. If she chooses the first option, it'll make her seem weak. If she chooses the second, I'll play tattletale to Dreven and he'll probably force her to take it. Either way, we win that round."

His smile widened. "Second, we'll make the attack look like it came from the people hunting us. We'll have a third party whip up identical gear and wear it to destroy the witch. That'll push the suspicion off us and make Sarah and Dreven focus on them, which will keep them on their toes."

Sloan's concern—which had risen steadily since the revelation of the discovery of the bugs—reached its peak as the man said his next words, ones he'd feared would come.

"And then, I'll reveal the existence of the listening devices. That should be the straw that sets Sarah off. We'll point her at the group that's hunting us and let them fight it out. We'll either help her or abandon her, depending on what looks like the most useful choice at the time. And once it's over, she'll be broken and back down the ranks and I'll be the one in charge."

He raised his mechanical hand and suddenly, it transformed and reshaped into a wicked-looking blade. "Or, if necessary, we'll kill her and deal with her replacement." He smiled at Murray and Sloan. "Either way, we win, and all the rest lose."

CHAPTER TWENTY-ONE

Diana was hiding out in the fifth-floor conference room, as she had taken to doing when she needed space to think while at the headquarters building. More agents and a second tech had stolen most of her other sanctuaries. Now and again, she sat in the lobby and watched the freelancers and other coworking clients wander through from behind the anonymity of her illusion necklace. Sometimes, she simply wanted to feel like she wasn't the epicenter of everything.

Her inner voice snorted at her. *"Arrogant, much? May I get you some cheese with that whine?"*

Shut up.

"Wait, I have another one. I'll call you Copernicus from now on since you're clearly the center of the universe."

I swear to heaven I will see a therapist or a surgeon or something and have you excised from my brain if you do not shut the hell up. It cackled at her as it faded, and she heaved a sigh. *Sadly, as usual, mental Diana is closer to right than to wrong.*

She had been a little too trapped in her head lately. Call it fallout from the fight at the Core, or a reaction to Taggart, or getting to spend less time with Rath and Lisa, or even—*ewww*—missing Bryant, she'd let self-pity gain a foothold. She sipped her coffee slowly, which she'd brewed extra strong and extra bitter. *Well, that shit stops now.*

Her phone buzzed, and her glasses displayed Bryant's face—the goofy picture of him from his official ARES file. She grinned and said, "Accept," and the device connected to her comms. "Hello, Bryant. How's the weather?"

He laughed. "Who the hell knows? I'm indoors like twenty-four-seven."

"Any news about Carson?" She couldn't keep the hope out of her voice, but at least it was actually hope talking, not fear pretending to be something more positive.

"Not yet. The doctors say his body is healing and the brain scans show no issues, so they're not sure why he's still out of it."

"Magic?"

"I went so far as to escort Kienka to the hospital so she could examine him in case the ARES and government magical medicals missed anything. But there's nothing there."

Diana laughed. "Magic medic. I want one."

He chuckled in response, and it warmed her to hear it. "I know you do, honey."

She raised an eyebrow, impressed. "*Raising Arizona.* Rath would be proud of you."

"I do have a smattering of pop culture knowledge, you know. It's not like I grew up under a rock."

"Okay, then, answer me this. In what movie is George Carlin a priest and Alanis Morissette God?"

"Please. *Dogma*. Give me something difficult next time. However, as much as I'd like this to be a social call, it isn't one."

She sighed. "It never is. This wasn't quite what I had in mind when I invited you up to my hotel room, you know. The 'I have to work in the morning' excuse is one thing, but this 'I have to work all the time' is something else entirely."

He laughed again, as she had intended. "Well, this might make your day a little brighter. We have a lead on someone who's apparently tried to suborn several Senators. Our person in the NSA passed it along since it's far from public knowledge."

"So she's still there, huh?"

"Yep, received another promotion and everything."

Diana shook her head. ARES had many impressive contacts but getting one of their people hired by the NSA was a coup. The fact that she climbed the ladder to get deeper and deeper access was a testimony to her abilities and served both organizations involved very well. "I hope you've set up a good landing for her if something goes wrong."

"Pre-written pardon, arranged by the vice president and renewed by each new resident of the Oval Office."

"Dang. Nice. Can I get one of those?"

He chuckled. "No, you'll simply have to behave. If that's even possible for you."

"Bite me."

"Tempting."

She rolled her eyes. "Did you call for a reason other than simply to annoy me?"

"Only to share the information, because two of those senators being targeted are acquaintances of ours. Janet and Winston."

"Wow, big surprise."

He laughed. "I know, right? If it would be anyone, it's logical that those two jerks would be involved. The person who's pursuing the senators has ties to Chinese intelligence, but they were reasonably easy to find so must be taken as clearly suspect."

"This, right here, is why I never wanted to be a spy. It's so much easier to be a federal agent. Get told where criminal is, investigate criminal, confirm criminal status, kick criminal ass."

"Yeah, that describes you pretty well, Sheen."

"So, now that you've given me this information, what do you want me to do with it?"

The line crackled and inspired a worry that someone might listen in on their calls. *It's something to ask Kayleigh about, anyway.* "Merely grist for the mill. Add it to your collective brains and see if any connections emerge. The usual stuff."

She smiled. "You could have done this via email. You wanted to talk to me. Admit it."

He laughed. "I always want to talk to you. But now, I must run. Duty calls."

"Yeah, yeah. Will you make it to Pittsburgh soon?"

"You know it." He hung up and left her with a grin on her face. She looked around at the mostly empty conference room and the completely empty coffee pot. *It's time to get out of my head and back into the action.*

She swept into the lab where Kayleigh and Deacon worked busily as she'd expected, and crossed to where her housemate sat on the opposite side of her raised work surface. "Okay, people, new information for you. Someone from China is apparently trying to run a scam on Cyphret and Tomassi."

Deacon swiveled in his chair with an odd look on his face. "Cyphret and Tomassi, you say?"

She nodded, and the tech looked at his partner. Kayleigh sighed. "We didn't want to add this to your plate until we knew more, but we've found trails that suggest China is involved with Zachariah Greene, one of the other members of the oversight committee."

"I haven't met him yet." The words were faster than her brain, but once it caught up, she continued. "It's weird that China would set its sights on those three in particular. Maybe they're part of a bigger operation?"

The blonde tech shrugged. "Anything's possible. But it doesn't feel that way. I think—we think—it's probably someone high up in the Remembrance using the Chinese connection as a cover. That doesn't preclude a legit nonmagical thing going on with some of them, but my guess is that these three come with a little added bonus."

"And the rest of the committee?"

Deacon slid into a seat across the worktable from

Kayleigh. "They haven't been targeted, as far as we know. Have you heard anything?"

Diana raised her hands in a gesture that communicated, "Who knows?" much more effectively than words ever could. "What can we do to eliminate some of this impressive lack of knowledge we have going on here?"

The two techs exchanged a look which told her they'd already started. *I love having good people.* Kayleigh said, "We've dug into Greene fairly hard and tried to trace his network back. This will give us a little more to go on. We thought we might insert some stuff into the communications to see if we could get him on our hook as well. Ideally, we want to do the same with the Chinese connection."

"And the magical side, too," he added. "If they're smart, they have protective layers in there, but I should be able to find my way through them. Hopefully."

Diana tapped her nail against a tooth while she considered this. "What if we had Bryant share misinformation with the committee? Not in person but in a report so they'd all receive it? If it was spicy enough, they might feel they had something to bring to the table. That would at least tell us who's already taken the deal from our earthly foes."

The techs both nodded. "It sounds like it could be worth trying. We might want to wait until we have a little deeper penetration on the people talking to Greene, though."

She stood and stretched. "I'll leave this in your capable hands. I'm more an investigator than a spy." She waved as she left the room. *Okay, now we're starting to turn the tables on these bastards. Once we have the next level up in our sights, we can sweep the scumbags up in this town, get Sloan back, and go after bigger fish.* She smiled and pressed a button on her phone. Rath picked up immediately, his greeting happy.

"Hey, buddy, what do you think of a fish sandwich at Wholey's?" His reply was as enthusiastic as she could have hoped for. *Yep, it's all coming together.*

CHAPTER TWENTY-TWO

D reven materialized at the edge of the property his
master had claimed as his own. In former days, it
had been a castle, part of the distant past of Oriceran's
ever-brewing battle between those who possessed real
power and those whose might was purely symbolic. To
wed the two—to put one who knew how to rule properly
onto a throne rather than trust in the vagaries of heredity
—was truly a goal worth fighting for.

Here, or on Earth. Either way. Once accomplished in one
place, the other would follow that much more easily.

The castle was not all it had once been. There were
fallen stones where pillars had once stood, and an entire
wing had been lost as the hillside beneath it eroded. Nonetheless, the main part of the structure still remained and
overlooked the flatlands for miles around. Blocks that
started out white were grey and black with age, and what
would have been well-trimmed lawns were overgrown
with plant life of all kinds. Yet a clear road ran between

them and twisted its way up the hill to the front door. That path was his goal.

Unfortunately, it was currently blocked by the cold iron fence that demarcated the perimeter of the property. The gate that opened onto the proper route was closed, and none of his entreaties thus far had convinced it to open. Dreven considered simply launching himself over it with a burst of power, but he held the owner in high regard and would not want to risk disappointing him. Plus, he knew there would be guards against such things, very likely quick to react and lethal in nature.

No, he would wait, if waiting was what his master desired. He positioned himself squarely perpendicular to the crease that separated the two halves of the gate, slid his hands into the opposite sleeves, and bowed his head. The cowl of his robe fell forward to keep the wind and sun from his face. His thoughts spiraled inward as he used the opportunity to meditate and refresh his energies.

He had stood for an unknown time when the gates parted slightly. He dashed through them as soon as they were open wide enough to fit his body, and it slammed shut immediately after, so quickly that it snagged his robe. He spent several moments in an attempt to free the trapped cloth, but it refused to budge. A wave of his wand and a murmured word summoned a shadow blade that sliced the offending fabric away.

He swung toward the castle, took a moment to recapture his full awareness, and marched forward at a steady pace. This wasn't his first walk along this path and he knew that its twists and turns made the transit take significantly longer than the eye would expect. On his first visit, buoyed by excitement and high hopes, he had traveled only halfway before his energy had begun to flag. This time, he husbanded his strength and expended it only when essential to ease his progress. Otherwise, he relied on his body's resources to propel him. He needed as much magic as possible to face—or to serve—his master, whichever the case might turn out to be.

After almost an hour, he arrived at the entrance to the building itself. Two-story-high wooden doors stood before him and one side glided open silently at his approach. He slipped through the gap, and it closed behind him with a whisper and a click. Dreven paused to allow his eyes to adjust to the interior gloom before he proceeded. The last time he had been there, one of his master's underlings had been present to escort him down the wide red carpet that marked the path from the door to his superior's working room. Now, it appeared he was on his own.

He walked on, careful to confine his steps to only the crimson fabric as he had during the previous visit at the behest of his host. On that occasion, he hadn't known why. This time, he still didn't know why, but it didn't matter. There was a very real sense of a threat that stepping off the path would result in a death too horrible to imagine. In this large, empty, echoing space filled with the remembrances of battles past, those imagined demises held great power indeed. He shuddered involuntarily. *From the cold, only from the cold. My mind is too strong to be influenced by these minor things.*

He walked through corridors with tapestries on both walls depicting scenes of violence and lighting fixtures dangling above with flameless candles fueled by magic. It was one of the petty vanities of his master that he possessed the power to spare to spend it on such mundane purposes. *Of course, once you see behind the image he projects and realize that energy has been stolen from others, it's even more terrifying.*

He crossed the threshold into his superior's office and stood at the end of the carpet, not daring to approach closer. The room was deep but not particularly wide, with the working desk at the far end surrounded on three sides by bookshelves packed with tomes. Closer to the entrance was a comfortable discussion nook with two formal couches arranged in an L and several large chairs. In the middle ground were matching cabinets facing one another across the room, one loaded with liquors and other vices, and the other a display case for magical items that would make any visitor envious.

The deep rasp of his master's voice filled his ears as if the man stood beside him. "Dreven, come forward." If a snake were able to speak, it would likely use the same long pronunciations of words as did the other wizard, that single choice alone enough to create tension in the listener.

He obeyed and concentrated on keeping his stride steady despite the concern—*not fear, no, surely not*—that accompanied each step. His master had bent his head to his work, apparently uninterested in charting his progress across the room. He stopped two feet before the edge of the desk and clasped his hands behind his back where they couldn't be seen twitching toward his wand.

Lechnas set his pen down and aligned it carefully alongside the heavy paper he'd been writing on. He was not a big man, nor a thin one. Neither tall nor short. If not for his aura of power, he would have been unremarkable in a crowd, at least until one saw his face. Two scars traced from each temple to the opposite jaw. The story he told was that they were the reminders of what trusting anyone other than one's own kind brought. As if to further embed that reminder, he had arranged to have the raised lines tattooed in deep scarlet on his pale skin. The color matched his strange eyes, which seemed to burn with the might coiled within him. Long, straight black hair was swept to one side of his head to keep it out of the way of his work.

He wore black or red exclusively, and today had chosen a combination of the two. A red shirt drew the eye away from the black waistcoat and trousers. Dreven had never failed to feel underdressed around him. He held his tongue as the wizard rose and those eyes drilled into his own. He tried to read something in them—any clue as to the reason for this summons—but found nothing he could comprehend.

When his master smiled at him, Dreven knew he was in trouble. "Please, sit." A chair scraped from the side wall to slide gently into the back of his knees, and he obeyed. Lechnas brushed his hair back and tucked it behind his ears as he sat in his own chair. "I must say, I am disappointed in the results you have provided so far."

The dryness in Dreven's throat made it difficult to swallow, and it took a few attempts to find his voice. No particular menace radiated from the other wizard, but the room still felt thick with danger. "I am, as well. Most particularly the loss of several of our minions during the prison break." His superior stared at him without speaking.

"So…uh, yeah. That's the bad news. However, there is good news."

Lechnas raised his index finger and moved it from side to side in negation. "You have not finished with the negatives. Allow me to list them. We have lost an artifact, last seen bonded with your human associate. Your personal power base has been damaged by the death of Nehlan, who also failed in his task. Finally, all the people you claimed you would kill to cut the head from our human enemies are still alive."

Dreven nodded. "And yet, master, we have retrieved Rhazdon's Defense, which is a more than equal trade." He cringed and hoped the other wizard shared his opinion of the value of that accomplishment.

"And I permitted you to use it at the prison and still, the humans live."

He sighed. "You are correct, as always, master. But there is good news as well. Our message resonates with groups across the humans' planet, and each day, more and more turn to what they believe our cause to be. If we remain visible and continue to take action against those in power, those numbers will increase all the more."

"I agree."

He blinked, shocked by the simple affirmation.

The wizard waved his hands and a bowl of sand on his desk surrendered its contents. The grains swirled in a gentle arc to the center of the surface and formed themselves into an image of a sword and a pair of daggers. "We must work on two fronts. First, you must find Rhazdon's Vengeance. If the humans should discover the blades first, or if one of our other enemies should, it could lead to disaster."

Dreven bowed his head. "I am already pursuing this, master. We will find them."

"See that you do." He slammed his palms down on the desk and dispatched the sand to its container. "And we must initiate more actions against the humans and bigger ones. They must learn to fear us. Every day they believe they can resist, their will grows stronger. We must cause them to lose that belief. It is my place to do this on Oriceran, and I am accomplishing it. You only have to do it on Earth, where it should be far easier."

He stood and his subordinate bolted to his feet. Lechnas pointed a long finger at him. His master's face was as pale as ever, but both the scars and his eyes seemed to have filled with blood and blazed at him. "Fail me again, and it is the end of you. Mark my words as I swear this shall be so."

Dreven opened his mouth to speak, but before he could utter a syllable, he was thrown from his feet and into a portal that deposited him in the grass outside the iron fence surrounding the castle. He stood and brushed his clothes off, then sighed and let the fear the other wizard instilled in him fall away. *It is time to make the rest aware that any failures will be met with death, at my hands or at Lechnas'.*

CHAPTER TWENTY-THREE

C ara and Anik were at the range, one of her favorite
ways to relax. She'd already fired a box of rounds
and now started on her second. His pace was slower as he
worked on quick-firing from a hip draw. They didn't
converse much as the giant ear protectors were an impedi-
ment to that, and they'd chosen not to bring ARES comms
along to make it feel more like they were on an
off-duty day.

She shot a smiley face into the target ahead of her,
swapped the magazine, and added hair. One more round
provided the finishing touch—a final hole in the center of
the forehead—and she left her lane. Anik finished shortly
after, and they returned their ear protectors to the owner.
He was an older man, overweight and with a biker's vest
and a long grizzled grey beard. As near as she could tell, he
was always happy and continued to be so as he waved them
out and told them to have a fantastic day.

Anik joked, "Any day you get to shoot things is a
fantastic day, right?"

She nodded in agreement and climbed into the passenger seat of the SUV they'd borrowed for the afternoon. He drove toward the city and they spent the first few miles in silence. Finally, with the air of someone who'd wanted to ask for a while but had been afraid to, he said, "So, what the hell is up with you, anyway?"

She burst into laughter at the question. "Why do you think anything is up?"

He grinned. "Huh. Let's see. You normally seem much happier than you have been, you're always ready to bite someone's head off, but most of all, I'm reasonably sure I saw you muttering the word 'die' over and over as you practiced at the range."

Her eyes widened in alarm until she realized he was holding laughter back. She smacked him on the arm, and he let the mirth free and she was forced to join in. When the joke had run its course, she sighed. "Yeah, you're right. I suck lately. Too much time spent in my own head. The thing at the prison messed me up for a while, and somehow, everything since has kept me from getting back together."

Anik split his attention between her and the road. "What can we do to make that better?"

She shrugged. "Time will help, I'm sure. Visiting the range helped. Hanging out is good." She smiled at him, and he returned it.

He raised an eyebrow. "I'm good at giving massages, you know. They are supposed to be very relaxing."

"Soft pass. Maybe a raincheck? I'm not really in a gentle place at the moment." He nodded and she cut him off before he could say something about non-gentle options.

"Let's eat there." She pointed at the restaurant that was well-hidden on one of the side streets, a place specializing in an enormous variety of hot dogs. Her favorite was the Korean with Kimchee and red pepper paste.

They got their orders and sat at a small booth near the window. Anik's ever-present kindness was soothing, and she told him so. He sighed once and set his half-eaten food down. "Look, Cara, I'm bad at relationships, historically speaking. So, I'll simply put this out there. When you're ready, I'd really enjoy discovering if there's a real thing between us. I feel like there is but that the time is only right for an instant before something gets in the way."

She set her own food down to give him her full attention. It seemed like he had more to say, so she simply nodded. "Go on."

"I'm not pushing. I don't have a timetable here, and heaven knows, you have to be patient in order to work in demolitions." She laughed and he chuckled with her. "But I don't want you to think I'm not interested, that's all. Because I am. Very."

She bought time with a long, slow sip of her iced tea, then sighed. "Honestly, I had those same thoughts before the prison break. Since then, though, my brain's been a mess. I don't know what I think or feel, only that I have to attack it until I break through the junk. But I will and I'm happy that you're interested in being there when I do."

He took the hand she stretched toward him. They sat in silence for a few moments until she pulled away. "Okay, enough feelings. Ewwww."

He laughed. "Right. Boo on feelings. Be tough. Like stone."

"Like steel."

"Like diamond."

Anik groaned. "Okay, you win. But if I can find something harder than diamond, we'll revisit this conversation."

She grinned around the bite of Korean vegetables in her mouth. "Deal."

Despite the nice afternoon with her potential future romantic partner, Cara was glum and moped as she cleaned her already spotless gear until Hank stopped by. That wasn't particularly noteworthy, as he tended to be in and out at odd hours in general. Upon arriving in town, he'd become involved with a local car restoration and racing group, and they met at seemingly random times based on when they could get access to whatever they needed at that moment—a garage, a race track, a frame bender, or anything else, he'd explained.

She felt his eyes on her as she ran a cleaning rod through the chambers of the Ruger. "What?"

He laughed. "If you clean that any more, you'll wear it away to nothing."

"Yeah, yeah. Go build a car or something, will ya?"

"Nah. I have a better thing happening tonight. And based on the way you've limped around like a wounded animal lately, I think you should come along. If I hadn't found you here, I wanted to give you a call."

She clicked the cylinder closed and turned to face him. "What is it?"

He shook his head. "Nope. First, you agree. Then you find out."

"What kind of messed up rule is that?"

"My messed up rule."

She sighed. *It's not like I have better plans for the evening.* "Will it require me to talk to anyone?"

"Not if you don't want to."

She stared at him. "Will I enjoy it?"

"I promise."

"All right." She stood. "What should I bring?"

He grinned. "Only your tiny little self."

She punched him in the arm. "I'm not that small, you know. You're merely mammoth."

They drove the half-hour out to one of the city's less affluent neighborhoods in Hank's rebuilt Eagle Talon. The original car wasn't anything amazing, but the man had invested enough love and elbow grease to transform it into something spectacular. The weird miniature stick shift had been replaced by a better version, and the vehicle hummed as he wove it expertly through the back streets.

Finally, they reached their destination and pulled in between the other cars, new and old, and a line of motorcycles. Hank had refused to share any details but based on the vehicles, she was sure she'd feel right at home. *As long as it isn't some kind of alpha-male poetry jam or something.* She snorted at the idea of him and poetry coexisting in the same place. It wasn't that he was dumb. Far from it. He was one of the most intelligent people she knew. He merely tended to live in the physical rather than the metaphysical.

When he pulled the door open to let her pass, the sound of yelling assaulted her ears. She walked into the dilapidated warehouse to find bleachers set up to create a square. A few people were seated there, but more stood and cheered in front of them. The smack of leather on flesh revealed the purpose of the gathering, and she grinned. For the first time in a long while, her heart pumped faster.

Cara turned to see him staring at her, and he grinned in satisfaction. "I knew it."

"You are a good judge of character, Hank. But how the hell did you find a fight club?"

He shrugged. "There's a crossover with car people, actually. Thrill-seekers."

She pushed through the crowd for a view of the people in the middle, both of whom were bigger than she was. One used traditional boxing techniques and the other was kickboxing. Unfortunately for him, he wasn't as fast as his opponent, who would dart in, deliver his blows, and retreat before the kick caught him. She felt Hank slide in against her back and kept her gaze forward but turned her head a little so he could hear her. "House rules?"

He shrugged. "You can fight anyone who's willing to fight you. No weapons other than the ones you were born with. Eyes and necks are off limits. It ends with surrender or unconsciousness. No killing. No magic."

"Not even yours?" She chuckled.

He growled before he replied, clearly eager to get into a battle. "Especially mine. That would be a serious abuse of trust in this place."

Cara nodded. "Does gender matter?"

She caught the shake of his head out of the corner of her eye as the match they watched ended with a knockout. The loser's skull banged on the mat fairly hard, but there was a medic there immediately. She noticed a vial at his belt with surprise. "He has a healing potion?"

"Yep. Everyone pays to play, and the organizers use the funds to rent the places, pay the doc, and have the potions as a backup plan." He paused as the next bout was called, then continued. "To your earlier question, only will matters. Gender, sex, sexuality, color, race, ethnicity—not a damn one of them is relevant inside the circle. Only who's stronger or who's better."

She grinned wide. "This is my kind of place."

He laughed. "Told you."

She'd watched several rounds, including one where Hank fought a man even bigger than him. The two of them had battered each other with real enthusiasm, and at the end, it came down to who could absorb more abuse as the exhausted fighters traded punches without even attempting to dodge or block.

Then, finally, it was her turn. She had challenged a tall man who looked a few years younger than her, and he'd accepted without a hint of disrespect. They had chatted for a few minutes, and she'd learned he was an EMT who regularly pulled sixteen-hour shifts to save up to buy a house. He couldn't relax on his days off because he'd become an action junkie, and cars, fighting, and sex were the only things that worked for him now. Cara had claimed to be a security consultant and shared some of her background.

Hank, now fully conscious again after the judicious application of smelling salts, helped her with the MMA-style gloves. They'd cushion the punches but allow her to grapple and grasp if needed. Her style didn't depend on it, but she wasn't fully sure that her opponent's wouldn't. He moved like someone with martial arts experience, though, so she was sure he'd be a decent match.

As the fight began and he circled, her grin widened. His experience showed in the way he remained relaxed and his eyes stayed defocused, ready for an attack to occur from anywhere. She launched a slow roundhouse, and when he tried to grab it rather than block it, she yanked it back. He gave her a nod to acknowledge her information-gathering effort and followed it with a charge led with a right hook.

She ducked and spun away from the blow and one leg trailed into a whipped sweep that he skipped over with ease. The expected kick barely missed her back when she darted in the opposite direction from his motion. *He's quick and smart. Excellent.* She rose and expected him to circle again, but he'd already pushed in. A front-kick led the way, and she retreated into a fighting stance to let it slide past her. When it dropped, he was close, and she fired two rapid jabs into his ribs. The third deflected from his elbow block. She sensed the incoming reverse punch as he shifted his hips, but it was faster than she'd anticipated and caught her on the ear as she jerked her head aside.

Cara hopped back, her ears ringing. If he'd wanted to kill her, he would have followed through, but he clearly enjoyed the sport and strategy as much as she did. He gave her time to recover before he circled again. There was a purity to the fight as she couldn't switch to weapons or magic and only had this one thing to think about. It calmed all the voices in her head and allowed her to simply be in the moment.

They made several more passes and exchanged kicks and punches, and while most were blocked, some made it through their defenses. Blood was visible on both combatants. Her opponent had caught her with a heel on a spinning hook kick far faster than any he'd demonstrated previously and opened a cut on her cheek. His lip had split from a headbutt when he'd raised his chin to protect his nose.

He changed tactics completely and lunged directly at her, ready to grapple. She tried to evade but wasn't quick enough, and he held her in a hug and forced her back to topple her. In an actual battle, she would have chopped him in the throat on the way in or crippled him with a kick to the knee or taken advantage of one of the many other openings for lethal or permanently damaging counters. Here, though, she lost her breath as he landed on top of her and drove his forearm into her solar plexus.

When he grinned, there was no malice in it, only shared energy and excitement. She threw a hook with her free hand, but he ducked under it and the angle prevented her from connecting. The little sparkles at the edge of her vision were welcome friends. Finally, she was able to draw a breath, but by that time, he had her arm in a wicked lock and her legs trapped between his. She gasped the words. "I concede. This time."

He let her up, and the surrounding crowd replied with a mixture of claps and groans before they were separated by their friends who corralled them in different directions. She looked at Hank, who had a broad grin on his face. "Thanks, man. I needed that."

"I know you did, and you're welcome anytime." He rolled his neck and had an almost lustful look in his eyes. "Now, it's my turn in the ring again."

CHAPTER TWENTY-FOUR

R ath leapt into space from one of the tallest buildings in the city, sixty-three stories up. Gwen provided a visual display of the air currents for him to use, and he focused on maintaining height and speed as his AI scanned the streets below for trouble. Each time he used the wings, he became better at controlling them, and his patrol partner gathered data so Kayleigh could improve them. The ones he wore were the second iteration, and the improvement from the first was impressive.

The troll banked and spiraled around the top of the newest skyscraper in town, which was also one of the greenest buildings on the planet. He'd initially been confused since the structure looked black and grey and blue, but Diana had explained the alternate meaning. That clarified, he was glad to hear that such things mattered. Small improvements added up. *Which is why I'm flying around downtown instead of sleeping. Well, that and because it's fun.*

He had tracked one target in particular for several

nights. Pittsburgh wasn't exactly a hotspot for illegal drug distribution, but there was one person who seemed to be near the top of whatever chain was present. He'd noticed him on multiple occasions, and Gwen had searched through all the information she had access to. There was a strong correlation between acts of gang violence in the city and the man's presence. Whether he was the direct cause or merely part of an overall increase in aggressiveness that happened when he was in town, he was interesting because of it.

Last time, he had been able to get close enough to tag his mark, and they'd followed him until after sunrise to track his movements. The techs currently worked on upgrading all the city's surveillance—invisible to the actual owners of the equipment, of course—so they could be used to detect the lightly radioactive substance as well. But, for now, they had to do it the old-fashioned way.

Gwen identified the target on a traffic camera and threw the image up on the right side of his goggles' display. A map appeared on the other side to indicate the best route to take to reach him. Rath followed it, descended to lower air currents that quickened in the channels created by the tightly packed city structures, and landed in a skid on top of one of the building on the main street heading northeast from downtown. If there was a specific location within the city limits where trouble tended to congregate, this was definitely it. The troll included the area on every patrol because of its popularity with the criminal element.

Below him, the man entered an alley and left his line of sight. Rath dashed across the rooftop and stood at the brink to look at the building opposite him. It was two stories higher than he was. The bricks were rough enough that he could probably climb them but fortunately, he didn't have to. He raised his arm and triggered the grapnel attached to it. The arrow rocketed to the top of the next structure, the tines deployed, and it latched onto the edge. He activated the winch mounted on his harness and was hoisted up to the top of the other building, where he strode to the lip and looked down.

The target and his underlings stood in a semicircle around another man, with Rath's target at the center of the group. "Gwen, amplify and isolate." The sounds in his headphones changed as the AI improved the resolution of what he wanted to hear. It wasn't perfect, but it was definitely better. *Need to get Kayleigh to design throwable sticky bug.* He eagerly anticipated his initial training session with Lian Chan, and most of his thoughts now turned first to throwing things as a combat option.

His target growled a threat at the huddled figure, who shrank against the wall and seemed for all the world like he tried to crawl through the solid substance. The troll was finally close enough to have a closer look at the man he'd tracked. He wore a dark suit with a grey fedora. The tips of his shoes were barely visible from above, but they reflected the minimal light that filtered into the alley from the street. His voice was gruff and hoarse as if he had to fight to force it out of his throat. "I said you had one last chance, dirtbag. And what did you do? Did you change your ways and sell the stuff like you promised you would?"

The cringing man said something in protest, and his harasser lashed out and kicked him back against the wall. He dropped to the damp asphalt with a cry of pain. Rath's target stepped forward to tower over the fallen figure. "No. You locked yourself in your filthy hidey-hole and used it instead, exactly like last time. And for that, you die here tonight. I can't let the others think I've gone soft." He crouched, careful to keep his trousers from touching the ground, and the words that followed were barely audible. "Plus, you're a scumbag who pollutes my world with your very existence."

He rose and dusted his hands off. The troll knew what would come next and leapt into space. It was a five-story drop, but Gwen made it easy and provided an aiming circle and a countdown. He fired the grapnel, it seized the edge of the roof, and the winch slowed his descent so he didn't hurt himself when he landed. The criminal he struck, however, fared less well. His feet intersected with the back of his neck and drove him face-first into the ground in the same moment that the man in the hat gave the expected order. "Kill him."

His henchmen were busy dealing with a three-foot gymnast troll, however, and couldn't obey. After he'd landed on the one farthest to the right, Rath had yanked his batons out and stunned the one beside him to disable him, at least for a while. He'd launched himself into a series of flips to close the distance to the other pair, ignored the boss, and evaded the bullets that they hoped would stop him. When he reached the closest man, he feinted high with his batons, then smashed them into the outsides of his knees. His opponent wailed and fell.

Rath felt the leader react and growled. He hadn't finished with the others yet and wasn't ready for the main man. He threw his left-hand baton into the air, snatched the flashbang on his chest bandolier, and threw it over his shoulder before he caught the baton cleanly. Gwen dimmed his vision and dampened his hearing at the pivotal moment, and when it returned, the man in front of him reeled and waved his gun around in an exceedingly dangerous manner. The troll jumped into a forward flip and stabbed him in the leg and the shoulder with his batons as he landed.

He turned to survey the field. All four underlings had been disabled, and his target simply stared at him. He grinned. "What? Never seen a troll? Maybe should get out more."

The man scowled. "And I hope to never see one again. You'll leave now if you know what's good for you, little freak."

Rath twirled his batons. "Ouch. Words hurt. Be nice."

Faster than the troll would have anticipated and almost faster than he could see, the man drew a gun from beneath his coat and aimed it menacingly. It was large and silver and glinted with the occasional glare from a car that passed on the street. Rath processed and discarded plans and finally decided the grapnel was his best bet. He shifted his arm subtly to align it with the man's throat and knew full well he'd only have one attempt. His assailant's trigger finger tightened as he deactivated the safety. His face was disgustingly smug beneath his ugly hat. "Any last words, vermin?"

Before the troll could react, a bullet bored through the man's skull and plowed into the street behind him. Rath jerked his head up. "Gwen, find the gun." She drew potential locations into his goggles and eliminated them one by one as she processed the available data. He redirected his aim, fired the grapnel to the top of the building, and launched himself forward. It was a simple matter to grapnel up and fly forward several times until he was higher than most of the buildings around. The AI had pinpointed the most likely location. He landed on that building, ready to investigate, when an outline appeared in his glasses. A dark figure with a large rifle across his back ran along a rooftop several buildings away.

He dashed at top speed to the edge and launched himself into space. Focused on the pursuit, he gained slowly on the running figure and realized he was likely to reach him before his quarry ran out of rooftops. Rath felt a sudden thrill of worry. *What will I do when I catch him? Seems like an excellent fighter.* He shrugged mentally. *Can use fighting mode. Should be good enough.*

The man stopped unexpectedly and turned to face him. In an instant, the gun was in his hands and aimed at the flying troll. He heard the sound of two shots in quick succession and felt the impacts as they struck and ruptured the ballistic fabric of the wings on his right side. He immediately careened in that direction as the ones on the opposite side worked as normal and he was forced to press the button to retract them. It was a ten-foot drop to the rooftop, and when he landed, he rolled to absorb the momentum. He scrambled to his feet. The man simply stared at him, the gun now out of sight.

Gwen's voice sounded surprised, which was, in itself, unexpected. "We have a comm request. It's on a near-band frequency, which probably means it's him."

The troll frowned. "Can we isolate everything else so he can't get into it?"

"Easily."

"Okay, do it. Anything seems weird, cut off."

"Affirmative."

The man's voice had the same electronic disguise as he'd used before. "Hello, friend."

"Friend probably not the right word, Amadeo."

He laughed. "Perhaps in time. But there's no reason for us to be enemies."

"You shot the Pirate Prince. And hat-man."

"Both criminal scum and both a sickness in this fine city."

Rath shook his head. "Doesn't give the right."

In the distance, the figure raised his hands to the sides. "And what gives you the right, hmm? What makes you better than me in this regard?"

He couldn't reveal his connection to a government agency, of course. "Don't kill. Only capture."

Even through the processed version of his voice, the troll heard his belief. "Some people warrant killing. And can you truly say you have never been involved in causing someone's death? Given your nightly pursuits, I think it is unlikely. Besides, I'm not paid for captures." There was an accent there that reminded him of one of the Rocky movies. "In any case, it is time for me to depart. I would urge you to stay away from me, but somehow, I don't think you would listen. So, we will have to agree to disagree."

The man turned and immediately began to run. Before the connection dropped, he offered one last piece of advice. "But don't follow too closely, little troll. If you leave me no other option, the next bullet will not hit only your equipment."

Rath lowered himself to sit cross-legged on the rooftop and watched as Amadeo sprinted into the distance. Finally, he was lost to sight, and the troll sighed. "Gwen, that person is scary. Let's keep an eye out for him. A very well-hidden eye."

CHAPTER TWENTY-FIVE

The summons to visit the lady of Stonesreach came in the form of the emissary who appeared in sight of the building. Diana had no idea how long he'd been there when the systems alerted her to a person who watched their headquarters. She was immediately suffused with guilt over the fact that she hadn't paid a social call to the ruler of the Kemana in some time.

She scurried out the front door wearing her illusion necklace and ran to where he stood. He inclined his head as she slowed to a halt before him. "Agent Sheen."

"Emissary."

"You are summoned, along with those whose counsel you prize most. The lady wishes to discuss matters of mutual concern." The level of gravity he conveyed eclipsed anything she'd previously seen from him.

She nodded. "May we have permission to portal onto the grounds in front of the entrance?"

"You may. Bring no weapons. We are aware that several of you possess magic, and of course, that is fine. But nothing else may be carried into the lady's presence at this time."

Diana nodded again. "Understood. When would she like us there?"

"As soon as possible, Agent Sheen."

She sighed inwardly. "Within the hour, then."

"That will be sufficient." He gave a graceful tilt of the head that resembled a shallow bow and vanished, his departure veiled by magic as before. She looked around to see if anyone was watching and was glad she'd had the foresight to wear the illusion necklace. She'd need to find a quiet place and portal into the base, though, to avoid connecting the emissary to the coworking building.

Diana pulled her phone out and instructed Friday to call Rath and Cara in immediately, then headed to the riverside at a run. *There should be cover under one of the bridges to portal from.*

They stepped through the rift that linked the hallway that led to the garage to the broad expanse of white stone that made up the entrance area of Lady Alayne's castle. Cara had visited previously and did not react to the elegance of the space. Rath had not and made a noise of appreciation that echoed the one she left unspoken. *There is no way to come here and not be awed by what they have created.*

The doors flanked by the elves in armor had already swung open and the emissary beckoned them forward. They had taken most of the allotted hour to prepare. Diana had portaled to the house to change out of her grungy office clothes into better ones. She'd selected high black boots over denim of the same color and an asymmetrical electric blue top that hung down on one side to her thigh. She'd corralled her hair into a ponytail, then gathered Rath up. The troll had simply brushed his fur to be ready to go.

They'd met Cara at the base. She'd chosen all black as well, with shorter boots, black denim, and a black tech top under a looser dress shirt. Her second-in-command was more relaxed than the last time Diana had seen her, and she was overjoyed at the change. *That's a good sign for what is to come. Things are on the right track. Well, other than the fact that we have a homicidal vigilante for rent in town.* Rath had told her about the man who had shot the Prince, but she was overcommitted already. The troll didn't seem to want help, anyway, and only wanted to be sure she knew.

They strode inside quickly and followed the emissary along the pale stone floors. He escorted them into the throne room, where Lady Alayne awaited them. She was dressed similarly to the last time they'd seen her in rich green robes and an abundance of sparkling jewels. There was a frown on her beautiful face, and Diana felt sadness well at the thought that she might have something to do with it. The elf's otherworldly attractiveness struck at a level much deeper than conscious thought. She closed her eyes briefly to banish the effects and focus her mind.

"Lady, thank you for the invitation to visit. How may we serve the good of the Kemana?"

She inclined her head at them. "We believed it might be useful for you to know that the trials you face above have come to roost here in our fair city as well."

Diana frowned. "I'm unhappy to hear that, Lady."

"As are we, Agent Diana Sheen. It appears that the messages the Remembrance has seeded above have also taken root here. My people who watch for such things report that there are five separate groups of sympathizers, at a minimum, and that the word is spreading. They believe there will be more and fear it may eventually lead to action."

"That is deeply unfortunate, to be sure. How can we assist?"

The elf shrugged. "The cause of this lies on the surface. You must be more vigilant in eradicating it."

She held her disbelieving laugh inside. Cara, however, did not. Her second-in-command kept her voice neutral when she replied, "We are doing so the best as we can, Lady Alayne. Do you have suggestions as to how we might improve?"

A stern look appeared on the elf's face, and Diana discovered that she had begun to take offense at the woman's attitude. "Our perception is that you have made things worse, rather than better, by your actions. You've empowered their message of resistance and failed to stop them from acquiring powerful artifacts and freeing their captive members. In short, Agent Cara Binot, Agent Diana Sheen, you must now succeed where thus far, you have failed."

She'd expected Cara to be the one to bristle, but it was Rath who growled. He stepped forward a pace, then stopped as the emissary caught his eye. He looked at the elf. "You overstep, Lady Alayne. If you wish things above ground to improve, consider joining us there. Otherwise, do not criticize my friends."

Diana blinked. She'd known Rath's speech patterns were choice rather than anything else and had teased him with the clip from *The Office* where one of the characters asked why one would bother using lots of words when "few word do trick." At the time, he'd merely given an inscrutable smile and changed the subject. But this was an impressive display, both of language and of devotion. She stepped forward and rested a hand on his shoulder.

The elf blinked as well and inclined her head again. "Perhaps I have been overly insulting. Please accept my apologies, all of you." She looked directly at the troll. "We've not been introduced, although I have heard stories of your accomplishments on the lips of many. I am Lady Alayne."

He nodded. "Rath."

"Pleased to meet you, then. But my concern remains. Often, situations that exist on the surface in diffused form are far more concentrated here in the Kemana, which can lead to actions erupting here first."

Diana nodded. "We hear you, Lady Alayne. Please know that we are doing, and will continue to do, all that we can for you and for the people of Stonesreach."

The elf stared at them as if to take their measure. The moment went on longer than was comfortable, and then longer still. Finally, Lady Alayne nodded and turned to the man standing several feet away to one side. "Please give it to them."

The emissary frowned slightly. "My Lady, are you sure?"

The elf sighed, clearly torn. "I am not. But that is not a decision against, on its own. Give it to them."

He held his hands out before him and an ornate scroll case appeared in them. He walked forward and offered it to Diana, who accepted it with appropriate reverence. As he returned to his position, Lady Alayne explained. "Inside is all our knowledge about Rhazdon's Vengeance to assist you in your quest."

Diana frowned. "How did you know?"

Lady Alayne smiled. "There is very little that happens in this place that I am unaware of, Agent Diana Sheen, especially when it involves as pivotal an individual as Nylotte."

She shook her head in appreciation of the elf's machinations. "Indeed, Lady."

The woman waved. "Off with you. There is no time like the present to begin improving our situation."

The emissary escorted them out. As they prepared to step into the portal, Cara looked at Rath. "You're something else, you know that?"

The troll laughed. "Sometimes, people need to be reminded of who they are."

That inspired an unexpectedly wide grin on her second-in-command's face. "I couldn't have said it better myself."

As they stepped through the portal, Diana had the distinct impression that she was the only one missing some important key to understanding the conversation. *But really, what else is new?*

CHAPTER TWENTY-SIX

S loan stood in a bus shelter half a block away from the Italian restaurant, close enough to see the sign proclaiming "Homestyle" but far enough that he would be unlikely to be recognized by anyone going in or out. He sent a text to Mur. - **No Action Yet** -

The other man replied with an hourglass icon, or in other words, "Wait." Marcus had decided that he wanted to be a part of the event but had chosen his right-hand man, Murray, and detailed him to find a couple more to help out. Mur had successfully argued that only those already in on the plan should be involved, so it was left to the three of them.

The initial hope had been to get the witch alone, but after several days of surveillance, they had realized that Wysse spent no time by herself. She lived with roommates and traveled in a group. There had been as few as two accompanying her. Tonight, there were four. They'd decided that to attack her after a late dinner—when the witches would all be tired and hopefully, a little slower—

would offer the most potential for any unexpected events to go their way. It had the added bonus of being fairly dark and given that it was a Monday night, not too busy.

According to the plan, he would shadow them to the parking garage, and the attack would take place in the lobby. Mur had taken position on the stairs leading up, out of the line of sight, and Marcus was one floor up, ready to race down. They'd rigged the power box with a small explosive to short it, and Sloan would detonate it with his phone to start the action. His job was to act as the spotter and join in as quickly as he could once things began.

The witches emerged from the restaurant, Wysse in the lead. Sloan's stomach twisted. On the one hand, she was a criminal who would kill him in an instant if a reason presented itself, and he'd already seen her kill others. On the other, being responsible for setting her up to be eliminated didn't sit all that well with him. He'd tried to rationalize it away, aware that someone else would do it if he refused and also knowing that even if this effort went wrong, they'd try again until they succeeded. None of it assuaged his guilt, so he decided it would be best to accept what he couldn't change and get on with it. Staying undercover always involved compromises.

The witches were a little tipsy, and their observations about the humans they passed were loud enough to offend those being discussed and to make him feel less regret about what was to come. As they entered the lobby, he triggered the explosive and ran behind them into the suddenly darkened space.

They'd agreed that gunfire would be a bad idea, so Mur had brought a large pipe and Marcus would rely on his fists and arms. By the time he arrived, his two comrades had evened the odds with their surprise attack—three witches versus the three of them. One of the fallen women was bleeding from her skull, and another looked as if she'd received a high-intensity electrical blast from Marcus's arm, judging by the wisps of smoke that drifted from the vicious burns that marred her skin.

Wysse was still standing and launched an attack as he reached the door. Shadow tentacles reached out from her wand to capture Mur, lift him, and hurl him through the window and out of the lobby. Blood stained the glass, and Sloan hoped the man hadn't cut anything vital. The nearest witch fired a force bolt at him, and he dove to avoid it with a shout and made sure to angle toward the third witch. She faced Marcus and had summoned a force shield to absorb the lightning that cascaded from his metal limb.

Sloan rolled to his feet and barreled into her from the side, where she had no defenses. He led with a left hook and drove a knee into her stomach. As she doubled over, he dropped an elbow to the back of her head, and she collapsed. He spun sideways in time to take a force bolt in the chest. It flung him against the wall, and his head impacted with the polished stone hard enough that his vision doubled, then doubled again. He slumped, unable to get his bearings, and focused all his will on not throwing up from the way the world dipped and wavered around him.

The rest of the fight played out like a movie as he concentrated on one of the four rotating images he saw. Marcus circled to put the witch with the force attacks between him and Wysse, which forced the witch's tentacles to retract. He skipped in and punched the other in the throat with his metal arm, and it returned bloody and pointed in sword form. *Damn, he can do that fast. I wonder how it happens. Like, servos or something maybe? I should ask him.*

He realized his mind had gone off on a tangent and yanked it back to the moment. His vision had resolved into only two images, one apparently from his left eye and one from the right. Wysse was speaking, but her words didn't make any sense as they reached his ears. He thought he heard her say "Sarah," and maybe "Punish," but that was all he could discern. In reply, Marcus extended his arm toward her. She flinched and cast a shield between them, and the leader of the Remembrance humans adjusted his aim and blasted the witch Sloan had downed with lightning to kill her instantly.

The man smiled at Wysse, who cowered behind her magical barrier. It was difficult to tell what her plan was, but it seemed clear it wasn't working. Her words came into resolution as she tried to negotiate with him. "I'll go away. You'll never see me again. There's no need for any more killing." She sobbed. "Haven't you done enough?"

He walked in a predatory circle around her, which forced the witch to turn to keep her defenses raised toward him. He laughed at her fear. "No, dear Wysse. You thought you were my equal, and worse, thanks to Sarah's whispers in your ear, you thought you were better than me because I'm supposedly only human and you magicals are so much more."

She shook her head. "No, that's not it. I only did what I was told. It was all her. Blame her."

Marcus grinned. "Oh, sweetheart, believe me, I do. And she will get what is coming to her, have no fear. But first, you need to give her a message."

"I'll tell her anything you want me to."

His grin grew wider. "I know you would. Sadly for you, it's not that kind of message." He raised his arm again. Sloan expected to see the slot on the top rise to deploy the lightning-stun cannon and was surprised when a different one opened on the bottom. The man raised his wrist so the barrel that extended would be unobstructed, and the weapon discharged with a loud pop. The witch's eyes widened as the single bullet drilled into the center of her chest. Her mouth formed an "O" as she looked at it and her shield fell with the distraction.

Sloan consoled himself with the idea that she was already unconscious as the lightning savaged her while she fell. Her killer ran it back and forth across her body and laughed in a not entirely sane way before suddenly, it cut off. He frowned at the arm and muttered, "Damn battery." The agent slid into darkness after that and only roused when Marcus slapped his face and lifted him.

His knees buckled immediately, and the man moved in to support him and put his metal arm around his shoulders to hold him up. He gazed at the lobby and saw that their leader had done a good job of making it look like ARES had executed the attack by spreading a few shell casings, a baton dipped in the witch's blood, and most telling, a pair of discharged grenades identical to the ones the team used. Mur's truck pulled up outside with a man he didn't know at the wheel. Marcus set him in the bed reasonably gently. A moment later, Murray joined him, still bleeding and frighteningly pale. Sirens howled in the distance, and the vehicle accelerated sharply as it headed to the road and the highway beyond it.

The thought crossed his mind that what they'd done would be the start of some significant trouble, but he spiraled into unconsciousness when the truck hit a particularly hard bump and his head bounced off the metal. *Ah, dreamland, how relaxing...*

CHAPTER TWENTY-SEVEN

E manuel's shop was on the path to Rath's training appointment, so he and Max made their way down the streets toward it and enjoyed the summer sun. The dog noticed a rabbit across the grassy lawn and whined, and the tiny troll laughed and gripped his collar ring tightly. "Go, Maxie!" With a joyful bark, the Borzoi dashed through the intervening space, headed for the startled animal.

It ran, and the dog followed, zigging and zagging to match its movements. There was no way he would actually catch the bunny and he really didn't try hard enough. It wasn't about the catching, it was about the chase. Rath grinned. *Kind of a metaphor for some of the stuff we do. Although I would like to catch that Amadeo and put him on a train to a different city.* The rabbit raced toward a small pond and ran near the ducks. Max was immediately distracted and began to play with them instead, bending over his front paws and hopping around like a goofball.

Rath spent the whole time laughing more freely than he had in weeks. Finally, after the ducks had been replaced by squirrels who chattered from their branches above, the tired dog and gleeful troll made their way toward the shop. They'd left early enough for distractions, and he still had a half hour before he had to be at Lian Chan's. He tried not to let his mind wander into imagining what the place or the training might be like as he didn't want to ruin the reality of it with false expectations.

They bounded inside to find the owner sitting in his usual chair, sipping tea and reading a tome that looked very old. Rath ran onto Max's nose and said, "Launch," and was flung upward. He did a flip and landed cleanly on the table beside Manny.

"Well done, my friend." The elderly man laughed, slid a bookmark into place, and closed the book. "How nice of you to stop by. Get this—I had a customer earlier." He looked proud.

The troll clapped with the right amount of enthusiasm. "Excellent. What sell?"

Manny shrugged. "I didn't say he was a buying customer." They laughed together. "But he'll be back, I'm sure. It takes a first visit to get used to the place."

He nodded, then sobered. "Have information. Need to share."

The man shifted his position so he could look at his visitor more comfortably. "Go ahead, then."

"Vigilante in town. Amadeo."

"Like a Batman kind of vigilante?" He frowned.

Rath shook his head. "Assassin of bad guys."

Manny put a hand over his mouth. "That's not good at all. Are you in danger?"

Warmth surged through him at his companion's first concern. "Not if I stay out of his way."

He chuckled nervously. "Well, you should definitely do that."

The troll nodded and looked at the clock on the wall. "Max, Ready." The dog stood from where he'd been resting and Rath clambered down the table leg to jump onto his back. He waved at Manny as they headed to the door.

He called, "I'll let the others know about the vigilante." As they left, Manny muttered loudly enough that Rath could make it out. "Amadeo...Amadeo. Why do I recognize that name?"

They arrived at the location on the card two minutes before the appointed time. Their travel had taken them along a street they'd not been down before, filled with shops under signs he couldn't read and scents and items he couldn't identify. It looked ethnic, but not Chinese or Japanese. He didn't know anything about it at all, other than it seemed pleasant.

The address was a narrow door to the right of a tea shop of some kind, where the patrons sat at the narrow tables in the window and used cups that would have been small for his three-foot form, much less their full-sized bodies. He rang the doorbell and the door buzzed, so Max pushed it wide with his nose and they entered a long corridor. It appeared to run the full length of the shop and then open into a space behind it. The Borzoi padded cautiously down it, kept his head low, and made inquisitive snuffles.

At the end of the passage, the room opened up to the left into a large box with minimal furnishings. Two garage doors made up the back wall. There were targets on the wall nearest him, and Chan sat on a folding chair in the far corner. The man was looking away as they entered but turned immediately. Rath wondered how since he couldn't hear, and the question must have shown on his face. "Vibrations, young troll. I felt you probably about halfway along the hallway."

He grinned. "Hard to sneak up on you."

The man returned the smile and his dark almond-shaped eyes crinkled into laugh lines at the edges. "Very difficult indeed, unless you can fly. But, from what I've heard, you know a little about that, hey?"

Rath laughed. "A little."

Chan gestured toward a case on a table at the center of the wall opposite the targets. "Take a look and choose where you'd like to begin."

He hopped off the dog and grew to his three-foot size, then snagged a chair and pulled it over to stand on top of it and peer into the open container. It was all wood, about two feet wide and one long. Nestled in a rich scarlet fabric were an assortment of weapons, each made of silver metal and featuring at least one sharp edge, usually more. On the far right were darts, ranging in size from tiny to long. Beside them rested throwing stars with various numbers of pointy ends. Next, throwing knives, light, thin, and about hand-sized. The final section held the truly unique items. There was a bolo, several spheres of different sizes, things that looked like jacks from the child's game but with wicked edges, and a couple of others he couldn't even hazard a guess at.

He turned to the man who would be his teacher. "Any best to start with?"

Chan shook his head. "Whatever calls to you is best. The teachings are adaptable as all good lessons should be."

Rath regarded the choices before him and decided that the throwing knives were the most logical first choice. He selected a pair and carried them to his instructor. The man straightened and tilted his short-bearded chin at the weapons. "Examine them. What do they tell you?"

He angled them to the light and saw nicks on the blades, along with scratches and smudges. When he examined the other edge, he found a slight bend in one of them. "They have been used before and not cared for properly."

The man broke into a smile. "That, my friend, is the perfect answer. You are correct on both counts. All these weapons are for my students, and all my students are instructed to leave them unrepaired when they finish. Can you guess why?"

The troll thought about it but could only come up with one response. "Training?"

He laughed, and it was soft and gentle and inoffensive. "Close, but not quite all the way. Yes, for training, but specifically to teach you that you must care for your things if you wish for them to care for you. Those weapons are now your responsibility, my friend. We shall practice with them today, and you will take them with you. When you return for your next lesson, if they are not in perfect condition, I will refuse to teach you."

Rath nodded. "I understand. I agree."

Chan tilted his head at the targets. "Throw."

He positioned himself and tossed one of the blades. It was remarkably light and well-balanced and felt good in his hand and as it left. It missed both the target and the cork board around it and struck the wall a foot to the side. Worse—or maybe better given the terrible throw—the handle impacted first. He looked at his teacher with a regretful expression.

The man smiled and chuckled. "That is nothing to be ashamed of. Everyone starts somewhere. What's important is where you finish and what you do along the journey." He stood and walked over to stand behind him. "Okay, get into position to throw again."

During the next half-hour, the man adjusted many little things about Rath's throwing. His stance had been slightly off balance, the way he brought his arm down had been too rigid, and other corrections big and small made all the difference. By the end of the session, he hit the cork board every time and the target itself once in a while. He'd lost any feeling of self-doubt or anxiety and merely enjoyed hurling the metal.

Finally, his teacher clapped once. "Collect your blades, and I will see you here in two days at the same hour."

Rath did as he was told but paused before he left. "May have time conflicts. Helping friends."

Chan nodded. "There is no greater purpose. If you must reschedule for such a thing, then reschedule we shall."

The troll grinned. "Thank you, Chan."

"You are welcome, Rath."

As he walked beside Max out to the street, his mind already thought about how to integrate the knives into his equipment kit. He turned to the Borzoi. "Let's go see Kayleigh." The dog's enthusiastic bark was all the confirmation he needed.

CHAPTER TWENTY-EIGHT

Since her visit to the Kemana, Diana had half-anticipated and half-dreaded her next training session with Nylotte. The knowledge that the Remembrance had gained strength in Stonesreach was something she would have expected the Dark Elf to share with her, and yet she had not. Combining that with the reminder that the woman had known Nehlan, the bastard who'd kidnapped Lisa as leverage, left her feeling strangely awkward toward her.

Not angry, exactly, nor upset. But it felt as if a foundation she'd thought was solid was suddenly sand, ready to shift at the touch of a wave she couldn't see coming. *Maybe disappointed is the better term, but that would be stupid, right?*

So, when the word came that the Drow needed to see her immediately, it carried with it a bag full of worry. Still, she didn't delay. At this point, the need for responsiveness had been reinforced many times over with sharp words and longer than strictly required lessons. She stepped through into the training space, expecting to find her teacher there, but the cellar was empty.

Scraping sounds came from above, and Diana climbed the staircase slowly. As she reached the door at the top, it swung open, accompanied by the Dark Elf's impatient voice. "About time, Diana. I have someone for you to meet."

She pushed through and found herself in the presence of another Drow. *Huh. I wonder what you call a group of Drow? A dirge? A dram? How about a despair of Drow?* She nodded at her teacher's guest, and the woman nodded in return. Nylotte said, "Kienka, this is Diana. Diana, meet Kienka. She knows your boyfriend quite well."

The agent rolled her eyes. *She never misses a chance, does she?* "Is this about Bryant?"

The two Dark Elf women laughed, which drew a frown from her. Her teacher shook her head. "She has assisted in the search for Rhazdon's Vengeance, as her contacts on Oriceran are different than mine."

She was interested despite herself. "How so?"

Kienka's voice was dark and matched her skin and her hair perfectly. It held a subtler sarcasm than Nylotte's. Bryant had told her once that his magical supplier had been one of the first to cross over, so perhaps she'd learned to hide her arrogance better than her counterpart. *Or maybe my teacher simply doesn't care what we think of her. It's probably that.* "Mine tend to be less accomplished than hers —closer to the ground, one might say."

Her teacher chuckled. "Or, to put it less gently, mine inhabit higher social circles."

The other woman nodded. "True. But mine found the clue you needed. There's a lesson there."

Nylotte gave her a sour look. "As if I need teaching from you, crone."

The other woman's laugh was overly loud and fully mocking. "You need a great deal that you do not wish to acknowledge."

Diana feared that the conversation was about to go to unproductive places, at best, and dangerous places, at worst. "What clue?" she interjected.

Her teacher sighed, clearly exasperated. "We know where Angel and Demon are located." Kienka raised an elegant black eyebrow, and Nylotte growled softly in irritation. "Are *probably* located."

The agent's excitement level went from zero to sixty in an instant. "Where? How?"

Kienka replied, "To the latter question, one of my contacts who specializes in finding powerful antiques—"

Nylotte interrupted. "Stealing powerful antiques."

The other woman frowned. "Let's say acquiring powerful antiques. In any case, that person knew the right being to bribe for information. At great cost, she was willing to share the suspected location of the daggers in return for a present reward and a promise of future consideration."

Diana didn't much like the sound of that deal. "What kind of consideration?" Both women waved their hands in an almost identical fashion that she'd come to interpret as, "Trouble down the road, don't worry about it now." She shook her head. "Okay, fine. Where are they?"

Kienka gestured at Nylotte, and her teacher said, "Oriceran. In a tomb."

She sighed. "Of course they are. Why wouldn't they be?"

Kienka had departed after several rounds of tea and discussion. It appeared to be an expectation or a ritual, as neither she nor Nylotte truly seemed to enjoy it and spent the time taking verbal shots at one another.

When the other woman was finally gone, Diana had considered the ramifications of the Dark Elves' contacts in her mind for too long to remain silent. "Can you explain the social circles thing?"

Nylotte shrugged as she collected the cups and placed them on the serving tray. "Like here, there is a criminal element—or an underworld if you wish—on Oriceran. It consists of big fish and little fish, friendly otters and vicious sharks, and all the variations in between. I swim most often with the bigger sharks. Kienka makes all the sea her own but tends to spend more time bottom-feeding than I do."

The woman loves her metaphors. "Should that worry us?"

Her teacher sighed and paused her cleaning to look her in the eye. "You seem to bring a wealth of preconceived ideas to this subject. There is no absolute path of purity, only an ongoing question of how much of your precious idealism you might sacrifice in the face of necessity. Kienka and I are long past concerning ourselves with others' moral expectations. I am entirely comfortable with who I am and what I do, and if it is practical for me to know those whose objective morals are, shall we say, disappointing to most, I will do so."

She brushed her hair out of her face and tossed her head to flick it back. "And before you become all self-righteous, remember that you seek to steal items which do not belong to you and use them against others who, like you, believe they are doing the right thing. I fully believe that you are an objectively better choice to possess them, which is why you have my assistance." She lifted the tray and left the room, headed for the small kitchen in the back corner of the main floor.

Diana considered the woman's words. Her teacher had definitely captured the line of her thoughts and body-slammed it to the ground. But she was right. There was a continuum in place, and on one side were those who sought to hurt others, and on the other, those who sought to help others. Between these two extremes, the path intersected with legal and moral concerns of every kind. She asked herself, as she had many times before, if her purpose was just. And, as she had many times before, concluded it was. Mental Diana materialized in her vision and stood with her arms folded as she shook her head. *"Well, then, perhaps you should climb off your bloody high horse and get some work done, rather than worrying endlessly about who knows who?"*

She snorted rudely, and the image vanished. When she followed the Drow into the kitchen, she found her rinsing the cups out and setting them to dry next to the teapot inverted on the draining rack. "I apologize. You are absolutely correct. I hereby renounce my position as Morality Sheriff."

The Dark Elf's stiff back softened as she chuckled. "Very good, protégé. You are able to learn. Before our time together is finished, perhaps you will even understand yourself a little better."

Diana laughed. "Let's try to keep our aspirations reasonable, shall we? There's no reason to go crazy here."

Nylotte turned with a serious expression. "You should realize that in our fight against the Remembrance and whoever leads them, I may need to contact people far less savory than those we have already engaged."

She nodded. "I get it. No worries."

Her teacher answered with a loud clap. "Excellent. Now, gather your magical colleagues together. We're headed to Oriceran to cause trouble and steal stuff."

CHAPTER TWENTY-NINE

She and Rath had picked Cara up, and they'd driven to the headquarters building to get ready. The vehicle was, as always, a pleasure to drive, and Diana enjoyed each and every twist and turn along the way. She squealed the tires in the garage and skidded to a stop perfectly within the lines of the space that she'd targeted.

Her second-in-command stared at her like she was crazy. "Showing off much?"

"You gotta take the fun moments where you can get them." She laughed.

Cara nodded. "Amen to that, sister."

"Why so serious?" Rath interjected. His impression was good enough to draw laughs from each of them. As they passed through the tunnel, Diana realized that not only was she pumped up about their mission to locate the blades, she felt happy about it. Whatever internal concerns had bugged her had been banished. One look at the bounce in Cara's step showed that she felt the same. And Rath...

249

well, he could always be depended on to see the bright side of life.

They traded jokes while they changed into their tunics and strapped their armor on. She and Cara packed exclusively anti-magic rounds since the one thing they could absolutely count on would be magical opposition of some kind. Grenades were another matter, however. She stared at the selection and found no clues forthcoming as to what might be the most useful. With a shrug, she selected one of each type other than incendiary and slid them into the open slots on her belt and left thigh.

Cara replaced her in front of the grenades as Diana retrieved her carbine from the wall and strapped it on. Her AI collar lay around her neck, but she wasn't sure how well it would work on Oriceran. She had a notion that some of the processing and data access was offloaded to headquarters via the comm device at the back of her belt and assumed it wasn't designed for interplanetary communication. The comms would function without a home connection, though, as the redesign after the museum battle had eliminated the need for a base station in favor of distributed networking.

She noticed Rath peering down at his vest in search of something and sat beside him on the bench. Since he stood on it, the arrangement put them more or less eye-to-eye. "What's up, doc?"

He grinned. "Duck season."

"Rabbit season."

The troll extended two knives to her, and she accepted them and held them up to the light. "These are sharp. A little misused, though. Where did you get these?"

"Training. Friend of Professor Charlotte."

"A Griffin?"

He laughed. "Not officially. Sometime maybe. Good at throwing things."

"Excellent. You can teach Cara a thing or two."

From the other side of the room, her second-in-command replied, "I heard that." After a pause, she added, "And you're not wrong."

Rath gestured toward his vest. "No sheaths."

Diana tapped his arms to get him to raise them and looked at the vest. Sure enough, it lacked any open slots to put the knives on. "Wait a sec." She turned and rummaged in one of the miscellaneous gear bins and found a strap. It was too long, so she looped it before running it around him between his ribs and his stomach and grabbed gaffer's tape to secure it in four places. She attached two knife holders at the appropriate angles, and he slid the weapons home with a grin.

"Thanks."

"Don't mention it. But please, don't stab me, 'kay?"

Cara chimed in, "I'll give you five dollars to stab her."

She shook her head. "Traitor."

After a couple more minutes, they were as prepared as they could be. Diana concentrated and opened a portal she'd only done once before. On the opposite side, the bedroom that formerly belonged to Nehlan could be seen through the wavering rift. She turned to her teammates. "Ready?"

They nodded. Neither appeared concerned and both looked as happy as she felt about the quest for the artifacts.

Of course, once they find out it's in a tomb, they might feel differently.

Good choice not to tell them, then," her internal voice replied,

She grinned. *Well, you know how it is. Sometimes, Drow are jerks.*

———

Nylotte waited across the room when they arrived. She was dressed in leather from toes to collar, all of it black except for the tight jacket she wore, which was a deep shade of purple. She'd pulled her white hair back in a braid, which gave her the most martial look Diana had ever seen on her. The satchel she'd carried before was strapped across her chest again and rested on her right hip. Nods and greetings were exchanged.

The Drow turned to her. "Are you and your team ready to do this?"

"We are."

"Very well." She waved her arms in a circle to conjure another portal, this one leading to what looked like a darkened hallway. Diana went first, followed by Cara and Rath, and Nylotte stepped through and closed the rift behind her. A cavern surrounded them, seemingly natural stone that had been carved into a rough descending staircase. Light was provided only by occasional flickering lanterns hung from spikes pounded into the walls.

Cara peered around with her hands on her hips. "Lovely place."

Rath nodded and sneezed. "Dusty."

Diana knelt and examined the floor, which had several footprints of differing sizes visible in the grime. "But not as secret or hidden as we thought, apparently. People have been through here. I would guess recently, too, although there's no way to know how old these are."

Nylotte studied them over her shoulder. "At least one is a dwarf or a gnome. Or maybe a mid-sized troll."

She stood quickly. "Onward?"

The Drow nodded. Diana led them forward carefully and left herself time to react to any mundane traps or hints from her magic danger sense. They found one not too far down the path, a tripwire and dart mechanism. It had already been sprung, and the walls were covered in tiny needles. There was no gap to indicate that they'd hit anything. Again, it offered no information on when the trap had been triggered, but she felt an increasing certainty that they were not alone in the space.

That feeling was confirmed when they reached the next trap, which had found a victim. It apparently used some kind of acid, because a humanoid figure lay on the ground with most of its face disintegrated. The surrounding blood had not seeped away completely, and that which had collected in the cracks and crevices remained damp.

Nylotte grunted. "This place is more dangerous than I imagined it would be, which increases the probability that Rhazdon's Vengeance lies within."

Diana chuckled darkly. "Or about a million pissed-off wizard skeletons or something."

Cara coughed. "Wait, what?"

Rath grinned. "Skeletons. Groovy."

She laughed and held her rifle up to the troll. "This is my boomstick."

He dissolved into a series of quiet laughs while their teammate stared at them and Nylotte shook her head. The Drow tilted her head toward Cara. "She may have become my favorite student."

Diana snorted. "Just because you have no taste in movies doesn't mean you should be jealous of those of us who do."

The other agent tried again. "Are you saying we're in a tomb? Like, an underground crypt filled with dead things lying around?"

Nylotte offered a wicked grin. "Or no longer lying around, as the case may be. But yes to the first part."

Cara pointed a finger at her boss. "We'll discuss information sharing later, boss. It's a thing. Look it up."

A loud crash sounded from deeper in the tomb, and they all sobered in response. Diana kept her voice at a whisper barely strong enough to reach the Dark Elf in the back of the formation. "Onward. I'm first, then Rath, then Cara, then Nylotte. As long as we can be sneaky, we do it. If we find someone we absolutely must engage, we try to keep it quiet. Maybe we can get near these other bastards without them realizing we're here."

She advanced along the hallway until it reached a pair of open doors. There were signs that others had passed through recently in the dust that covered everything. She paused and searched for traps but detected none. Her attention was caught by a sarcophagus that rested at the front of the chamber, supported on an ornate table and illuminated by a chandelier that hung above it. The room widened as she walked forward, and she shifted her gaze deliberately around the space—left, right, up, and down.

Even so, she found it difficult not to be distracted by the object ahead. The stone was intricately carved, and as she traced the designs up from the base, she realized that the lid wasn't on. *Great. It's probably a mummy that'll attack us. Or a Lich. That'll suck.* Ever since her early experiences with the *Tomb of Horrors* module, she feared liches with a deep and abiding passion.

Perhaps the overall abundance of sensory input was to blame for her failure to notice the waiting ambush. Time slowed, and she jerked her head back to barely avoid the needle-thin line of flame that slashed across her vision to sear into the left-hand wall. She threw her body back and down to avoid a possible swing of the weapon that would behead her. A curse sounded from the right, and feet pounded rapidly away down the hallway in that direction. She flipped up and raced in pursuit. Nylotte reacted quickest and was on her heels in a moment. Ahead, the figure darted through an opening and a huge door began to descend from the ceiling with spikes on the bottom. Diana shouted and slid beneath it with space to spare. She twisted and heaved a block of force under it so the Dark Elf could make it through, but the enormous weight of the grid slammed it shut before the others could arrive, which left them on the opposite side.

Diana spoke into her comms but received only silence in response.

Cara tried again. "Boss? Are you there?" She shook her head at Rath when no reply came. "Check around and see if there's a switch or something." She joined him in the search, but they found nothing useful at all. "Well, damn."

The troll grinned. "Guess we go left."

She nodded. "I guess so. I'm gonna be honest, I liked the odds better when there were four of us."

"Never tell me the odds."

Cara groaned. "I walked right into that one, didn't I."

"Yep."

At least I'm entertaining the troll. That's a plus. She led the way into the room with the sarcophagus and peered into it. The empty space within did nothing good for her anxiety. "So, do you think they never actually put anyone in there?"

Rath jumped up and shook his head. "Nope. I think it woke up."

"That's really not possible."

He shrugged. "Magic. Wildcard."

"Yeah. You're right, there. You never know what those crazy wizards, witches, elves, other elves, dwarfs, and Kilomea will get up to."

"Don't forget gnomes."

"Right, gnomes."

He grinned. "Or Willen."

Cara rolled her eyes. "Let's stop now." He laughed and followed her as she moved down the hallway leading from the left side of that room. It turned to the right and curved right again, then led to a space that would have been immediately behind the chamber they'd entered earlier. Judging by the way the space in front of her seemed to open up, it was a mirrored arrangement to the other, although no corridor extended in the direction Diana had gone. *Dang. That's one hope dashed.*

She paused as an unusual shuffling noise emerged from the area at the end of the hall. She raised her rifle and rushed forward to discover six skeletons that lurched awkwardly into motion, but their movement seemed to become smoother with every step. Rath skidded in behind her, and for a moment, neither of them reacted as they stared ahead.

"Do you see this too?" she asked,

The sound of his batons extending to full length accompanied a nod. Her glasses verified that they had no heat signature at all. They were, literally, the walking dead. Or, maybe for clarity and with due respect to zombies—*please, don't let there be zombies*—the walking really dead.

She raised her barrel and sighted down it. "Watch out for whoever's waking these jerks up. Logically, they've gotta be around here somewhere." Inside, a part of her brain that still shook its head in disbelief suggested that logic had nothing to do with what they faced. She pulled the trigger, and the skull on the nearest shattered. Naturally, that didn't stop the rest of the body at all.

Rath darted in, hammered the closest skeleton on the right side, and his batons struck it in the knees. They shattered and it fell. He looked up with a smile, but she shook her head. "Look again." He did and grimaced when the skeleton dragged itself toward him. He regained his cheerful demeanor as quickly and leapt up to land on its back and break the brittle bones before he finally dispatched the skull to the rear of the room using his baton in a golf swing.

Cara grinned. *You know, this would make a good VR game. I need to talk to Kayleigh about that.* She let the rifle fall and attacked with her fists and feet, weaving her way through the slow-moving assailants and literally disarming them, then making another pass through to remove other important limbs. Rath raced her on the opposite side as he disabled his targets one by one and pounded them into the ground. A skull whizzed past her head, and she glared at him. "Careful, there, Arnold Palmer."

He laughed. "Hail to the king, baby."

It was a passable impersonation, and she laughed. While she'd been engaged with the skeletons, she'd remained alert and wondered if and when the person who'd raised them would appear. They had finally dispatched the last of the bony warriors when a witch in a red dress with scarlet ribbons in her blonde hair suddenly winked into existence. She pointed a wand at Cara and shadow energy extended toward her. It expanded into a larger and larger cone as it approached in waves that reminded her of the ocean. For a moment, they were almost captivating in their slow roll, then she recovered her wits and flung herself to the side to avoid them.

Rath ran at the witch with a battle cry, and the cone vanished as their enemy pointed the wand at him. She released a much faster thin bolt of shadow, but the troll simply vaulted over it. Cara took an instant to perfect her aim and fired three bullets at the woman's chest. She staggered back but didn't fall. "Dammit. Vests, again. It's like they're standard dark side issue these days." The fact that they'd made it to Oriceran didn't shock her. *Criminals love discussing how to beat the authorities.* She raised her aim and fired at the woman's head, but she dropped out of sight behind another one of the tables that, fortunately, didn't have a coffin of any kind on it.

The snap of Rath's batons echoed through the space, and she dashed over in case he needed help. He was on top of the witch and stabbed his weapons into her again. Her eyes rolled back into her head and she slumped, as boneless as the skeletons they'd destroyed. She bent to zip-tie her wrists, and Rath did the same to her ankles. That done, she snatched the wand up and threw it far across the room while the troll connected the two ties with a third, which would keep her immobile.

Cara stood and peered around the room now that she had time to notice the details. Ledges extended from the walls, three on each side, for the skeletons to rest on when they weren't sent to kill intruders. Two were at rib height, and the middle was at eye level. All of them were empty. The chamber had only one exit other than the one they'd used to enter, and that again led to the left.

She shrugged and headed toward it. "C'mon buddy. Maybe we'll find some zombies or vampires to play with."

The troll skipped up beside her with a grin. "Hope so. Fun."

The agent laughed. "You know, this once, I'll have to agree. I hope Diana doesn't face anything worse."

At that moment, in a different section of the labyrinthine crypt, Diana made a hasty retreat as a giant golem—at least twelve feet high and enormously wide—lumbered out of the pit where it had been hiding. It was a hideous creation, an amalgam of pieces of bone and bodies in various stages of decay. In its hand was a broad club formed of overlapping bones held together with what looked like razor wire. Closer inspection revealed it was actually some kind of sinew with teeth embedded in it.

Her stomach fluttered as she turned to Nylotte. "I hope you have a good idea because right now, all I can think to do is run screaming."

CHAPTER THIRTY

Nylotte shook her head. "Even in my experience, this is an abomination. I have never heard of such a thing."

A mocking voice spoke from outside the portcullis that had fallen to block the front exit from the room. Matching grids had descended to cut off the room's other exits. "Foolish Drow. You should have been quieter, like we were, and avoided waking the beast." He was barely visible from their position and seemed shorter than average.

Nylotte scowled. "Ushev, is that you?"

He laughed. "Yes, my old friend. It is so sad to see you in such dire straits." His voice suggested that it wasn't actually sad but rather a cause for celebration.

"When I get out of here, know that I will not stop until you are dead unless you release those gates immediately."

He snapped his fingers loudly. "You're a merchant, right?" The growl that came from deep in Nylotte's throat indicated that she didn't approve of that description. "How about we make a deal? You kill the annoying human accompanying you, and we will open the door to allow you to depart."

"And the weapons?"

Another laugh from their foe. "Those belong to us, I'm afraid. After all, we are the ones preserving the ideals of Rhazdon." Diana thought she heard sarcasm in the words.

Her teacher sounded smug. "So, you are Remembrance. Thank you for confirming that for me, Ushev. With instincts like that, I imagine you're on the bottom level of the hierarchy."

He snarled. "Very well, witch. Enjoy the rest of your short life."

The Dark Elf shook her head and returned her eyes to the mutated monster in front of them. "He's an underground gnome and likes to pretend he has power. Our paths have crossed once or twice."

The golem took a step toward them, and the vibrations echoed throughout the space. Diana moved away instinctively and was encouraged to see that her companion did as well. *At least I'm not the only scared one in the room.* "Okay, so, back to the question at hand. How do we destroy that?"

Nylotte's smile held the anticipation of a predator about the strike. "We deal with it the same way that humans and Oricerans have done since the earliest days. We burn it to cinders."

The agent raised her hands and discharged a wash of flame at the monster. Nylotte did the same, and the creature shrieked in response, perhaps from pain or perhaps from anger. It threw the bone club at the Drow, and her attack faltered as she ducked to safety and barely evaded the sharpened teeth that encircled it. Diana frowned. *It's strange that he discarded his only weapon.* He reached down and she noticed the giant link hooked onto a spike in the floor for the first time. The monster grasped it and yanked with a bellow, and the rest of the chain appeared over his shoulder and streaked toward her position. She dove to the left and narrowly avoided decapitation.

Her teacher had begun her attack again but this time, she hurled individual fireballs instead of a sustained blast so she could stay on the move. Her pattern was simple—fire, reposition, and repeat. Diana raised her rifle and sprayed rounds at the abomination. They appeared to penetrate and stitched a line from his chest to his forehead. The creature looked less concerned with the bullets than he was with his determination to destroy the Drow with the chain.

The Dark Elf shouted, "Anything vital is so deep in there that the gun won't reach it. Think, my student."

She sighed and let the rifle drop. The fire attacks seemed to bother it, but they didn't do much damage. Eventually, she and Nylotte would tire, and if they hadn't killed the atrocity, he'd have an overwhelming advantage. She scanned her surroundings for options and studied the objects in the room—coffins, candelabra, and a heavy table. *Nothing useful, dammit.* When he swung the chain at her partner again, she released fire toward him in a thin stream and channeled her strength with it to try to push it deeper into him. She saw the wound penetrate and the cauterizing effect of the flame kept it from closing or healing. Most of the bullet wounds had already vanished.

"I have an idea," she yelled. "It's a terrible one. But be ready to shoot something with your fire." She couldn't use the timer, because getting it in position would require adaptation based on how he moved. And it wouldn't work unless it was all the way in the channel. She withdrew the fragmentation grenade from the holder in her hip and held it up, then used a force blast to direct it at the monster.

"You're an idiot," her teacher yelled, but she also sent a distracting wash of flame at the golem to give her room to work. She remained still, focused on the projectile, and nudged it telekinetically to keep it on target while she pushed it forward with her force magic. He shifted and she adjusted the trajectory as she noticed as if from a distance that the chain arced over his head in a determined effort to obliterate her.

She shoved the grenade into place, hurled herself aside with her telekinesis, and narrowly avoided the blow from the metal whip as she sprawled in the middle of the room. "Now!"

Nylotte's timing was perfect, and she detonated the grenade buried in the golem's flesh. The fragments erupted from his body in every direction, and he fell to his knees, then collapsed with an uncomprehending look on his face. Diana lay still and simply took a moment to rest. Her teacher hadn't spent much time training her in precision magic, and she'd now discovered that it was entirely exhausting. She must have lost focus for a moment because suddenly, the Drow's boot tapped the ground right in front of her eyes. "Get up."

"No. Can't. Tired."

The other woman gave an exasperated sigh. Magic wrapped around her and hauled her into a seated position, and she felt the metal edge of a vial on her lips. Her teacher allowed her several sips of the energy potion—maybe half —but removed it before she could finish it. Relief flooded through her and she bounced to her feet. The world swirled for a minute, and her companion had to support her until she returned to normal.

"*Damn*. I do love that stuff."

The Drow sounded amused, maybe even fondly amused. "Try not to fall asleep before we return to Earth. Do not doubt that I'll leave you here."

With a screeching sound, all three portcullises raised at the same time. From the front left corner of the room, Cara and Rath appeared. They looked at the fallen golem and then at the two women. Her second-in-command shook her head. "I'm glad we missed this. Rath and I have had fun knocking out skeletons and necromancers."

The troll added, "And zombies."

"Right, and zombies. Slow zombies, though, not fast zombies. Fast zombies are terrifying, leading to a significant reduction in fun."

Diana gestured at the fallen monstrosity. "Well, you had the better end of the deal."

Cara nodded. "I can see that. I'm glad we missed it. Is that…a skeleton sticking out of its arm?"

Nylotte's condescending tone was back. "It's an undead golem. What do you think they'd make it out of?" She strode toward where the gnome had been. "We must push onward. Ushev and his people are ahead of us. We mustn't let them retrieve the weapons." She walked out of the room, doubtless assuming they would obey and follow without objection.

The others intercepted Diana as they all moved toward the door. Cara asked, "What's an Ushev?"

"Gnome."

Rath asked, "Which kind?"

Diana blinked. "There are kinds?"

He laughed and busied himself with retracting and holstering his batons as they followed the Drow. The tunnel curved and turned, and more than once, she used force magic to activate traps ahead of them. When they reached the end of the passage, it opened into a chamber at least four times as large as any they'd seen in the crypt thus far. The ceiling climbed to several stories above them, with large black metal chandeliers hanging from it. Pillars dotted the space and reached up to support the roof. It all appeared to be carved from the natural stone, not constructed.

Cara commented on that fact, and Nylotte nodded. "Most of these were. Magic has always been used for actions both spectacular and ordinary here, as it is constantly being replenished, unlike on Earth where we must conserve our fuel."

Diana shook her head. "The things we could accomplish with that kind of power. It boggles the mind."

Her teacher sounded wistful, the first time she'd ever heard such a tone from her. "If only people could focus on building up instead of tearing down, it could be a utopia. But, as history shows us repeatedly, that is never the way. Not on the two planets we know about, and doubtless not on any others, either."

The lead agent peered ahead to a double set of stairs on the far side of the room, both of which curved inward toward an altar. She triggered the magnification in her glasses and the twin silver daggers wavered into focus. "The blades are on the altar." She tensed in preparation to move, but Nylotte laid a hand on her shoulder.

"Beware. Our enemies reached this place first but are not up there yet. Either it's an ambush, or there are traps that they cannot overcome. Or possibly both."

She nodded. "Rath, how about a bird's-eye view?"

He grinned and crouched. She lifted him gently and used a mixture of force and telekinesis to raise him up a dozen feet before she positioned him alongside the nearest pillar so that he would have protection. After a quarter of a minute or so, she lowered him. He knelt and drew in the dust on the floor. The area quickly took shape, and he marked three places with an X. The first was immediately to their left, the second was halfway up the room on that side, and the third was ahead of them at the base of the steps. He pointed at them in that order. "Kilomea. Witch. Gnome."

The Drow added, "And that doesn't mean there aren't traps waiting."

Diana frowned, then sighed. "It's time for something stupid again, I think." She turned to her teacher. "Can you drop Cara on top of the Kilomea?" When the elf nodded, she looked at Rath. "Wait for a moment while I clear any traps, then go after the gnome."

The Dark Elf added, "I will also take the gnome."

She nodded. "I assumed so. That leaves the witch for me." To Cara, she said, "I hesitate to say this since it's not the most efficient way to deal with it, but you probably want to preserve your magic power if you can. There's no way to tell what we'll face after we deal with these three."

Her second-in-command grinned. "You're telling me to defeat a Kilomea hand-to-hand? Hell, I'd pay for that opportunity."

"Then let's do it."

CHAPTER THIRTY-ONE

C ara rocketed toward the Kilomea, her Bowie knife held reversed along her right forearm. He reacted when she was about three feet away and flinched to the side in a dodge that took him out of her path. Instead of the anticipated collision, she landed cleanly, spun quickly, and held the blade up in a block.

The impact of the ax blade with her knife launched tremors up her arm. She ducked and the creature's other ax whipped over her head. Using her momentum to her advantage, she turned the duck into a roll and moved out of the corner to make space in which to move. When she found her feet, the giant stalked toward her and the axes swayed gently at the end of his long arms. His voice was as growly as she'd expected it would be. "It's about time you arrived. Waiting was boring."

"Aww, you were waiting for little old me? How flattering." She feinted a front kick, and his axes twitched in the direction of a block. The minimalism of his reaction and the look on his face communicated that he was still bored and clearly didn't respect her as an opponent.

"Waiting for someone. Was hoping for a challenge. But you'll have to do."

"Cruel, cruel words. You hurt my heart. Allow me to return the favor." She stepped in and swept the blade across in a slash. He brought the ax up to block, and she twisted to deliver a side kick, whipped around, and planted her heel into his chest. He didn't move, and she dropped and rolled away before he could counter. *Shit, it's like kicking a boulder.*

He advanced without replying and slashed with his axes, a fluid combination that she struggled to mostly evade and block when necessary. She failed to catch the last blow in the flurry cleanly and blood trickled down her right arm. He pushed forward and now aimed at her head with every second or third blow. She managed to evade them all and finally dashed behind a column and kept it between them.

Wait a minute. No one said anything about conserving bullets. In her reactivated enthusiasm for hand to hand combat—thanks to Hank's nocturnal entertainment of choice—she'd immediately thought it would be fun to go up against a Kilomea when the opportunity presented itself. *And, on another day, with less on the line, maybe it would be.* She backed up to give him an angle to attack, and when he emerged from behind the column at a run, it was to find her with her pistol drawn.

She feared his chest might be resistant after her kick had failed so spectacularly, so she aimed for his legs, emptied the magazine, and achieved several successful strikes. He groaned where he had fallen as she reloaded, then she stepped closer and delivered a ringing shot to his head. She knew the one blow wouldn't have been adequate on its own, but the shock surge put him out. Cara holstered her gun and raised her rifle, then stalked forward along the left-hand side of the room.

Rath and Nylotte took different paths toward the gnome. The Drow had warned him not to underestimate the creature and that he was a formidable opponent, and he had taken the advice to heart. He held one of his throwing knives in his right hand, ready to throw, and had the other ready for a swift transfer and throw. He moved around the pillar in a crouch and took a quick look around, but the gnome was still focused on the noise coming from the far corner of the room, which allowed the troll to creep forward.

When he finally judged that he couldn't get closer without revealing himself, he stepped out and threw the knife at his opponent, grasped the other, and tossed it a moment later. His form was much improved from his first effort with the grape, and the blade flew true. His accuracy still wasn't perfect, though, and what was intended to be a strike to his chest instead hit the gnome in the leg.

A shield snapped up immediately to deflect the second knife, and Rath hurtled around the corner. Ushev growled a curse and pointed a finger, and a huge piece of rock detached from the wall nearby and careened toward the troll's head. He yelped when he saw it, threw himself to the side, and managed to avoid most of it. What did strike him hit hard, though, and he scrambled dazedly toward cover.

Nylotte intervened before the gnome could press his advantage. She had circled while he took the direct route and blasted their enemy from that side while his shield faced Rath. Ushev staggered as her tiny fireballs battered him, a continuous flow of small impacts that nonetheless prevented him from being able to counter. When she had him pressed against the wall of the cavern, she extended tentacles of shadow and wound them around him to immobilize the gnome. One covered his mouth as a gag, which also prevented him from using verbal magic.

She looked at the troll. "Are you okay, Rath?" He nodded and staggered to his feet, his head ringing. She beckoned for him to join her, and when he got there, she reached into the satchel and handed him two potions, one red and one blue. "Red is healing. It's customized for a troll. You probably only need about a third of it." He drank without hesitation, and his head cleared immediately. He grinned.

"Thank you."

She nodded. "It's good to make sure one's..." She paused before she continued, "Partners are at full strength. We still don't know what we might face before we're safe."

Diana had made a furious initial attack on the witch and hoped to overwhelm her, but that effort had failed. The first salvo of bullets, fired before she'd revealed herself, should have succeeded, but the woman in the tight black dress with the plunging neckline had reacted quicker than she would have thought possible to simply redirect each bullet past her with twitches of her wand. *Which is really damn impressive. That kind of precision is—no, I'm not jealous. Shut up.* Her inner voice chose to remain silent.

The agent stepped out with her rifle raised. A new magazine now replaced the one that hadn't brought the desired results. "Hi, there...uh, Elvira. Love your show. How about you put the wand down and no one gets hurt?"

The witch grinned, her obvious beauty another annoyance. *I would give a lot for her skin.*

Now, her mental voice did chime in. *"Phrasing."*

Diana rolled her eyes, then turned her attention to the woman, who finally spoke. "You must be Agent Diana Sheen. Dreven has described you before. Congratulations on avoiding his clumsy trap."

She blinked in surprise. "Yeah, sure. Okay. Thanks. Drop the wand."

Her adversary laughed, and her appeal doubled. "I'm afraid not, Diana. I will leave with those blades. If you wish to live, you'll leave now."

"So, the hard way." She pulled the trigger and again, the bullets failed to reach their target. The witch countered with a blast of force, but she conjured her buckler and the attack rebounded to its source. Again, a small gesture with the wand protected her. She tried lightning next, and Diana relied on her vest to protect her as she lunged forward. Magic crackled around her as she moved into range and channeled all her energy into a front kick at the woman. Her foot passed through the illusory figure and she fell heavily.

The real witch stepped out of an alcove behind the image—which explained how the attacks seemed to authenticate the illusion—with her wand extended and she covered Diana in shadow. She summoned a shield but knew immediately that she wouldn't be able to hold it for long under the brutally powerful attack. Despite the drain on her energy, she tried to focus and investigate the woman's power, but it was too strong for her to tease out any part to try to separate from the rest. The pressure increased as her anti-magic deflectors were consumed, and she groaned in pain. She forced her eyes open and saw that the portion of the floor the woman stood on was cracked.

Encouraged, she siphoned off the tiniest amount of energy and let it build for a few moments, then launched it in an assault on that damaged area. The floor crumbled, and the witch was thrown off balance. The assault fell away briefly, and Diana shouted with relief. She levitated two slabs of rock in front of her in time to block the next shadow assault. The witch tried again, but a slight adjustment of the rocky barrier deflected the onslaught. The agent saw Cara out of the corner of her eye and grinned, then yelled, "I can do this all day, witch. Is that all you have?"

Her second-in-command took advantage of the distraction and fired triple groups of anti-magic bullets at the target. After the first, Diana released the shield as the woman lurched awkwardly, regained her balance, and suddenly raced away. The agent pursued but skidded to a stop as a section of the tunnel her quarry had fled down suddenly crumbled. Cara halted abruptly beside her and gestured at it with her chin. "Backup plan. Smart."

"Right?"

They returned to the main portion of the cavern to find that Nylotte and Rath had trussed the enemies and dragged them out to the center to make it easier to retrieve them on the way out. Diana looked at the altar and the stairs leading to it before she faced the Drow. "Suggestions?"

Nylotte shrugged. "No, actually. Nothing that I've found or that Lady Alayne provided you has anything to say about this."

Cara said, "I call left side."

She laughed. "We head up together. Nylotte can stay here to rescue us if things go wrong."

It was a shock to all of them when everything went right. Moments later, the two women and the troll stood at the table and stared at the blades. Diana shook her head. "They look so ordinary."

Cara replied, "They're beautiful."

Rath nodded in agreement.

"So, there's every indication that these things have a mind of their own." Diana gestured at the weapons. "It's probably safe to assume they'd have a preference as to who gets to use them. Nylotte is more of an attack from the back sort, and Hank's magic doesn't lend itself to this fighting, so it's down to the three of us."

Her second-in-command sighed. "It has to be you, then, boss."

"No, I don't think so. How about this—we each put our hands over them and see what happens. Maybe they'll let us know. If not, we'll decide from there."

Rath nodded. "I'll go first." He stretched his hand out and remained motionless for several seconds. She looked at him with a raised eyebrow, and he shook his head. "Nothing."

Diana moved forward to try next. She closed her eyes and tried to reach out to the weapons but failed to feel any kind of connection.

Cara took a deep breath and stepped forward. As her hands moved closer, a sense of active magic permeated the platform and the daggers changed. Color crept over the blades and washed slowly from the point to replace the silver. One transformed to pure white, and the other deepest black. She gasped as they leapt into her palms. The woman's voice was filled with wonder. "They're...talking to me."

Around them, the cavern began to shake. Nylotte raced up to the platform, barely ahead of crumbling pedestals and a collapsing roof. Diana saw the stones fall upon their trussed prisoners but couldn't feel too much regret about them facing the ultimate consequences of their actions. The Drow summoned a portal to her workshop, and they all dived through as the crypt fell in on the space they'd abandoned.

CHAPTER THIRTY-TWO

"I can't believe you went to another damn planet and you didn't invite me." Hank spoke loudly from across the yard where he stood near the grill with Cara. There had been much jockeying for the position of grillmaster but ultimately, her second-in-command had claimed it and selected the newest agent to assist. Diana didn't have a dog in that particular fight, as long as she didn't have to do it.

There had been an incident. Kayleigh and Rath still teased her about it. *Well, hell, how am I supposed to know that fish flakes like that and gets all over the place? And oh, by the way, it certainly wasn't my choice to do fish, anyway.* Fortunately, they had stuck to proper grill food for this gathering—burgers, hot dogs, Kielbasa, and chicken.

It was the first time most of the team had been to the house she shared with Rath and Kayleigh, and the teasing had started in the first minute with the first guest—Tony—and hadn't stopped since. Her standard reply was, "Welcome, have a beer, go out into the yard, and shut up about the house." But it was said with a smile.

Now, looking at them all with a drink in her hand and the sun starting to work its way toward the horizon, she was filled with satisfaction. Her team had come together spectacularly well. She was reluctant to discuss business for fear of breaking the spell of pleasure, but there were things she needed to say before everyone became silly later. And silly was inevitable—it was part of the requirements for attending. The lawn darts had been hidden away and replaced by a few setups of the Midwest version of horse-shoes, which involved beanbags and an inclined target with a hole in it, and she expected the competition to be fierce.

Her first stop was Sloan, who watched Rath and Max. He was still processing recent events, but when she'd asked him whether he could continue, he'd merely shrugged and given her a smile. "It's what I do. I'll be fine. I've been here before. No worries." She tapped him on the shoulder to get his attention and asked the question she'd promised herself to put to him at least every second day. "Hey, Face. Time to come out?"

He grinned at her. "Oh, hell no. There's way more trouble I can cause for these jerks before I fade."

She laughed and moved on to her next target, Tony. The former detective argued with Anik about which variety of hotdogs was better, chili-cheese or Chicago. The demolitions expert was in favor of the latter, and Tony seemed personally offended by his stance. "Seriously, man, all the deliciousness of chili on a hotdog. How can you not see the glory?"

Diana stepped in before the other man could answer. "Hey there, Stark, what's the deal on Starsky and Hutch?"

He wiped his mouth before he answered. "Vicki is the

better of the two, but they're both quality. I think we can continue to use them for support. I'd like to give them some investigative stuff, too, if their chief signs off. And since she's an old friend of mine, I'm sure she will."

She nodded. "Good. Keep me in the loop but do as you think best." She turned to Anik. "What do you need that you don't have?"

He kept a straight face as he replied instantly, "A vacation." She laughed with him at the joke, and he took a pull of his can of Lawful Evil Double IPA. "Seriously, though, it's all good. I'm working up some specifications for an expanded demo kit based on what we've faced and should be ready to start putting it together soon."

Diana put a mock look of fear on her face and turned it into a grin. "Excellent plan. I can't wait to see it when it's done."

She circled to the tech table, which was a corner of the picnic bench that Kayleigh had insisted on having in their back yard. In retrospect, it had been a solid idea. The duo held down one end of it, and the rest was covered in foods of various kinds, wrapped to keep them warm or cool, whichever was required. She smelled the corn on the grill, and it made her mouth water as she took a seat beside Deacon.

"So, trouble twins, is everything good?"

The new team member laughed, and the old one simply rolled her eyes as always. He said, "We need better computers. This off-the-shelf stuff is crap."

Kayleigh added, "Crap for work, super-crap for gaming."

Diana laughed. "Work hard, play hard. Try not to break

the bank, okay? Or, you know, find a bad guy's offshore account and spend their money." She'd meant it as a joke, but the way their eyes lit up told her she'd probably opened a door better left closed. *Actually, maybe it's time to start kicking doors down all over the place.*

She paused beside Rath and Max. The troll had put a target on the fence that ran along the back property line and threw small discs of grilled Kielbasa at it, launching each with deep concentration. After he'd reviewed where the missile impacted the man-shaped silhouette, the Borzoi would dash forward, barking, and snap up the fallen weapon before he returned to Rath's side. She'd noticed that everyone made it a point to stop and talk to them. She grinned at the memory of going to the shelter with Rath to adopt the dog. *That was a great day.*

"Not too much extra food for Maxie, Rath." She pointed at him. "He seems like he's gained weight. Perhaps you need to take him patrolling more often."

The troll looked shocked, then stared at his partner and knelt to run his hands over him. "Maybe a little. Max must train harder. Starting tomorrow." The dog gave a snort and lay on the grass to watch his sausage-throwing friend with attentive eyes.

Diana laughed as she finally made her way around to the grillers. Anik hadn't seemed at all tense about them hanging out together, so she assumed Cara and he had come to some kind of understanding. A bystander might assume she and Hank were a couple, but the body language was definitely more locker room than ballroom. *Or bedroom.* She stepped rudely between them and turned to face Hank, completely eclipsing her second-in-command. "So, new guy, what do you think?"

He coughed once on the combination of beer and laughter at whatever Cara did behind her. "All love. Love the town, love the people, love the action." He got a suspicious look in his eye and she threw a hand up to stop him.

"One word, only one, about anything involving more than four wheels and I will throw you over that fence. And I think my elderly neighbor would find you very attractive as she nurses you back to health. What are your feelings on jello salad on a daily basis? She puts grapes and marshmallows in it."

He drew an imaginary zipper across his lips, and she nodded and spun without warning. Cara had been giving her bunny ears but put the hand behind her back with a look of complete innocence. She coughed once. "Hey, boss, nice party."

Diana stared at her with angry eyes, then relented. "You, of all people, need relaxation. Everything good with...you know?" She looked at the woman's boots. Kayleigh had customized an off-the-shelf pair with sheaths for Cara's new knives, and the woman had taken to wearing bootleg jeans until they found a better solution. The single time she'd tried to leave them behind, she'd only made it about ten feet before she fell to her knees with her hands clutching her head.

The woman nodded. "Yep. We're moving toward an understanding. Right now, I can only manage about a half-hour at a time of talking to them without becoming exhausted, so it's slow going. But progress is happening."

"They're not trying to turn you into a zombie?"

"If they do, rest assured, your brain is the first one I'll come for. It's bound to be fluffy and delicious and not dense at all. You know, since you don't have much packed in there."

She rolled her eyes. "Yeah, I had it from 'fluffy,' thanks. Your burgers are burning." They weren't, but she enjoyed the way the other woman startled.

Her rounds made, she sauntered over to stand in the doorway to the house and watch her people. Finally, the pair of clicks she'd waited for caught her attention as the front door opened and closed, and she turned with a smile. Bryant dropped his suitcase and came over to wrap her in a hug. She dug her head into his chest and breathed his cologne in. Her words were muffled by his clothes. "I missed you, chucklehead."

He laughed. "Good party?"

She grinned. "It is now. Shut up and kiss me, you fool."

Once again, he obeyed orders like the excellent soldier he was. Her last thought before she let her concerns slip away was, *Shit. I gave the techs the green light to steal money from bad guys. I hope they don't talk to Cara and Hank about the semi.*

CHAPTER THIRTY-THREE

Iressa limped angrily into the small den she used as her private office. It was sparsely decorated as she always tried to limit the demands she placed upon a host. It made manipulating their minds so much easier if there was less for them to object to. Switching hosts regularly increased the difficulty level for those who might be interested in tracking her.

That, plus the use of illusions and a persistent habit of checking for watchers at all times and in all places kept her safe while her plans inched toward the moment when everything would come together.

She paused to corral her emotions. When one of the falling rocks had struck her leg and broken the bone, she'd been upset. When the healing potion failed to restore it fully, she'd been irate. The healer she'd used had cowered beneath her passionate anger and made excuses or explanations that she wasn't interested in hearing—something about it only needing a day or two to mend due to her unique nature.

Naturally, she'd killed the woman for bringing it up.

The witch lowered herself into the seat behind the desk and set the disc before her. Some hours before, she'd alerted Sarah of the need to speak, and the time was at hand. She cast the communication spell, and vapor emerged from the small object to show the other witch in her office on Earth.

Her minion spoke. "How may I serve you?"

Iressa snarled, "Better than you have thus far, I hope." The report of the authorities' attack on the woman's subordinate was beyond troubling. If they possessed that level of knowledge about the Remembrance, it threatened all of them, especially if they'd abandoned restraint as the escalation to executions suggested.

If part of her anger was directed at herself for failing to kill those present in the crypt, well, that wasn't something her pet witch needed to know.

Sarah cringed at her words, and whispered, "Yes, master."

She sighed inwardly. The woman wouldn't have been her first choice, but she'd have to do. "What is your status now?"

The woman straightened. "Dreven has insisted on daily communication with Marcus and I." A sneer slid over her face. "He directs us to engage in small actions, which the humans support fully. I feel it's beneath us and distracts from our ultimate goal, but he doesn't want to hear my protests."

She grinned. "Our dear Dreven is likely under some pressure from his master to do so. The fact that they scurry about like this means they do not have a clear path forward, or that this is only a part of it. We must plan for either eventuality." *But we mustn't eliminate darling Dreven yet. Let them think they are safe and in control until the moment we are fully ready, and then they can share Ushev's fate.* The irony was that if they had succeeded in reaching the blades, she would have killed the gnome herself to claim them.

"How do we do that, master?"

Iressa's grin widened. "We do it in three ways. First, you ensure that the magicals in your city's Remembrance are completely loyal to you. Do anything you need to do. Money, magical items, vices, violence, whatever. They must be yours."

The glow of satisfaction that suffused Sarah was exactly what she'd intended. "With pleasure."

She nodded. "Second, you seek to turn these small acts into larger acts, especially when they involve the local authorities. That will put pressure on the group that killed your underling." The witch flinched at the mention of that and revealed her own anger about it, which served her superior's purposes perfectly. "Finally, we plan a strike against these people who are after you. We find out where they work, where they live, and where they go for fun. Then, we kill them, one and all."

Sarah grinned. "Yes, master. Thank you. It is beyond time that we had real leadership."

Suck-up. Iressa waved, and the connection dissolved. She steepled her fingers and defocused her eyes, turned inward, and considered the days to come. A distant corner of her mind suggested she might not be safe in her current location, which drew a sigh. When that voice spoke, she listened.

She pushed herself up from her seat and winced at the stabbing pain in her shin. Thanks to the beauty she'd been blessed with and the powers of persuasion she'd developed over many hard and pain-filled years, there was a list of men dying to claim her. Little did they know the ultimate result of that particular desire. She considered the timing and decided she didn't have to act immediately. *First, a long, hot bath to make this accursed leg stop hurting.* She exited the room and called for the house's servants to prepare it for her. *I'll wait until tomorrow to kill my benefactor. Then, it's on to the next.*

The story doesn't end here. Follow Diana, Rath and FAM's adventures in Agents of Order.

CONNECT WITH TR CAMERON

Stay up to date on new releases and fan pricing by signing up for my newsletter. CLICK HERE TO JOIN.

Or visit: www.trcameron.com/Oriceran to sign up.

If you enjoyed this book, please consider leaving a review. Thanks!

AUTHOR NOTES - TR CAMERON

WRITTEN JUNE 27, 2019

Seriously now, thank you.

Thank you for reading the *fifth* book in the Federal Agents of Magic series, and for continuing on to the author notes! I continue to find great emotional support in the reviews and comments about the prior books – I'll respond to a couple notable ones below, stealing shamelessly from Michael Anderle's early approach to author notes. I'm deeply honored to be able to continue to share this ever-sprawling story with you.

This book was big fun to write. After the culmination of the first arc in book 4, it was time to start making life difficult for the characters again. Hopefully you enjoyed it, and feel like things aren't *too* easy for them!

The next three books will challenge the Agents further, and push several of the characters against, and through, their existing boundaries. I think we're done with adding new good guys for the time being, but I wouldn't swear to it. Sometimes inspiration strikes and suddenly you just have to add someone! After those ones, books 9 and on are in the planning stages, and so far all signs point to big fun ahead.

My daughter and I climbed two small mountains (but still, legitimate enough to be recordable) with friends this month. And playing with VR quickly required acquiring our own system. I loved Guitar Hero and Rock Band when they came out, and Beat Saber is *such* a worthy successor.

I'm 73% complete on the Spider-Man videogame, which has a great plot, and have just started Red Dead Redemption 2. I'm not feeling that one yet. I live for story, but it feels like the gaming is sacrificed for long conversations and setups. But it's still early days, I could be very wrong.

Plot details for book six are almost complete, so I start writing tomorrow. For those who might be interested in my process, I average two chapters per day of new content when in the writing stage, six or seven days per week, and then have to do a *lot* of cleanup. I am an extraordinarily messy first-drafter. The revision process is pretty rewarding because of it, where I can say "Oh, that was a nice idea, but I can totally make it better."

New characters, as promised! What do you think of Hank, Deacon, and Chan?

Quick response to Lcashless1, who said: "The only thing I do not like is the fact that Diana is developing her powers very slowly." It's true. On the one hand, I'm trying to avoid the Captain Marvel effect, where nothing can defeat her. On the other, gotta keep her development interesting, as you've pointed out. There will be more to come in the upcoming books, and I really appreciate the insight.

To Fussyforfurkids, who said: "Not as good as Liera."

That's a high bar you're setting! I loved those books too. I'm glad you have room in your reading schedule for both.

Finally, there seems to be an interest in a dual-troll adventure. I'll ponder on that one – it's a pretty challenging assignment!

Quick media notes: I loved *Detective Pikachu* again when the kid demanded we see it a second time. Yes, I was surprised too. The latest Expanse book is in the rear view, and it made me sad. It was wonderful, but you know, a little dark. *Deadwood* movie was good. *Good Omens* was great, and I'm into my second watching. *Fleabag* was phenomenal if you're into that sort of thing, and *Killing Eve* season one was strong if you're into *that* sort of thing. I'm still looking forward to *Watchmen* and *American Gods*. And breathless to see *Endgame* again when it's released to digital.

If you want to chat media, the books, or whatever else, I check in pretty often on Facebook. Just search TR Cameron Author to find me. Or, less reliably, thom@trcameron.com.

Now, back to smacking flying boxes in *Beat Saber*. Until next time, Joys upon joys to you and yours – so may it be.

AUTHOR NOTES - MARTHA CARR

JULY 2, 2019

Here's a question I ponder all the time. It's even inspired me to start The Peabrain Society to help others climb their mountain.

What stops people from going for the very things they dream about?

That can have a dozen answers – hence the need for an entire movement (which, by the way starts in September – it's gonna be amazing). I'm willing to start with one thread that's pretty common and unravel it a little here. It'll also give you an idea of what we'll be doing in the new Society, kind of...

Here we go.

We tell ourselves a narrative that we dug around for in the first place and then we adopt it as if it were fact. I'll give you an example.

My late sister Diana's house sold this week. It was a relief for about five minutes and then sadness. It's the last thing that needs to be done for her and then she is just memories. I was sitting in my office and realized, I feel sad...

But instead of stopping there, I searched my brain for events to come up with a justification and the narrative begins. I feel sad because... More searching, checking in for what sets me off more. Aha! Her last days were so tough and I could have done more, if only I'd known. It all seems so futile.

And we're off and running. The narrative (or story) becomes the way I distract myself from feeling so uncomfortable. It's like I believe that naming it can make it go away faster. It gives me something to overcome and rise above and get back to other things. Even seems noble, right?

But this is the very thing that can get in the way and weirdly, put roadblocks to my own success, my own personal happiness. I ignored the opportunity to learn something.

Instead, I can ditch the narrative and just say, I feel sad, and stop there. But wait, there's more. I can not only just be sad without explanation, I can invite that sadness to come and sit down next to me. I can ask, what are you here to teach me? And then, I can let the answer come to me.

It's reverse engineering at its best.

I let go of control and a fear that sadness can park itself and stay and I let it sit next to me like an ally, instead of the enemy.

Sometimes the answers find me almost right away, sometimes its weeks and I'm walking down a grocery store aisle when it hits me. But when it does, it's deeper and more profound and helps me see a new view of the world.

Some old fear loses a little bit of ground. Some old belief that's no longer serving me slips away and is replaced by a new one with some life in it.

And instead of fighting and pushing against life, I'm telling myself that the universe is to be trusted. Even the hard events are here in a loving way to show me something. Give it room, let it linger, good will come from this.

When I've been able to do this – and generally it includes conversations with others on a similar path – my life has changed in weird and wonderful ways, opening up to what seems like unrelated dreams. I still don't know what the sadness is here to teach me, but I'm okay with paling around for a while, getting on with life until the answer appears. I'll let you know.

That's just a taste of what we'll be working on come this fall. I'm so excited! More adventures and dreams to follow.

AUTHOR NOTES - MICHAEL ANDERLE

JULY 10, 2019

THANK YOU for not only reading this story but these *Author Notes* **as well.**

(I think I've been good with always opening with "thank you." If not, I need to edit the other *Author Notes*!)

RANDOM (*sometimes*) THOUGHTS?

OH MY #$@@# the Vanilla Bean Frappucino at Starbucks is *FREAKING COLD!*

Ok, half the fault is mine (one could argue all of the fault is mine for sipping it too fast, but I'm the only one arguing and I can't get better than 50/50.)

I'm setting up my new little 12" Macbook (arrived the same day Apple stopped selling them) and so far, I'm happy.

I need a laptop this small for writing and working outside of the condo, and especially while traveling. The 15" Macbook I use has been a good machine, but frankly my (old and getting older) back doesn't want to keep carrying that hunk of metal everywhere. I would rather stow it in the rolling suitcase and carry the dinky Macbook for on the plane.

The only trouble I expect is when I go into Mexico. I have had the agents question my need for two laptops before.

Normally, I'm all about having the fastest, most powerful machine I can afford. While this little machine is expensive, it is not the fastest most powerful by any stretch of even my prolific imagination.

Now, since the MacBook Air is now the beginning Macbook again, I suspect we won't see this model again until they place the same CPU chips they have in the iPad Pro bodies into this form factor.

Don't think it will happen? Well, Apple is releasing a desk-top class browser and mouse support for the iPad Pro so most of the pieces are being put in place to make it happen.

I think it is just time until Apple uses their chips inside of this hardware. I've no idea if we are talking 18 months or 36 months, but I do believe it will happen.

AROUND THE WORLD IN 80 DAYS

One of the interesting (at least to me) aspects of my life is the ability to work from anywhere and at any time. In the future, I hope to re-read my own *Author Notes* and remember my life as a diary entry.

Starbucks off 15 South next to Silverton Hotel and Casino.

The sun is setting to the West, not yet behind the mountains, so the front door to the Starbucks has the full sun shining in and it's July.

So, freaking hot in Las Vegas.

Inside of this Starbucks the walls are a form of brick (yes, I did just scratch one to make sure it was rock - I'm curious that way.)

The inside here feels like a new version of a rustic cabin in Arizona. Slate floors, brick walls, wood ceilings, and large joists running up the ceiling. Black air-conditioning vents and black iron work on all of the wood.

Cool.

In other notes, I've purchased an XBox One X (that's the latest, right?) and I've only played one game.

It was...ok. I'm looking for something a bit different, but I'm willing to continue (it has to do with dinosaurs on an island, and little walking cats as partners.)

I'm in the mood to find a game that has incredible eye candy, and I can just walk around and see new and cool stuff.

Not interested in games I have to put a lot of time into to become good enough to enjoy playing.

If you know of any of those games, check us out in the Kurtherian Gambit group for fans and authors and hit me up.

Eventually, I'll get to play more games again.

FAN PRICING

$0.99 Saturdays (new LMBPN stuff) and $0.99 Wednesday (both LMBPN books and friends of LMBPN books.) Get great stuff from us and others at tantalizing prices.

Go ahead. I bet you can't read just one.

Sign up here: http://lmbpn.com/email/.

HOW TO MARKET FOR BOOKS YOU LOVE

Review them so others have your thoughts, and tell friends and the dogs of your enemies (because who wants to talk to enemies?)... *Enough said ;-)*

Ad Aeternitatem,

Michael Anderle

OTHER SERIES IN THE ORICERAN
UNIVERSE:

SCHOOL OF NECESSARY MAGIC
SCHOOL OF NECESSARY MAGIC: RAINE CAMPBELL
ALISON BROWNSTONE
THE DANIEL CODEX SERIES
THE LEIRA CHRONICLES
I FEAR NO EVIL
FEDERAL AGENTS OF MAGIC
THE UNBELIEVABLE MR. BROWNSTONE
REWRITING JUSTICE
THE KACY CHRONICLES
MIDWEST MAGIC CHRONICLES
SOUL STONE MAGE
THE FAIRHAVEN CHRONICLES

OTHER BOOKS BY JUDITH BERENS

OTHER BOOKS BY MARTHA CARR

JOIN THE ORICERAN UNIVERSE FAN GROUP ON FACEBOOK!

BOOKS BY MICHAEL ANDERLE

For a complete list of books by Michael Anderle, please visit

www.lmbpn.com/ma-books/

All LMBPN Audiobooks are Available at Audible.com and
iTunes. For a complete list of audiobooks visit:

www.lmbpn.com/audible

www.ingramcontent.com/pod-product-compliance
Lightning Source LLC
Chambersburg PA
CBHW031643100726
47898CB00006B/1953